Bamboozled

JANE FLAGELLO

ZIG ZAG PRESS LLC

ISBN-13: 978-0-9961237-0-9
ISBN-10: 0996123709

Cover design by WickedSmartDesigns.com
Interior formatting by Author E.M.S.

Zig Zag Press LLC
Williamsburg, VA
2015

Published in the United States of America

Dedication

This book is dedicated to Carolyn who midwifed it into existence. A mere thank you is not enough. You believed in my story. Your muse-like gifts helped me flesh out my characters and the plot twists. Thank you.

Attribution

"Help us find the courage to make our lives a blessing" are lyrics Debbie Friedman (1951-2011) wrote in 1988 based on the Jewish prayer for healing, the Mi Shebeirach, developed during the 16th century.

Prologue

Thursday, October 3

They are real!

Rachel stared at the stones sitting in her lap—eight dullish rocks, about the size of walnuts, with just a hint of sparkle. She knew what they were—diamonds—uncut diamonds. Memories of afternoons spent listening to Aunt Lil's stories about a young girl and her two brothers' journey to America so many years ago flooded into her mind. Her pulse quickened. She knew her life was about to change forever. These were diamonds and their value…priceless!

Tears slipped down her cheeks and crossed her lips. Their salty taste captured the sadness deep in her heart at the passing of her favorite aunt. Two years ago another death had rocked her world—her husband David. One moment he was alive—the next—he was gone. She had turned to Aunt Lil for comfort. The memory of Aunt Lil holding her, stroking her hair, and telling her that she was not to worry remained vivid. She closed her eyes. Aunt Lil's voice filled her mind.

"Everything will work out fine. You'll see, my little Rachel. Things will be different for you now that David has gone to live with God. You'll be okay. And when I'm gone, all that I have will be yours. You'll be fine. I lost my beloved Abraham long ago, and I'm still here. You are strong, just like me. You will survive. More than that, Rachel, you will thrive. Trust me. Sweet times will come again."

That was Aunt Lil. All strength and courage, packed in a five foot two body, calmly facing the crap that life threw at her. Aunt Lil embraced the very essence of life, the sweet moments as well as those times and events that challenged you to your very core. She was the glue that held everything and everyone in this family together. Who would assume that role now that she was gone?

Rachel reached into the old suitcase and picked up the pile of letters wrapped in a frayed blue ribbon. In faded black ink her aunt's maiden name, Lillian Hershenburg, was still legible. The aged green postage stamp featured Lady Liberty. She smiled at the three cent marking on the stamp.

There must be fifty letters here. These must be from Uncle Abe. How like Aunt Lil to save them. She slid the top letter from under the ribbon and opened it. The date was June, 1940.

My dearest Lily,

It has been so difficult being away from you for even a day. And now, a week has passed without me seeing your smiling face, talking to you, holding your hand. I do not know if I can endure our separation much longer. You are my first love and when you told me that I was yours, my heart soared. You asked about my apprenticeship. It is very interesting and demands great concentration. Mr. Golden is an incredible craftsman, the likes of which I have never seen before. I am learning more and more each day. Some day I will be just like him, a diamond cutter without equal. And for you, I will cut and polish the most spectacular diamond, though no stone could ever shine as brightly as the precious love you are to me. Let's plan to meet at our special place in the park on Sunday afternoon. I will be there at one and wait for you. Come if you can get away.

Always yours,
Leo

The shock at seeing a name other than Abraham hit Rachel hard. *Who was Leo?* Rachel pulled the bottom letter from the pile and opened it. It was dated June, 1941. The ink had smeared in several places leaving blotches on the paper. *Had Aunt Lil been crying when she read this?*

My dearest Lily,

My heart is broken as I know yours is too. Our parting last night was so painful. I know I hurt you deeply and I am so very, very sorry. Mr. Golden has been so good to me during this first year of my apprenticeship. There is no way I can refuse his request to marry his oldest daughter. It is the only favor he has ever asked of me. We knew our being together was a dream. In time you will forget me. You will find someone to love you. Together you will build a wonderful life filled with the laughter of children. I will never forget you. You will be in my dreams every night and in my heart forever.

I will always love only you,
Leo

A gasp left Rachel's lips. Sitting on the edge of the old rocking chair, staring down at the untold riches in her lap, holding letters from her aunt's first love in her hand was almost more than she could bare.

Rachel remembered the stories. Aunt Lil and her two brothers had left Germany just in the nick of time. The Nazis were beginning what they called the final solution, the extermination of the Jews of Europe. Their father had been prescient, seeing the full scope of Hitler's plan. He sent his children away to save their lives. He could not save his own or that of his beloved wife, Rachel's namesake.

Aunt Lil had arrived in America with nothing but the suitcase that now lay open at Rachel's feet. She worked as a seamstress in the fledgling garment district until she met and married Uncle Abe. He had been a warm loving man and they always seemed happy together. These letters told of someone else—someone before Uncle Abe—who clearly loved her aunt very deeply. Had that love been allowed to grow Rachel wondered how her aunt's life would have turned out. That they had not been able to marry hurt Rachel's heart.

A squeak on the stairs pulled Rachel's attention back. She dropped the letters back into the suitcase and quickly hid the stones, wrapping them in the tattered pink blouse that had hidden them for so long. Holding it tightly, lest any of the precious treasure be revealed, Rachel stood to find Jimmy Raconti, the next door neighbor's son, at the top of the stairs.

"There you are, Rachel. Mom sent me to find you. That lawyer guy just got here. He said he's ready whenever you are," said Jimmy.

Her skin prickled. *This guy really creeps me out. What the hell is a thirty-two year old man doing still living with his mother?* She pushed the thought aside. Jimmy had been there Sunday morning when Aunt Lil died. He said he heard a crash and turned to see her hit the floor. He'd called nine-one-one. The paramedics arrived too late.

For the last few days, he seemed to pop up everywhere. Every time she turned around, there he was. Bringing food.

Cleaning up. Getting more chairs. Handy man to a fault. An unsettling feeling gripped her as their eyes connected. There was something about Jimmy, the ever helpful neighbor, that did not ring true.

"Thanks. Let me just put all this stuff back. I'll be right behind you."

Jimmy turned and went back down the stairs. Clutching the diamonds tightly, she slid the stones back into the purple leather pouch that had hidden them for so long and stuffed the pouch safely into her pants pocket. Her loose-knit turtleneck sweater would hide any telltale bulge. Bending down, she shoved the pink blouse and letters back into the old suitcase. She closed the lid, latched it and pushed it back into the corner behind her old doll house.

There are so many details to death.

Chapter 1

Sunday, September 29
5 days earlier

Rachel stared into the bathroom mirror after she finished brushing her teeth. She planned to enjoy a quiet, fall Sunday exploring her new hometown after her noon check-in call to Aunt Lil. Maybe a walk on Duke of Gloucester—DOG— Street, the main street in Colonial Williamsburg. Perhaps roaming through one or two of the many consignment shops. For a small town, the number of places you could buy used furniture and other people's cast-offs fascinated her. A late afternoon pizza at Sal's, then home to laundry, a good book, and a glass or two of Chardonnay.

Her morning routine had gotten easier these last few years. Without hormones, what was once coarse, frizzy hair fell stick straight, halfway down her back. Okay, perhaps there was a benefit or two that no remaining estrogen offered. Most women in their sixties simply did not wear their hair long. It made her feel young. It was fun.

Walking to her closet she surveyed its contents. It was

still filled with stiff, formal clothes from her days working as a paralegal at a law firm.

"I've got to bring these to Goodwill," Rachel said out loud to no one. She'd gotten used to talking out loud, to verbalizing what she used to only think.

Knowing her plans for the day, she pulled out slim leg jeans and a hot pink v-neck t-shirt. After pulling on Spanx, a godsend to every woman with a little extra flab, the jeans slid on easily. Giving herself the once over in the oak framed cheval mirror she found at one of the consignment shops, brought a smile to her face. She was pleased with her reflection.

"Damn good for sixty. Gravity, go screw yourself!"

Compared to many of the people she was meeting at Newcomers, the club that helped new residents fit in and make friends in her gated community, she did look damn good. Could easily pass for fifty. And during her walk in town yesterday, she managed to turn a few heads and garner a few second looks.

Okay, not hard to do with construction workers. Still, a definite ego boost.

Heading back to the bathroom to complete her make-up she found herself staring at her reflection. Critical eyes stared back. A pang of uneasiness surged through her. For a moment, her courage for embracing her new life wavered. She was starting over. Well, not over really. "Anew" might be a better term. Her eyes locked to her reflection.

Who is this person?

The lines, the wrinkles, the dark spots, thinning hair, all badges of honor earned in the wars of raising a family. With a little eye make-up here, a dollop of magic cream there, all of it would momentarily vanish.

That's all life really is, a connection of moments.

That was what she was really learning how to do, live

fully in all of the remaining moments of her life, no regrets.

Regret, like guilt, is a wasted emotion. Can't change the past. Just deal and move on.

Rachel had never really been alone. She had gone from her parents home to creating a home with David, the man Selma, the neighborhood matchmaker and busybody, brought around. She had hidden on the upstairs landing when Selma came that day. The words she overheard still stung. Selma had told her parents in a gravely, smoker's voice that *'it was a good match. David was a good man, would be a good husband. And besides what other prospects did Rachel have? She wasn't pretty or smart—and she wasn't getting any younger.'*

After Selma left, her parents told her it was done. She would marry. It might have been the late 1960s, but burning bras and the women's movement had yet to take hold in her little corner of the world. Her mother always reminded her that she didn't have much to offer. She was shy, not very pretty, and not very smart. Missing any sense of her own self-worth, David was the best she could hope for. If not him, she was sure to wind up an old maid. Back then, Rachel believed the relentless messages she heard every day from the one person who was supposed to love her unconditionally. She was not strong enough to revolt. She meekly surrendered to her pre-ordained place in the world.

Am I strong enough now?

And what about David? When she listened to her friends bitch about their husbands and how they cheated and lied, buried their noses in sports on TV, never spent time with their kids, she had to appreciate what she had. He'd been a good husband. He worked hard, never missed a day. He was an accountant for a large CPA firm. Tax season, from January to April 15 was one endless work marathon. It didn't really end that day. There were extensions, corporate taxes, IRS audits. But, he came home each night, never cheated to her knowledge, took care of the bills and made sure the kids had everything they needed. She hadn't been ready for him to die two years ago. Is anyone ever ready?

What more did she want?

That was the question that haunted her. *What more did she want?*

Once upon a time she had different dreams. As a young girl, when anyone asked, she told them she wanted to be a lawyer like Perry Mason. She saw herself in politics. Maybe Congress. They laughed. Women didn't do these things. They stayed home. Made babies.

June Cleaver and Leave it to Beaver were the role models. Graduate high school, become a teacher, nurse or secretary. Marry your "white" knight and live happily ever after—barefoot, pregnant and in the kitchen. Her happily ever after ended the night David died. After forty years of marriage, their plans for retirement at The Villages in Florida shattered. And now, alone at sixty, she found herself resenting the traditional wife role she had so meekly accepted such a long, long time ago. New questions about her own life blasted forth.

Shaking her head to end the mental replay, she understood that she both relished and totally feared tomorrow. *Crap! What do I want to do? Am I too late for me?* Out loud she recited her new mantra for life.

"Put one foot in front of the other. Take one day at a time. Live it fully. And breathe, always remember to breathe." That was the advice Aunt Lil gave her the night David died and her world went numb.

The ringing phone pulled Rachel back into the moment. She walked to the nightstand to grab it. For a split second, she hesitated. Her hand hung in the air.

"Hello."

"Mrs. Rachel Resnick?"

"Speaking."

"This is Dr. Samuels from Brooklyn Medical Center. I am so sorry to have to tell you that your aunt, Mrs. Lillian Steinmetz, passed away this morning."

Rachel's mouth went dry. Her heart started to beat so fast she thought it would burst from her chest. The room started to spin.

"Mrs. Resnick?"

"Yes. I'm here. I'm sorry. What did you say?"

"Your aunt, Mrs. Steinmetz, died this morning."

"That can't be. She wasn't sick. I was just about to call her. You must be mistaken."

"I'm afraid not. I am so sorry for your loss. Your name and phone number is on her medical emergency form as the person to contact."

"I…I…I'm not there. It will be hours before I can get there. I'll have my daughter, Jenny Silver, contact you shortly, if that's okay, and find out what we need to do."

"That will be fine. And again, I am so sorry for you loss."

"Thank you."

Rachel stifled her scream. A fist clenched and squeezed her heart. Slumping onto the edge of the bed, she bit her lower lip trying to hold back her tears. *This can't be happening. Aunt Lil…gone…I just talked to her yesterday…she sounded fine…joked that her doctor said she'd live to one hundred.* A beeping sound from the phone made her jump. She hadn't hung up. She pressed Jenny's speed dial number.

"Jenny, it's mom. It's Aunt Lil. She's gone."

"Oh, mom. I'm so sorry. I know how special she was to you."

"I'm on my way. Can you call the hospital—Brooklyn Medical—and get the ball rolling?"

"Don't worry. I'll take care of everything. You just drive carefully. See you tonight. Do you want to come here or meet at Aunt Lil's house?"

"Let's meet at Aunt Lil's. I'll stay there. We'll do everything from there."

The call to Jenny lasted only a few minutes. She would take charge and handle everything she could. *Busy hands kept the sadness at bay,* thought Rachel as she mindlessly filled her suitcase. Packing enough clothes for at least two weeks, Rachel grabbed jeans, t-shirts, sweaters, underwear, sneakers and good shoes. She packed black pants and several blouses to appear proper for the funeral and sitting Shiva, the traditional Jewish mourning time.

She was on the road heading north in under an hour. It would take eight to ten hours to reach Brooklyn. It was Sunday. She'd hit traffic later in the day. People returning from weekend get-aways. Right now, the sky was blue and the road clear. Humming along Interstate 95 heading north from Virginia, at a cruise controlled seventy-five mph, with Billy Joel playing in the background, Rachel let her mind drift.

How had she gotten here—alone on the road—driving home to Brooklyn—when everyone she loved was already there?

Thoughts of family flooded her senses. Although they talked every day, she hadn't seen Aunt Lil since the day before she left for Williamsburg—five months ago. The guilt of time passed, time never to come again, washed over her. She could feel a lump tighten in her throat as she forced back her tears.

Both of her children, Scott and Jenny, had married well and were living their own lives, doing their own thing in New Jersey. Helping them through the daily dramas of their lives was still part of her mother job—and it was rewarding.

And the grandkids! Two already here with another on the way. What more could someone want than to be near these precious little ones. Rachel knew that was the party line, what she was suppose to think and believe. And she did love them all dearly, but—there just has to be more.

Rachel wanted more than grandma duties for her golden years. She wanted the travel, the excitement, the adventure her more career oriented friend, Sara, always talked about during their weekly mah jongg game. If truth be told, that was what she missed the most since her move—Sara—girl time—and the game.

Five months ago she had taken the plunge. Against the loud cries of both Scott and Jenny, she had sold the family home, packed up and moved. Eight hundred miles seemed like a good distance. Not too far away and yet not too close to anyone and everyone she knew. A place where she could reinvent herself, become someone new.

"No, that's not right." Adamant words escaped her lips. "Not someone new. The person I really am. The person I locked away when I accepted someone else's plan about how I was supposed to live my life."

The house had to be sold. Memories of David were everywhere. His presence haunted the place. She could smell his Polo aftershave in the bathroom, feel him in the kitchen and almost see him sitting in his Lazy Boy. To create the new life she craved, she needed to distance herself from the comfort of the familiar, from memory.

Amazingly, even in a crummy real estate market, the house had sold in ten days. And why not? It was a great house, big lawn, country porch all around, backyard swing. It had done its job for her family. Now, it could do it for another family.

It had seemed like a good idea at the time. Now, as the

miles of asphalt and the colorful landscape slipped by, she was not so sure. The charm of Williamsburg had captivated her when Jenny was doing the college search thing. She hadn't chosen William & Mary which had really disappointed Rachel. So Rachel chose Williamsburg for herself, for her new life as an independent woman. Now, she had the time, all the time in the world, more time than she really knew what to do with. She was free in more ways than she could count.

Williamsburg was where she would make her mark. And the desire? Well, it was there. All she needed were the guts to go for it. That was the unanswered question. Did she have the guts to live free?

Rachel changed the music. Enough Billy Joel. Something lighter. She hit Sirius/XM button for the Margaritaville station, and Jimmy Buffett came on singing about cheeseburgers. *Sounds good*, she thought. Her plan called for stopping at Exit 29, grabbing some McDonalds and peeing. She would be on the other side of D.C., closer to Baltimore. Then it would be mindless driving until she reached the craziness and traffic of the New York Metro area.

Her mind drifted back to Aunt Lil. Even in her early nineties, she remained strong—a vibrant woman who loved life. Aunt Lil had always been there for her. She was Rachel's role model—her savior—her rock. As a young girl, Rachel had lived just down the block. She and Jake, her brother, had lived through their childhoods without the benefit of combat pay. Their mother was cold and distant, pitting them against one another at every turn. Their dad, who was one of Aunt Lil's brothers, did what dads did back then—go to work, bring home a pay check, pay the bills, say good night. In his mind, the mother took care of the kids. What he did not know, or pretended not to know or see, relieved him from the responsibility to do anything. Jake always kidded her that, when it came to mothers, they had gotten the fuzzy end of the lollipop.

A sharp horn blast drew her attention to the red BMW swerving in and out in her rear view mirror. *Where are the cops when you need them? This guy is going to get someone killed!* Grabbing the wheel more tightly, Rachel held fast in the center lane. As the Beemer passed on her right, a glimpse of the driver captured her attention. Slightly gray, suntanned and smiling. *Was that a wink?*

Beemer guy moved into the center lane in front of her. A slow moving pick-up truck forced him to hit his brakes. Rachel moved into the left lane and hit the gas. She easily passed the Beemer. Putting on her blinker, she moved back into the middle lane in front of the pick-up truck. A few minutes later the Beemer sped by on her left. Out of the corner of her eye, Rachel caught his broad smile and the salute he gave her.

This is so wrong, she thought. *Flirting with this guy on the way to my aunt's funeral. Not how I should be grieving. So wrong.* She let out a long sigh. *What could it hurt—a bit of fantasy? Maybe he would follow her to McDonalds? Maybe they would meet there, share a bite, two strangers on a road trip. Hey, it could happen. Only in the movies.*

Rachel looked ahead of her and then glanced in the rear view mirror, quickly realizing the red BMW was gone. *Shit!* Traffic was everywhere. It was going to take forever to get to Brooklyn. *Where did all these people come from? Where are they going? I've got to pee.*

Half an hour later Rachel pulled off at the Beltsville exit and made her way to McDonalds. She hit the bathroom first and then ordered a small crispy chicken wrap, fries and a Coke. As she put her tray down and slid into a booth by the window, her eyes were drawn to the red BMW parked next to her car.

Couldn't be.

"May I join you?"

Rachel looked up, directly into the warm, golden brown eyes and radiant smile of Beemer guy. He was tall, handsome, kind of a cross between Clark Gable and Omar Sharif. That touch of gray she had seen as he sped by her framed his face perfectly. And there was that wink again. He was wearing black Dockers and a red golf shirt that emphasized his tanned skin, opened just enough to reveal an alluring tuft of salt and pepper chest hair. Rachel experienced what she had only dreamed of—a man who took her breath away.

"Um, sure. No need to eat by yourself. Is that your car?" Rachel asked.

"Yes, guilty. My mid-life indulgence. Like it?"

"Love it! I lost sight of you on the road. Figured you were long gone. And yet, here you are."

Coincidence? Chance encounter? Whatever. Keep it light—have some fun—were the mix of messages trampling Rachel's usual, more conservative, street wise, instincts.

"Yep, here I am. The traffic's terrible today. Then again, it's always terrible on Sundays around Washington." He sat down across from Rachel and unwrapped his Big Mac.

Easy, cool, she thought, *like he sat down with strangers at McDonalds every day.*

"Only today? Do you make this trip often?" asked Rachel.

What am I doing? This isn't right. I'm in mourning. I shouldn't be enjoying myself, having lunch with a stranger. It isn't proper. What would people think? It's okay. What harm can one meal do? It's not like I'll ever see him again.

"Too often." he replied grinning and popping a french fry into his mouth. "I'm in software sales. I've got some really important clients in New York. Couldn't live there. Born and raised in Virginia Beach. Most times I fly, but this week I've got business outside the city so driving made more sense."

"Software sales. Sounds interesting," said Rachel bemoaning the amount of food she had yet to swallow and remembering her mother chastising her for always putting too much in her mouth at one time. Swallowing so she could finally talk, she asked, "What type of software?"

"Security. You can't be too careful, you know. Hackers everywhere. Sometimes it's kids, doing it just to see if they can get through the latest firewalls," answered Beemer guy, grabbing a napkin to wipe away the Big Mac special sauce oozing from his mouth. "And sometimes, it's more dangerous. Identity theft is rampant. You'd be surprised at how many people put the most intimate details of their lives, bank account information, social security numbers and all, on their computers. Stealing secrets too."

"Secrets? What kind of secrets?" Rachel found herself curious about the secrets. She knew people kept all sorts of secrets about themselves. "You mean what they post—like on Facebook?"

"Posts are one thing and Facebook's one place. But with the cloud—"

"Cloud?"

"Yeah. It's a newer way to store files on a shared server outside of your own system. You'd be amazed at what's out there," he said, swirling his finger as he pointed upward. "Formulas, design information, patents and new projects—just about everything and anything that we used to keep locked up in files and drawers is now out there in cyberspace. And my company keeps it safe—or at least that's what we tell our clients," he chuckled, his lips spreading into an inviting smile, revealing even white teeth.

Some dentist is smiling all the way to the bank, thought Rachel.

"Sounds interesting. I'm not too tech savvy anymore. Not that I ever really was. The gadgets change so fast, it's hard to keep up. My ten year old grandson knows way more than I do." Rachel started to cough, realizing that she had just divulged personal information.

He's so easy to talk to. So he knows I have a grandson. What harm can it do?

The conversation went on and on, mostly about security and the dumb stuff people and companies did on the internet. Some of his stories were so funny, she could feel her cheeks burning from laughing so hard.

"Oh my God! I've got to go!" Rachel said as her eyes caught the time on her watch. "I don't believe we've been talking for over an hour. I don't want to hold you up anymore and I really have to get back on the road."

"This trip is usually really boring. It's been nice—really nice having someone to talk to, even if I was the one doing most of the talking."

They stood together. He piled her empty food containers onto his tray, picked up both, and waved his hand as if parting the waters to escort her away from the booth towards the door.

"Your stories made me laugh and I really needed to laugh right now," said Rachel, turning to face him as he pushed the door open for her.

He sure is easy on the eyes.

"I'm sorry. Everything okay? Anything I can do?"

"No, just family stuff. My aunt died. I'm on my way to Brooklyn for the funeral."

"I am so sorry. The death of someone you love is never easy and when there is any distance to travel you are left with a lot of idle time to think." Holding out his business card, he said, "If there is anything I can do, give me a call."

Rachel took the card as her hand found its way into his.

First touch. Warm, strong hands. Her heart jumped—a feeling she had not experienced for many, many years—a feeling so very wrong right now considering the circumstances behind their meeting.

"Thanks for the company," Rachel said as nonchalantly as she could, stuffing his card into her pocket. "Safe driving. Maybe we'll pass again on the road." She watched him get into his car, back up and drive away. Pulling his card out of her pocket, she read his name.

"Mark Rogers. Nice name, Mark Rogers."

Following his lead, she headed out behind the red Beemer. She watched him pull into the gas station just before the entrance ramp to Route 95, and waved in his direction.

Mark Rogers waved to Rachel as she went by. He watched her car turn left onto the on ramp and pick up speed. Pulling out his cell phone, he punched number one on speed dial. A female voice answered after two rings.

"Contact made. Caught up to her just before she hit Baltimore. We had lunch. Just left her. Everything's good."

"Great. I'm at the house now. Met her daughter, Jenny. Funeral is set for tomorrow. We'll stay close. Make ourselves useful."

"Sounds good. Don't over play it. And keep Jimmy in line. He's the loose cannon in the plan."

"I know. Wouldn't have been my first choice. He's a hothead—got a short fuse. Time will tell if he can do this kind of work."

"We've talked about this already."

"I know."

"Dom is staying close in case you need him."

"Yes. I see his smiling face several times a day when he checks up on me. Where are you heading?"

"Back to Florida. I'll monitor things from there. Keep in touch."

"Will do."

Ending the call, he finished filling the gas tank, got in and started the engine. He turned right and headed south, back to a private airstrip adjacent to Dulles airport.

A long, dusty six hours later Rachel opened the front door of Aunt Lil's house and walked into memories—Aunt Lil's living room. Time warp. Nothing had changed. At least ten pairs of eyes turned in her direction and all conversation stopped.

"Mima, Mima." Little Abby, her granddaughter, raced into her arms.

"My how much you've grown. Look at you! Such a little princess," said Rachel, scooping Abby up and holding her tightly.

"Hi, Mom. We were beginning to get worried. A lot of traffic?" asked Jenny as she planted a soft peck on Rachel's cheek. "Everything is all arranged for tomorrow. Want something to eat? We've got deli. Scott's gone already. You know your son, he couldn't wait. He left about an hour ago. Said he'd be back in the morning. Uncle Jake called and said he'd be here tomorrow. I told him the time for services."

Jenny was off to the kitchen before Rachel could get a word in. That was Jenny. All business, all details, little emotion. She didn't inherit the warm fuzzy genes of either David or Rachel. And any she did have, she locked away and protected with a wall that seemed impenetrable. Rachel suspected that the pain of miscarrying twice had taken its toll on Jenny and Ted's marriage. Though they now had an angel of a child in Abby, Ted and Jenny seemed more distant from one another than ever.

"Deli sounds good to me," Rachel shouted after Jenny.

"Williamsburg isn't exactly the epicenter of Jewish cuisine. Any knish?" Rachel was hoping that Jenny had remembered to get knish, a heavenly mix of caramelized onions and mashed potatoes wrapped in a flakey pastry dough and baked to golden perfection. Her mouth watered at the thought.

Rachel looked around the room. There were two or three familiar faces, then strangers. Aunt Lil was one of the last surviving members of her era. Most of her friends had passed before her. Introductions were made.

Sara, her very best friend, came out of the kitchen arms outstretched. The hug was warm, and long, and being in Sara's arms felt like home.

"My, God, I've missed you," whispered Sara in Rachel's ear. "I'm so sorry. I'm here for you for as long as you want."

"Thanks. I've missed you too." Rachel held Sara tightly, giving the tears welling up in her eyes time to pass. There would be time later for crying.

Eat first. Then shower. Then sleep.

Tomorrow was going to be a very long and very emotional day.

Chapter 2

Monday, September 30

The small chapel at the cemetery was the perfect size. There would not be a large crowd. Jenny had done a great job with all the details. Rachel would have to remember to compliment her when they had a private moment. The cemetery was just over the county line in Queens and only a few miles from Aunt Lil's Brooklyn home. The service had been set for ten o'clock to allow any morning traffic rush to pass.

The service was short and sweet. Aunt Lil was interred next to her beloved husband, Abraham. Aunt Lil hated death and the rituals surrounding it. She always said that life was to be enjoyed and sorrow was there to help you remember and appreciate the good times. She wanted people to remember her in happiness, not be sad.

She had left detailed instructions with her lawyer about what was to take place, who was to be called, and that red, blue, pink and yellow were the colors of the day for the funeral. Anything but black. No black. Sit Shiva for one day—the day of the funeral—not the traditional seven days. Then everyone was to get on with their lives. She had established a trust account to take care of all the funeral costs. When it finally happened, the details fell rapidly into place like a well-oiled machine. Sunday morning's phone call to Rachel started the dominos falling.

Wasn't it just like Aunt Lil to plan her own funeral, thought Rachel.

Rachel fidgeted in her seat. Sara, who had somehow managed to sit next to her, reached out and held her hand. Sara was like that. Able to wiggle her way in so she would be where she wanted to be—needed to be. After two bad marriages and two ugly divorces, she had managed to find her feet and garner an inner strength to survive. Both husbands had become her friends after a time. That was the amazing part, that Sara had managed to befriend them both. Then again, to Rachel's way of thinking, Sara was one amazing woman. She knew what to do, what to say, how to stand her ground and stay calm when everyone else was losing it.

"Just a few more minutes and this part will be over," whispered Sara as she squeezed Rachel's hand.

"*Yit'gadal v'yit'kadash sh'mei raba,*" Rabbi Shapiro began to recite the Mourners' Kaddish.

"Amen," came softly from those gathered.

He continued as voices strained to follow the transliteration provided for reciting the prayers in long forgotten Hebrew. There were more prayers at the grave site. Everyone stood silently as the coffin was lowered. A shovelful of dirt thrown into the grave by each mourner symbolized the physical act of saying good-bye to Aunt Lil. Emotional good-byes would be harder and the people now gathered would process her death in their own way. Then it was done. As Rachel walked back to the limo, row upon row, mile upon mile of headstones met her aimless gaze.

Gone—all these people gone. Who remembers them? Who will remember me? Maybe Jenny and Scott will come by and place a stone on my grave—keeping me in their memory. What will they remember? I pray that they remember me well, as a loving mother, as someone who had the courage to make a difference in their lives and the lives of others.

Everyone was back at Aunt Lil's home by one o'clock to sit Shiva for the remainder of the day. Familiar smells wafted over everyone. Bagels, lox, tomatoes, red onions, noodle kugel, gefilte fish, turkey, salads—*the foods of her people,* Rachel thought, in good times and in sorrow. The caterer had delivered enough food to feed a small army.

Feeling lightheaded, Rachel headed for the front porch to get some air. Her route to the door was interrupted when a hand grabbed her elbow and spun her around.

"So, Rachel, tell me, how do you like your new home? Where are you living now?"

Face to face with a frumpy looking woman dressed all in black, Rachel searched her mind, working to link a name to this person. Something Italian, a pasta brand. Then it came. Mildred Raconti, Aunt Lil's neighbor. Rachel thought she knew all of Aunt Lil's neighbors, but she couldn't remember ever meeting this woman. No matter. Aunt Lil had talked about her, how nice she was, and how she came over each evening to have tea.

"In Williamsburg, Virginia, Mrs. Raconti."

"Please, Rachel, call me Millie." Millie took Rachel's hand in her own. "Your aunt was always talking about you. Worrying about you. You were her favorite, you know. Right up till the end, she would say, *'my Rachel, she's starting out new. I hope she finds someone to share her life with.' "*

And with that, the standard question came.

"So Rachel, have you met someone special?"

"No, Mrs. Raconti...Millie. I'm not really looking for anyone. I just want to get settled in and stop getting lost when I drive around town." Rachel pulled her hand away, suppressing the growing urge to flee from this woman.

"Give it time. You're pretty. You'll meet someone. You know, it's no good to be alone. My Mel, may he rest in peace, we did everything together. Now, it's Jimmy that helps me. He was always helping your Aunt Lil, too. You've met Jimmy, yes? Jimmy...Jimmy, come meet Rachel."

At the dining room table with a plate full of food, a young man turned his head as he heard his name. Unlike his mother who was all in black, he had clearly taken Aunt Lil's dictum about colors to heart. Wearing a bright blue shirt and Mickey Mouse tie, he grabbed a bagel to top off his bounty and headed their way. Rachel was taken aback by his burly appearance. Standing about five foot nine inches tall, he looked like an overgrown wrestler. Short dark hair, piercing brown eyes, with a prominent five o'clock shadow framing his face. There was something about him that sent an uneasy chill up Rachel's spine. He just didn't look like the type to own, let alone wear, a Mickey Mouse tie.

"Hi, Rachel," Jimmy said as he extended his hand. "Your Aunt Lil talked about you so much, I feel like I've known you for years."

"Hi, Jimmy. It's nice to meet you. I really want to thank you for being here for Aunt Lil. Whenever I asked her if she needed anything, she would tell me there was a nice young man next door that helped her with stuff. I guess that was you."

"Glad to do it. This is a great house. Really old, but it has so much potential. She'd call when the plumbing acted up or a bulb needed changing. My mom says I can fix anything and everything so anything you need, I'm your guy," said Jimmy as he stuffed a huge piece of kugel into his mouth.

"Good to know. Thanks. Excuse me, won't you. I just need a bit of air."

Rachel walked away without waiting for any response. Opening the front door, she pushed on the screen door and stepped out onto the porch, desperately wanting a few minutes to herself. Feeling woozy, she grabbed the porch railing. Taking a deep breath and trying to steady herself, she was disappointed to find the porch already occupied.

Crap.

"You okay?" asked the stranger.

"Yes, I'm fine. I'm sorry. I'm just a little tired I guess. The drive up. The people. I wasn't expecting so many people to be here last night when I got in. And today—"

"I'm Ben. Ben Collins. You're Rachel, right? I'm your aunt's lawyer. Well, really my dad was your aunt's lawyer. He died last year and I took over his practice."

Extending her hand, Rachel said, "It's nice to meet you. Aunt Lil talked a lot about your dad. She really liked him. Said he had an honest face." Rachel leaned back against one of the large white columns, hoping it would support her, like it did the roof above.

Ben reached out to steady her. His hand grasped her arm with a gentle strength. Rachel turned to look at the man preventing her from falling. Warm puddles of brown with flecks of honey gold and long lashes most women would kill for met her eyes. Not quite six feet tall, a mass of brown hair with a stray piece falling across his forehead, he was well built, someone who clearly took pride in his appearance.

"I think I need to sit down," she said as she headed for the steps. Ben backed away and disappeared into the house. Rachel felt the tears she had been holding back all morning rising and her throat tightening again. She held her face in her hands and let the tears flow, grateful for finally having a few minutes to herself.

The screen door swung open. Rachel bit her lip, resenting the intrusion into her few minutes of solitude. She could tell it was the lawyer. His tasseled loafers were a dead giveaway. Funny, her David wouldn't have been caught dead in shoes like these. On this guy, they somehow fit.

"Here," he said offering her a tissue, "and sip this." With perfectly manicured nails, he handed her a glass of wine. "I took a guess on white, but I can get you red if you want. Mind if I join you?" Ben sat down beside her without waiting for an answer. He stared out to the street for a long minute.

"My dad thought the world of your aunt. He used to say she was one of a kind, that they didn't make them like her anymore. Strong. Kind. A passion for living. He would tell me all these stories about her. And I would think he was making them up. Then last year when I met her, she started to tell me her stories firsthand. All the stories about her trip here, her family. She was amazing." His gaze never left the street.

"I spent many days, years really, listening to her stories too," said Rachel also finding a certain peace in staring off into space. "She encouraged me, inspired me to be someone special, to never stop chasing my dreams." Smoothing out an unseen wrinkle on her pants, Rachel drew in a long breath of air. "I guess I didn't really listen all that well. I stopped chasing my dreams years ago. I think that's what made her so mad at me. Mad in a loving sort of way. She thought I gave up. When I told her I sold the house and was moving away she was so happy for me. She knew she'd be alone, that I wouldn't be here to visit every day or so, but she was happy for me."

There was a long silence. Wisely, Ben said nothing.

"It's hard to remember your dreams in the heat of everyday life." Rachel's voice cracked. "One minute you're young and just starting out. You blink and it's all gone, done. You're old…too old to…."

Rachel abruptly stopped talking.

What am I doing? I'm spilling my guts to a total stranger. Who is this guy?

She turned and actually looked at Ben as if for the very first time. She worked to absorb the details of him. Her eyes made a circle of his face, isolating his features. Straight, very Anglo nose, warm brown eyes, chiseled cheek bones with just a hint of dimples. His cleft chin made his slightly crooked smile very appealing. Handsome man. He had a distinguished, very sophisticated air.

Feeling her face flush and an unfamiliar shiver along her spine, Rachel worked to give meaning to disparate sensations. Caution embraced her. She jumped up fast, so fast she spilled some of the wine over her hand.

"Shit. I'm sorry. Pardon my French. Thanks for the wine." She turned and walked into the house, feeling very naked, like she had just exposed herself in public.

The rest of the day was a blur of the usual platitudes— *'I'm so sorry for your loss'* followed by *'We'll miss her at mah jongg'* and *'I didn't really know your aunt very well.'* It was early evening by the time everyone finally left. What had been a crisp fall day slowly transitioned to night. The setting sun cast a warm pink aura around the infamous New York skyscrapers on the horizon. Rachel crossed her arms and pulled her sweater tightly around her as she stood on the porch waving good-bye to Jenny and Ted.

Only Sara remained. Standing next to her on the porch, Sara's reassuring hand found its way to Rachel's shoulder. Rachel laid her hand on top. No words passed between them. None were necessary. Sara silently slipped away into the house.

Thank God for Sara, thought Rachel.

That's what best friends do. Show up in good times and in bad. No one could have—would have—ever predicted their friendship. Two women with so little in common. Sara was all business, all career and ex-husbands. Rachel was stay-at-home mom until the kids were at school full time. The paralegal job she found was a few blocks from the kids' school. She took it with the stipulation that she would have the same hours as her kids.

When the kids got involved in after-school sports, Rachel had more time. She joined ORT, believing that fundraising for a world-wide Jewish educational outreach organization was a worthy cause. And with the work came two unexpected benefits. First, she learned how to play mah jongg, an ancient Chinese game embraced by Jewish immigrants on the lower east side of New York in the 1920s. She joined the mah jongg league from her ORT chapter and was now totally addicted to the game.

And benefit number two—Sara. As she and Sara worked on committees and played mah jongg each week, they shared their lives in ways that only women do. And slowly a friendship blossomed, one that now required no words.

Rachel was thankful Sara was there. Had Jenny stayed to help it would have been a calculated exercise in how quickly and efficiently everything could be cleaned up. With Sara, there would be laughter and talk and wine and the mess would somehow take care of itself, in its own sweet time rather than at Jenny's drill sergeant pace. That's what she needed right now—time—time alone in this house that held so many wonderful memories and had been her refuge as a little girl.

She thought back to her own childhood in what would now be labeled as a dysfunctional family. Having Aunt Lil living so close by eased the tensions in her own home. She always seemed to know just the right time to call with the invitation for Rachel to come for a visit. And Rachel would gleefully run down the block into Aunt Lil's embrace. They would play and talk and dream together. Aunt Lil always told her that she could be anyone she wanted to be.

Why hadn't I listened? Why hadn't I believed her? Why was the negative stuff—the constant litany of my shortcomings—easier to believe?

Locking the front door behind her, Rachel walked into the living room and stood silently, taking it all in. As she remembered, the room itself was the epitome of comfort. Aunt Lil wanted people to feel welcome and safe in her home. The flowered wallpaper had long ago lost its brilliance, appearing dark and dingy after so many years. The cream colored moldings had many layers of paint taking the edge off the intricate carvings that people were paying dearly to replicate today. None of that plastic covered furniture for Aunt Lil. There were two club chairs and two sofas in an eclectic mix of fabrics with deep cushions that you sank into when you sat down, and gold filigree lamps with hand-painted floral glass globes. Surely, these pieces would provide comfort to a new family.

Moving beyond the actual furnishings, Rachel's mind flickered from memory to memory as her gaze wandered around the room. There were family pictures everywhere. Holidays were celebrated here. She could still see a trace of the wine stain on the rug from that Passover when she, her brother Jake, and their cousin had swapped their grape juice for Manischewitz. At ten, she could not hold her wine. None of them could. They all got so sick. She and Jake had been punished when they got home, well out of Aunt Lil's hearing and her ability to intercede.

"Here." Sara handed Rachel a glass of wine. "Let's just sit awhile. All of this clean up can wait," said Sara, waving her hand at the empty plates and glasses scattered about. "How are you doing?"

"Numb really. She wasn't sick. We just talked on Saturday and I would have been calling her within the hour, before I went out. And then the phone rang. Sara, I felt it…when the phone rang…I knew something was wrong. How did I know that?"

"It's that Gypsy blood you're always boasting you have. Like when we play mah jongg, and you wave your hand over the tiles and say joker—joker—joker. You pick up your tile and I see that look on your face and I know you got one. Explain that and you can explain how you knew the phone call was bad news."

"It's just that she wasn't sick. She'd just had a physical. She told me the doctor said she'd live to a hundred. And then she keels over and dies instantly. It doesn't make sense."

"Doctors always say that. Death never makes sense. It comes too soon for some and waits too long for others. That's why you have to do the things you want to do. Not wait. Not hope. Just do."

"Isn't that the truth. Aunt Lil was always pushing me to strike out. There's a sign on the bulletin board at my gym— you know, one of those cutesy sayings—something like if you want things to be different, you have to do something different. Guess moving was the beginning of my push to bring something different into my life. Just wish I had been here when she needed me. She was always there for me. I feel like I let her down."

Sara held her tongue. There was really no response to what Rachel was saying. In time, she'd come to realize she had not let her aunt down. There they sat, wallowing in the silent comfort that only best friends can offer one another.

An odd squeak broke the silence.

"What was that?" asked Sara, jolting to full awareness.

"It sounded like it came from the kitchen." Rachel slowly

got off the sofa. "Stay here." Even as the words left her lips she knew that wasn't going to happen.

Detouring through the front hallway, Rachel grabbed one of Aunt Lil's sleek wooden canes with the brass head of a dog from the umbrella stand. Born cautious, Rachel also pulled her cell phone from her pocket. She held it tightly. Pressed nine-one-one. Her thumb hovered over the send button.

Slowly, she made her way down the hallway to the kitchen. Palms sweating. Heart pounding.

I locked the back door, didn't I?

"Oh!" A sharp cry left her lips as she confronted Jimmy Raconti in the small alcove just off the kitchen.

"Oh, I'm sorry I scared you," said Jimmy sheepishly. "Mom sent me over to check and make sure the heat went on. The furnace has been giving your aunt trouble. And the TV weather people said it was going to get cold tonight."

"How did you get in?" Rachel hit the red end button on her cell and slipped it into her pocket. She leaned the cane against the basement doorjamb. "I'm sure I checked that door a little while ago and it was locked."

"Really? The door wasn't locked. I knocked but when no one answered I figured you had already gone to bed. I was just going to check on the furnace. Then let myself out and lock it when I left."

Rachel stepped back into the kitchen to create more space between them. Something about this guy made her nervous. She could feel Sara's presence behind her.

Thank God for Sara!

"You know, this lock's been giving your aunt problems for years. It was on my list of things to fix, just didn't get around to it. You have to jiggle it to make sure the bolt goes all the way. Otherwise, it seems locked but isn't. That's probably what happened," offered Jimmy, hoping he was living up to his billing as a nice, helpful sort of guy.

Fighting the knot in the pit of her stomach, Rachel garnered her courage, took a step forward and reached around Jimmy to grab the doorknob. She opened the back door and put her hand on Jimmy's arm, guiding him toward it.

"Thanks for your concern, Jimmy. We're fine, really. I'm sure we won't get too cold and I know where my aunt keeps the extra blankets. I'll make sure we both have plenty before we go to bed. Good night. Thanks again."

With that, she maneuvered Jimmy out the door. Closing it firmly, she turned the lock. Rachel stepped back and stared at the door for a moment. She reached out, twisted the knob and pulled the door to make sure it was locked securely.

"What was that all about?" asked Sara. "I'm sure you locked that door."

"I am too. Did you hear him say he was coming by to check on the furnace and that the lock doesn't always catch?"

"Yeah. Sounded lame to me."

"There is just something about him. He gives me the creeps."

"Me too. That excuse—trying to be helpful? You have got to be kidding me!"

Sara walked back into the kitchen and pulled one of the straight back kitchen chairs away from the table. Dragging it into the alcove, she positioned it under the knob like she'd seen people do in countless movies.

Meeting Rachel's eyes, she said, "Just in case the lock doesn't work right, like he claims. First thing tomorrow, we call a locksmith."

Sara's hand reached for the light switch to turn off the porch and alcove lights. Rachel stopped her. Eyes met eyes.

Understanding arced between them like lightening connecting from sky to ground.

"Let's leave them both on. The more light the better tonight. I'm sure my aunt's estate can handle the extra electric bill. Want some tea?"

"The hell with tea. More wine please. Tomorrow is going to be another long day. You said the lawyer was coming Thursday to read the will?"

"That's what he told me before he left."

"I love will readings. Seeing the expressions on people's faces when they hear what they get. Or not!"

Laughing, the two women headed back into the kitchen to refill their glasses.

"That was fast," said Millie as Jimmy came through the back door.

"They were still awake and heard the door squeak. I knew I should have fixed that fucking door. They got me just as I was heading down into the basement. I made an excuse about the furnace. Really lame. What else could I do?"

"Now what? Any ideas how you're going to get into the house and continue to search it?"

Jimmy pushed past Mille, opened the refrigerator and pulled out a beer. "Don't know. Let's give her a day or two. Then I'll go back over and see if she needs any help. We don't want to be too pushy. She's not stupid."

Taking a big swig, he leaned back against the kitchen counter. He just stared into space, searching for divine insight. He needed a plan, a way to get back into the house. What he got was a replay of his crappy life.

Stupidity and poor planning got him caught on camera when he ripped off a mini-mart years ago. Fortunately, he never actually pulled out the gun he was carrying in his pocket. What the camera caught, and his public defender explained away, was a hand in a pocket with a finger pointing giving the impression of a gun. All for a crummy three hundred dollars! Didn't think the store would even have a camera or that the old man who owned it would be the father of a local cop. That was one pissed cop, furious that someone dared to rob his father. He was out for blood. He just wouldn't let go until the perps were brought to justice. Some justice.

His public defender was young, slick. Could probably have charmed the stripes off a tiger. The whole affair had been treated as a class A misdemeanor. Got six months probation and the lawyer finagled a way to get his records sealed.

That's how they met. The lawyer and the street kid. How it all started. Funny how both of their careers had blossomed. The lawyer left the PD's office and established a thriving private practice defending better paying clients. But he never let Jimmy forget that he owed him—big time. Since then he'd done a few jobs for the guy. More than a few really. Too many to count. He was the guy's go-to thief. And now he couldn't get out from under this asshole lawyer's thumb.

Millie Raconti stared too. There was a time when a different kind of life had been dangled before her. Or so she thought. Young, pretty and gullible—hallmarks of country girls who craved a life of fortune and fame in the big city. She believed the guy when he said that her high cheek bones and deep, exotic looking eyes were perfect for a modeling career. The photos he took trapped her into another kind of career. She freed herself from that life really fast. It wasn't pretty, but it was over, done. And, along with some carefully selected new found friends, a new life had begun.

Her eyes landed on Jimmy. Loser. Shit for brains. Sexy

swagger that the bimbos he hung with and slept with loved. His looks were fading fast. A growing beer belly was slowly replacing his six-pack abs with flab. She knew he saw this job as his graduation from petty street crimes to more involved cons. When they all first met to talk about the job, he had bragged that he had a lawyer guardian angel watching out for him at every turn. He got Jimmy off on the small stuff when he got caught. And when the going got rough, the lawyer would foot the bill so Jimmy could disappear for a few months.

"I'm heading out for the night. I'm stopping at the deli for a sandwich. Do you want anything?" asked Millie. "I can drop something off for you if you want."

"Nah. Just go. I'll see you in the morning. Will reading's Thursday. We'll be our usual helpful selves."

Glad Millie was gone, Jimmy sat in the dark for what seemed like hours. He hated it when one of his plans fell apart. Damn it. Why did the aunt have to wake up and see him? Scared the shit out of him when she screamed. Scared her, too—to death. Never believed you could scare someone to death. This old lady made a believer out of him. He'd looked it up on the internet.

What the fuck—it's really possible—someone can be scared to death. Who knew?

Fortunately, no one heard her scream. He'd had his hands full getting her down to the kitchen. Stood her up next to the sink and let her go so she'd drop to the floor in a more natural position. Smashed a tea cup next to her body so that the scene would match the story he'd tell when the paramedics arrived. Waited until a decent hour and then called nine-one-one.

Things would move quickly now. It could all get away from him really fast. After the will got read Thursday morning and everything got sorted out, he guessed it would be a short time between emptying the house of stuff and selling it. His window of opportunity was getting smaller by the minute.

Chapter 3

Thursday, October 3

"Let's get started," said Ben Collins.

Looking very professional in a beautifully tailored dark gray pinstriped suit, crisp white shirt, silver cufflinks, and marbled purple tie, Ben Collins stood at the head of the dining room table, reading glasses perched on his nose. They were honoring another one of Aunt Lil's requests; that her will be read in her home, not a cold lawyer's office and that it be done within the week of her death so that everyone could move on with their lives.

When he first entered the room, Rachel and Sara exchanged glances. Rachel knew they were thinking, or really fantasizing about, the very same thing. This is one good looking man. They were retired, not dead.

Jenny and her husband Ted, along with Scott and his wife April, were also seated around the table anticipating some small acknowledgement of their love and affection for their dear, now departed aunt. Rachel's brother, Jake, had called just before ten o'clock to say that something came up and he would not be coming. If Aunt Lil left him anything, she should send it to him. So much for family. Mrs. Raconti and Jimmy stood by the kitchen doorway.

Rachel was unsure why they were there. They both arrived an hour ago, arms full of bagels, cream cheese, and more deli; like they belonged in this intimate family gathering. Considering having food to serve after the will reading was a total oversight on her part, Rachel was grateful. But she could not shake a nagging feeling about the two of them.

Ben cleared his throat. "As you may know, will readings are usually done in a lawyer's office. I want to thank Rachel for honoring her aunt's request to have it here, in Aunt Lil's home. It is so fitting and more in keeping with the wonderful, loving woman that she was. My father was the lawyer of record when this document was prepared."

He began reading.

'I, Lillian Beth Steinmetz, being of sound mind, declare this document to be my last will and testament. This is the only will I have ever prepared. I appoint my niece Rachel Rebecca Resnick as Executrix of my estate.

I leave all of my property and all of my worldly possessions not already jointly owned by myself and my niece, Rachel Rebecca Resnick to said niece, Rachel Rebecca Resnick. She is directed to pay any and all taxes required by law. She is entrusted to make all decisions about the disposal of my property, now her property, in any way she deems fit. I am confident that her loving heart will guide her actions.

I have signed this will on this day, December 20, 2001. Lillian Beth Steinmetz.'

Silence.

"That's it, Rachel. Your Aunt Lil left everything to you." With a wave of his hands, Ben encircled the space. "The house and all of its contents, it's all yours."

"Jenny and Scott," said Rachel, drawing everyone's eyes to her, "rather than go back and redo her will, Aunt Lil prepared these gifts for each of you as a token of her love."

Rachel walked around the table and handed each of her children a crisp white envelope with their name clearly typed on it. Neither one opened the envelopes, just laid them down on the table.

It was done. As she walked back to her seat, Rachel pressed her hand against her side, feeling the presence of the secret stash that she had tucked safely in her pocket, close to her body less than an hour ago.

"Any questions?" Ben asked facing Rachel and moving around the table, making eye contact with each person.

Seeing no questions in the eyes of those present, Ben continued. "As you may know, your Aunt Lil had a separate account to take care of all funeral expenses so don't concern yourself with those. Handing Rachel a manila envelope, he said, "Here are copies of her bank papers, trust account records and other documents and your copy of the will. I'll file a copy at the court house later when I'm downtown. Thanks for coming everyone."

No one moved. An eerie silence hung over the dining room.

"I'll get the coffee," said Sara to break the silence. Standing up and heading for the kitchen she added, "Jenny come help me get things ready. Who wants decaf?"

As Sara and Jenny left for the kitchen, Rachel pulled out a copy of the will. She looked at the date. December 20, 2001—a few months after 9/11. Aunt Lil had been grief stricken as she stood on her porch and watched the towers burning. Coming down. All those people—gone. The horror of it all.

Rachel remembered talking to her that night. It was one of the only times Rachel could remember that her aunt had been so caught up in death and how fast it could happen. In the blink of an eye. Ashes to ashes. She had contacted her lawyer, Andrew, Ben's father, right after the disaster, established the trust, made Rachel a joint trustee, and made the will so there would be no questions about who got what or what to do. She knew Rachel would ensure her wishes would be followed.

Another two hours of mindless chatter came and went before everyone said their good-byes, gave hugs and kisses all around and left.

Enjoying the crisp fall air, Sara and Rachel again stood together on the front porch waving to Jenny and Ted who were the last to leave.

"How are they doing?" asked Sara.

"More of the same. Arguments, punctuated by long silences, followed by more arguments. It's not good. Something is very broken there. Ted's tried, but Jenny won't go to marriage counseling. Says it's a waste of money they don't have. I don't say too much. Don't want to interfere— have her think I'm taking Ted's side. Only time will tell whether what's wrong between them can be fixed."

As the car moved out of view, Rachel knew that Jenny would start a fight on the way home about what a waste of time this morning had been. She'd open the envelope and be disappointed that she didn't get more. Ted would defend coming, saying that being there was the proper thing to do. This would make Jenny even angrier.

Scott couldn't have cared less. How different brother and sister were. He and April had left right after the will reading was over. He distanced himself from most things that were family related. He just wasn't a family type of guy. Rachel could never really figure out why he had ever married, let alone had a child. And there was another on the way. And of course, her brother Jake, was his usual no-show self.

As she and Sara walked back into the front hallway, they heard noise coming from the kitchen.

The slump of Rachel's shoulders told Sara all she needed to know. She had not seen the neighbors leave. Mrs. Raconti and her son were still here, back there, trying to be helpful.

"Stay here. Let me. I'll get rid of them," said Sara with a tad too much glee in her voice. As she watched Sara walk down the hallway, Rachel was again grateful for her friend. The last thing she wanted to do right now was deal with the overly helpful neighbors.

"Mrs. Raconti, there you are," said Sara. "We really want to thank you so much for all you have done. Both of you. Rachel and I can take it from here. Cleaning up will give us something to do—Rachel something to do as she comes to grips with Aunt Lil's passing."

As she was talking Sara was corralling both of them towards the front hallway and the door. There was no way they could protest. She was good at this.

Rachel was waiting patiently to receive them at the front door. Her arms outstretched, she offered both a calculated hug. Placing one hand on each upper arm, each hug was respectful, but not too close.

"Thank you so much, Mrs. Raconti. And you too, Jimmy. Both of you have been so helpful."

"Millie, dear, call me Millie. And if there is anything you need, you just let us know. How long are you planning to stay?"

"I'm not sure at this point." Pausing for a moment, she added, "Definitely through the end of next week. I think I need to look around a bit and get a better idea of all that's here. Then I'll figure out how best to donate or sell what I don't want to keep."

"My Jimmy, he knows this house inside and out. He'll be

more then happy to help you move stuff and sort through everything if you want," offered Mrs. Raconti.

"Thank you. And you too, Jimmy. I'll be sure to call if I need anything."

With that she closed the front door for a second time. Now, they were finally alone. Thank God!

"Nothing. She left me nothing," said Millie as they walked around to the back door of their house. "All that time wasted. You would think she'd of left me a pin or other piece of jewelry. I'd dropped so many hints at the stuff I liked when I was helping her. But no. Nothing. Everything to Rachel."

"What the fuck are you rambling about? Quit your bitching. She's blood. You're not. And besides getting something in the will was never part of the plan. You know that."

"Rachel may be blood, but I'm the one who gave blood, sweat and tears to that old woman. Where was Rachel, or any of them for that matter, when she was lonely and needed someone to talk to, to listen to her stories, to have tea and keep her company and get her groceries. I'm the one who cared and what do I get for all my troubles? Bupkes! Nothing!"

"Shut up. I've gotta think," fumed Jimmy. "I've got to figure something out. See if you can get your friend on the phone in case he has any ideas about what to do now."

Looking at his face, his dark eyes getting tighter and tighter, she could almost smell the anger brewing inside him. Reckless, especially when he felt cornered, angry or challenged, it was only a matter of time before he took out his growing frustrations on whoever was in front of him. *Better to be out of his sight right now,* she thought as she watched him go inside. She had no intention of becoming his target of opportunity.

Now that the aunt was dead, his recklessness could become a huge problem. If they were not careful, it could get them both in tons of trouble. Time would tell about the success of this job. For now, let him think what he wants to about her. From the moment she met him, she knew he was wrong for the job. Bringing him into this con was a huge mistake—one she hoped did not have a tragic end.

Better to stay out here, enjoy the afternoon sunshine. Let him sulk by himself. She sat down on the top step and pulled her cell phone out of her pocket. Hitting number one on speed dial, she heard it start to ring. Time to call in with a status report and discuss new options.

Walking into the house, Jimmy grabbed a beer and headed for the back parlor. Sinking into the lone, old brown arm chair, he took a fortifying swig, grabbed the remote and started channel surfing. He stopped at Pawn Stars reruns on the History channel. Cradling the beer bottle to his chest, he settled in to watch people making deals.

That's what he saw himself doing, making deals. Already doing some small deals here and there. Spreading the goods he took around at pawn shops in Queens and Staten Island. Not too much in one place. Didn't need nosy people asking too many questions. The small items he had already pawned had proven to be quite lucrative in fact. Old people had great stuff. Lil's stuff definitely made him money.

And then there was the grand prize—diamonds. Lil was mentally sharp most times, but when she was tired and they got her reminiscing, she would slip into a time long ago, telling her stories almost like an out-of-body experience, babbling on, talking about diamonds. He wondered whether she really had the diamonds they were searching for. Did they exist or were they a figment of an old lady's imagination?

His search had been haphazard up to this point. A little here, a little there over the last few weeks. Every time she had called him in to fix something he would search. Millie would keep her company in the evening, crush up some Ambien or Lunesta and slip it into her tea. She'd sleep like a baby while he searched. Lil had not invited Millie over for tea the last few nights before she died. He couldn't figure out why. He kept forgetting to ask her, but it didn't really matter at this point. Lil was dead.

He'd done a cursory sweep of most of the main floor, but he needed to do a more thorough search. Every closet overflowed with boxes. Each one had to be checked thoroughly. If there were diamonds in that house, he needed to be more methodical and for that he needed time in the house. Time alone, undisturbed.

Chapter 4

Ben hit the road for Atlantic City after completing his official duties at the county clerk's office. Leaving on Thursday afternoon, before the Belt Parkway and the Garden State turned into ugly parking lots would shorten his drive time and give him more time at the tables.

He was feeling lucky. But then again, isn't that how every weekend started, with him feeling lucky. Brenda, his ex-wife, had nagged him relentlessly about his so called luck. That was then, when he was young, dumb and stupid. So much had happened since he and Brenda split.

"Don't go there," he warned himself out loud as he crossed the Verrazano with the lower Manhattan skyline in clear view off to his right.

The images of the towers falling haunted him. Elena, the love of his life, had worked in the North Tower. Meeting her had helped him turn his life around after his divorce. She brought out the best in him. He was becoming the man he always wanted to be with her at his side. His hopes and dreams crumbled that day.

Don't think about it. Keep your eyes on the road. Focus on the now. Don't think about anything but winning. And he was planning on winning big this weekend, getting lucky in more ways than one.

Ben knew he had a gambling problem. But he couldn't stop. His thinking was always the same. *This next hand will be different. This time I'll win.* Every time he got close to a big score and digging himself out, he'd go bust and get in deeper. He'd been in the hole for months—owed over three hundred and fifty thousand dollars to his financial benefactor, Alfonso D'Angeli, aka Big Al. *Financial benefactor, my ass* thought Ben. *Big Al's a loan shark. Like lipstick on a pig. No fancy title changes anything.*

At five foot seven inches and one hundred and sixty pounds, Big Al blended into the background like a million other middle-aged men. Most people would not give him a second glance. Translucent blue eyes were his best feature. At times, they were piercingly cold, cutting through you like knives. At other times, in the softest of light, they radiated their own unique glow, making you drop any guard you may try to employ. Big Al's craftsmanship—hurting people—was legendary, making him a very dangerous man to cross. Owing him money scared the shit out of Ben.

As Ben drove along the Garden State Parkway, his mind clicked into replay mode—last week's encounter with Big Al the feature film. A quick shower and change of clothes had Ben shedding his lawyer gig—mentally and physically. Refreshed and dressed in a white silk shirt, black slacks and tailored gray jacket, he headed out, ready for a night of gambling and fun.

The hallway had been deserted. After pressing elevator button, he positioned himself in front of the shiny brass elevator doors to admire his reflection. Just as the elevator pinged its arrival, the stairway door opened. He was no longer alone. Two muscular men literally lifted him into the elevator. He never saw them coming which proved to be the most unsettling part.

"If I might have a moment of your time, Ben," said Big Al as the elevator doors closed.

With these words barely out of Al's mouth, one of his companions depressed the red stop button. The other guy did due diligence with a swift pat down of Ben's person to ensure that he wasn't carrying. Big Al was all about perceptions and appearances. His companions were all about results.

"We have a little matter to discuss. I'm sure you can appreciate my position. It's been a few weeks and I've received nothing in the way of payment." Big Al's soothing tone belied the power of possible future actions.

"It's been hard these last few weeks, Mr. D'Angeli," said Ben, his mouth dry. Small sweat beads formed at his hairline. "You know I'm good for it. I've always paid my debts in the past. I just need a little more time. I'm feeling really confident right now. After tonight, I'll be able to repay the full amount."

"That would be nice and it would be a good thing for you to do—really—a good thing. You're a nice guy, Ben. I like you. But I'm sure you can understand. I'm a business man. And this," quipped Al with a flourish of his hand in the air, "well...it's just business."

The threat behind his words was real. Ben remembers thinking that no one overhearing what was transpiring in the now stopped elevator could have mistaken it for a normal business conversation. Then again, in Big Al's line of work, it was totally normal.

"Let's plan to meet Sunday afternoon, say around four o'clock, for a quick drink before you head home. That way we can complete our business and you can get on the road and miss most of the traffic."

Ben licked his dry lips. "That sounds like a plan. The lobby bar at four o'clock then. Wish me luck." What else could he have said? You didn't say *no* to Big Al.

Their private meeting was over in moments. The elevator jerked into motion, stopped at the next floor and Al and his companions were gone. Ben took a deep breath. His armpits were soaked. He remembered thinking he needed another shower. But the tables were calling his name.

Getting off at the diamond level, the private floor reserved for special players, Ben approached the tables. He ordered a double vodka martini from a passing hostess to calm his nerves. His plan to switch from baccarat to craps hoping his luck would change worked. An hour in and his chip pile stood tall. The dice were sizzling hot in his hands.

Sunday's meeting with Big Al went as well as could be expected. Money changed hands—two hundred and fifty large. While he wasn't out of the hole, as Big Al got up to leave he expressed confidence that Ben would be able to clear the remaining debt soon. Ben stayed behind. He needed a drink—a strong one.

Shaking his head, he stopped the replay. Speeding along the Garden State Parkway, he vowed that this weekend was going to be different. Applying some mental gymnastics, he shifted into a winning frame of mind. A broad smiled crossed his face. The big winner of the week so far was one very lovely lady named Rachel Resnick. She had just inherited a nice chunk of change. Thinking about her caused a twitch between his legs.

Her aunt, Lillian Steinmetz, one of his father's former clients, died last Sunday. He got the message when he showed up at his office Monday morning. Mrs. Steinmetz had left instructions that all details concerning her death were to be concluded quickly. He'd made a Shiva call Monday afternoon to pay his respects. That was when he met Rachel. This morning he read the will at a small family gathering at her aunt's home. Most of the family members gathered were very disappointed. They got very little. Rachel got it all.

Rachel…now there was one classy lady, Ben thought, the direct opposite of his Atlantic City weekend squeezes or his current lady love, Jolene. Could Rachel be someone he could cultivate a relationship with? It could sure solve a lot of his immediate financial problems, or at least give him more time to maneuver.

Wisely, her aunt had made sure that Rachel's name was on everything—everything jointly owned. No probate here. She was not going to get stuck paying all sorts of death and estate taxes to the good old state of New York. And while Mrs. Steinmetz was not loaded, she did have a sizable bank account, some stocks and, of course, there was the house and all of its contents. All of its contents—those actually seen and accounted for and those only hinted at.

Ben knew a little about Rachel from his visits with her aunt. What he had not expected were her good looks. Unlike most of the women of a certain age that Ben knew, Rachel had taken care of herself. While he was a sucker for redheads, Rachel's long, chestnut brown hair had enticing hints of red and gold highlights that reeled him in and captured his attention. He caught a whiff of jasmine when he rushed over to keep her from falling when she stepped onto the porch for some air after the funeral. And then there were those eyes—big and golden brown. He found himself mesmerized when she spoke and actually had to stare at something else to keep his concentration on what she was saying. Kind of a soft, vulnerable charm.

Older yes, but being with an older woman can have its advantages. Something he could exploit, perhaps. How could he make it work?

Ending his business arrangement with Big Al was his more pressing problem. How to actually do that—unknown. Once guys like Big Al had their hooks in you it was next to impossible to get out. There had to be a way—and a relationship with Rachel might prove to be his golden ticket. He'd have to be careful. Not too obvious. He could step in now and offer his services so he could continue in some small way to take care of Lil's finances. Minimize the number of curious eyes that reviewed her accounts. Keep control. That might work.

All thoughts stopped as he navigated the ramp from the Garden State to the Atlantic City Expressway. The colored lights of the hotel towers lit up the darkness, beckoning to him. Yep, he was feeling lucky.

Chapter 5

Friday, October 4

"Sara, you've been here almost a week. How much longer can you stay?" asked Rachel as she poured coffee for Sara who looked like she could use several more hours of sleep. They had both slept late. It was more like lunch time than breakfast.

"I'm here as long as you want. I'm retired, remember? Got nothing else to do. We can have some girl time, catch up, and see what we have here. Reminds me of my grandma's house. Way cool. What are you going to do with all this stuff?"

With that, Rachel burst into tears. Deep, guttural sobs echoed through the house. Her entire body shook. She was clearly crying for more than the loss of Aunt Lil.

"Come here." Sara's arms were around her as if somehow their mere presence could hold Rachel's changing world together. They just stood there, in the kitchen, clinging to each other, each swaying to her own private internal longings.

"This has got to look weird," said Rachel, as the tension eased and she started to calm down.

"Who cares?" Sara reached for the tissue box above the sink.

"God, that felt good," Rachel whimpered as she sat down at the kitchen table.

"You've been holding that in for a long, long time. Want to tell me about it?" asked Sara, handing Rachel the tissues.

"I can't remember the last time I cried like that. Not even when David died."

Sara remained quiet, leaning against the counter at the sink.

"It's so many things. I don't know where to start. David dying when we still had so many plans. Jenny's disapproval of me selling the house. Aunt Lil dying so suddenly. All this," she said, waving her hands through the air. "I feel like the walls are closing in. Like I'm in someone else's life and not having a very good time. I know I have to stop seeing everything through the prism of yesterday and simply enjoy my today's. Shit! That's why I moved. I want to start again. I want more time. I want my life back…but different"

"Yeah, we all want that—our lives to be all they could have been and not the crap we settled for. Knowing what we know now, if we had it to do again, we'd do it all differently." Sara stopped. "Or would we? We've become the people we are through the experiences that we've had. You wouldn't be you without your past. I wouldn't be me." Sara let her words hang in the air. "Want more coffee? Or something a little stronger?"

"Wine sounds good to me. Shit. It's five o'clock somewhere."

"Red or white?" asked Sara as she pulled two wine glasses from the drying rack behind her.

"White. Red gives me a migraine."

Sara filled the glasses and handed one to Rachel. Soon her nose was in the fridge.

"Yum. Leftovers."

She emerged with a turkey leg in her hand and one in her mouth. She handed one to Rachel.

"Be fair. You had a great life. David loved you and you loved him. Both of your kids are doing well. They've got their issues, but what married couples don't. Not like my bum of a son. Did I tell you Howie moved home again?"

"No. What's up with him?"

"Same old, same old. Lost another job. Nothing is ever good enough for Howie. Thinks he's the smartest guy in the room—in the world. Gets old fast."

"Sorry. They may move out. They may grow up. But your kids are your kids forever."

"Ain't that the truth. Anyway, you'll see. We'll do what we have to do here. You'll go back home and turn the page. The sadness will pass and you'll focus on the good memories of your aunt. You'll start a next chapter, not a new life because you are in the middle of the one you have, but a next chapter. If you want, I'll come down for a few days next month."

"That would be great. We could go shopping, play some mahj, shop some more."

Sara picked at the turkey leg.

"You know, a friend of my ex-husband, Marv, deals in antiques and buys estates. He's down in Philly, but I can call him to see if he's interested in any of your aunt's stuff or knows someone locally we can call."

"Sounds good. There are some things I need to find— special things I want to keep. And, we need to go through things—get a sense of what's here—carefully. My aunt always said that when she died nothing left the house without a thorough once over. She used to tell me stories about a friend of hers dying and her children finding money squirreled away everywhere."

"A guy I used to work with found twenty thousand dollars in cash hidden in the hem of an old blue coat when one of his aunts died," said Sara. "He said they tore the house apart after that."

"Great. There's nothing I like better in times of grief then a good treasure hunt. It'll give me something to focus on," said Rachel as she stood up, grabbed her wine and the turkey leg she'd been picking at, and headed into the living room.

"There's nothing like leftover turkey to bring out the hound dog in you," laughed Sara as she took another bite, grabbed two plates and some napkins, and followed Rachel down the hall. "At least the nosy neighbors were good for something. They brought the food."

"Good point." Rachel set her glass down on the old pie table near an overstuffed club chair. Stuffing the turkey leg into her mouth to free her hands, she pulled over the ottoman so she could put her feet up. Her immediate goal was to become one with the chair for a few minutes, to let it support her as she got ready for what lay ahead.

"First we drink," said Rachel, raising her glass in a toast. "Then we hunt."

"Is this you?" asked Sara, picking up the photo of a young girl hugging a cute little white dog.

"Yeah. That's Skippy. Not a very original name for a dog. He was a good boy. And then one day I came home from school and he was gone. My mother said the people who gave him to us wanted him back. And she gave him back. Never said another word about it. Definitely not Mother of the Year award material. I cried for days."

"What did your father say?"

"Nothing, like usual. He never said anything about anything. A Norman Rockwell family we weren't."

Sara put the photo back on the table and settled into the sofa across from Rachel. She wished she had not picked that photo. The last thing Rachel needed right now was to be reminded of the hurtful, mean things her mother had done to her as a young girl. No wonder Aunt Lil was so special to her. She was the loving mother Rachel never had.

"Families aren't easy. What's one of your favorite memories?"

"Of Aunt Lil? Oh, there are so many. She'd take me shopping and down to Coney Island and ride the carousel with me. And every spring we'd go to the circus together at Madison Square Garden. She bought me this beautiful doll house. I have to show it to you. I found it yesterday when I was up in the attic before the will reading."

"She loved you. Any one stand out more than the others?"

"Yes. Radio City Music Hall." Rachel's voice perked up. "We'd get all dressed up and go to the Christmas show every year. I loved it when all the Rockettes were dressed as wooden soldiers and did that kick line. I used to dream of becoming a Rockette."

"You, me, and a million other little girls."

"Yeah. Christmas was so special there. I loved it. We'd see the movie and the show. Saw Operation Petticoat with Cary Grant there. We went to the same Chinese restaurant every year. Then we'd go through the shopping arcade. She'd buy me a little glass animal from the same store every year. I still have them wrapped up for safe-keeping."

"Good memories."

Sara could see that other memories were churning through Rachel's mind.

"What? You have a funny look on your face. What's up?" asked Sara.

"Nothing." But the hint of a smile contradicted her

words. Nothing wasn't exactly nothing. It was something. A major something.

Rachel took another bite of her turkey leg and washed it down with a sip of wine.

"There's something I need to show you." Standing up, Rachel stuck her hand in her pants pocket and pulled out something purple, opened it and poured its contents into her hand. One by one she placed each treasure on the glass topped coffee table.

"Holy shit! Are those what I think they are?"

"That depends on what you think they are," said Rachel as she sat back in her chair, took a sip of wine and admired the bounty now on display on the table between them. "If you think they're just rocks, then you're wrong. If you think they're diamonds, uncut diamonds, then, bingo!"

"What the—how did you—tell me. Tell me." Sara slid off the sofa and onto the floor.

"I think these are the diamonds that my aunt used to tell me stories about," said Rachel. "She had a name for them. She called them life diamonds."

"What's a life diamond?" asked Sara, her curiosity piqued.

"She said they were diamonds that Jews kept so that when they were being persecuted—"

"And when aren't Jews being persecuted?" laughed Sara. "They don't call us the chosen people for nothing. Everyone's been trying to kill us off for centuries."

"True. Anyway, when they had to leave their homes fast, they'd have something of value to trade."

Sara gently lifted a stone and turned it around in her fingers.

"Diamonds were better than money," said Rachel. "They were easy to carry, easy to hide and held their value. Look at these. They look like drab, dull rocks to the unsuspecting eye."

"Can't judge a book—or a diamond—by its cover. Never

heard of life diamonds—but my Jewish education isn't as good as yours. I'm Jew-lite, remember"

"Too funny. Let me grab my laptop. We can Google it."

"Your aunt has Wi-Fi?"

"Yeah. She was one hip lady. That's how we stayed in touch most of the time. We'd Skype."

Sara unfolded her legs from under the coffee table while Rachel got her laptop. They both headed for the dining room table.

"Okay, let's see what pops up."

Rachel could tell Sara was excited about the find.

"Life diamonds," said Sara, spelling it out as she typed into Google.

"Life diamonds," repeated Rachel. "Don't you just love the sound of that? They were called life diamonds because they were able to offer Jews a new life in a new place. L'chaim," She raised her wine glass towards heaven. "How's that for beautiful?"

"Here we go. None of these seem to fit. Ugh, this first hit is about making a diamond from your dead pet's hair. Totally gross."

"Add the word Jews to the search. Let's see if that brings up something else."

"That worked. We've got hits. Looks like there's even a book about them. *Blood from a Stone: The Quest for the Life Diamonds* by Yaron Svoray. Wonder if it's available at Amazon?"

"Probably. Isn't everything available at Amazon."

"Listen to the Amazon description about the book. It says just what you said. *'They were known as Life Diamonds— rough, uncut diamonds of high quality held by Jews in Eastern Europe to use as passports to safety.'* Shit, girl, you're rich! These have to be worth millions." Excitement gave Sara'a voice a screechy high pitch.

"Ya think! I couldn't believe it when I found them yesterday morning. I was rummaging through the attic before Ben Collins got here—"

"He was something, wasn't he?"

"Focus, Sara. Anyway, I was feeling sad about Aunt Lil and the attic had always been my special place. I thought I'd be able to find some comfort up there. My old doll house was shoved in a corner. When I pulled it out, I saw this beat up old suitcase. I pulled it out. It wasn't locked so I opened it."

Sara noted the slow, methodical way Rachel was recounting her actions from the previous morning.

"It had some old clothes in it, and this flowery pink blouse. When I held it up, a pile of old letters tied in blue ribbon fell out. And that purple leather pouch. I felt something hard inside the pouch so I opened it. There they were."

While Rachel was speaking, Sara had gone back into the living room to get the stones and now placed them reverently on the dining room table. There were eight stones in all—about the size of walnuts.

"I don't understand. How did she get them? What are they doing in a crappy old suitcase in the attic and not in a safe deposit box?"

"Got me. She used to say that her father had given her a secret treasure. Not even her brothers knew about it—but a treasure nonetheless—that would ensure their safety and security in America. She promised to tell no one and only use it when she had to."

"That's a lot to put on a little girl. But why uncut diamonds? That would present her with all sorts of problems, the least of which would have been who to trust to cut and polish them," said Sara.

"I guess her parents, my grandparents, thought that she

would wind up in a Jewish community and that there would be people who knew people who could help her. And Sara, trust is what I am placing in you." Rachel scooped the stones into her hands. "Tell no one and I mean no one. Until I figure out what to do next, no one can know about these. Yes?"

"Yes, totally agree. These are need to know, and no one needs to know."

"Look at these, Sara." Rachel moved the stones between the palms of her hands. "They look like rocks, pieces of quartz, maybe. When I found them yesterday morning I knew immediately what they were from Aunt Lil's stories even though she'd never shown them to me. Funny, I always thought her stories were a figment of her imagination."

"Some imagination! Do you know how much these are worth?" asked Sara.

"No. But I plan to find out really fast. Carefully— quietly—and quickly." Rachel's eyes dug into Sara's. "Our little secret."

"Amen," confirmed Sara.

Chapter 6

The door bell startled them both. They had been working hard for most of the day, not even stopping for lunch.

As soon as Rachel saw the Asian delivery guy at the door with two bags full of food, she knew that something was up. A minute later she had her answer as a familiar car turned the corner. Ellyn's two-seater red Mercedes 460 SL was truly a sight to behold. Her husband, Mark, had done a great restoration job. It was beautiful. And although Rachel had never owned one, she had a thing for red cars, and this car topped her list of all time favorites.

"Sara, is this your doing?"

"Of course! All work and no play is not in my vocabulary. Hey, we've played mah jongg together on Fridays for over twenty years. Why should this Friday be any different?"

"My aunt died."

"Minor detail." Sara paused realizing the impact of her words. "Sorry, not so minor. Anyway, playing mah jongg may not be the most appropriate thing to do right now, but you've always said your Aunt Lil told you that God wants you happy. Mah jongg and the three of us

63

make you happy. Besides, it'll take your mind off things."

"You are one awesome woman! I love you!"

"I know. I love you, too."

Rachel rushed out to greet her friends while Sara paid the delivery guy. Seeing her best friend smile was worth incurring a little of God's wrath, Sara thought. Playing mahj during what should be a week of sitting Shiva was not exactly kosher but Sara was confident He would understand and cut Rachel some slack. And she knew Aunt Lil was smiling down from heaven just watching all of this.

"Wow, it's so good to see you both," cried Rachel as she hugged Beth, the first to get out of the car.

"I'm so sorry for your loss, honey. I know how much you loved your aunt," said Beth, hugging Rachel tightly with no apparent intention of letting go.

"My turn…my turn," said Ellyn. "We've missed you so much. How are you?"

"I'm fine. Better now that you two are here."

"I'm so sorry I couldn't get here for the service, to be with you and help," said Ellyn "but Mark had to have a little procedure and I needed to be there."

"He okay?"

"Yeah, everything is fine," said Ellyn. "Not that he would have told me if I hadn't overheard his conversation with the doctor. Husbands! Can't live without them. Can't kill 'em."

With that, suitcases and more bags of food were lifted and everyone headed into the house. Rachel followed her friends. She felt lucky to have friends like Sara, Beth and Ellyn. Classy ladies. The years had certainly been good to all of them. More important to Rachel, however, was that the three of them had opened their hearts to her. Somehow they each knew what she needed, when she needed it. Separately and together, they had made room for her in their lives years ago.

This was good. Just a few days ago this house was full of sadness, in mourning. Tonight, it was going to have at least one more night of food, fun, and friends. Aunt Lil would be happy thought Rachel as she closed the door behind her.

"You help everyone get settled and I'll get things ready down here," said Sara.

It had been a long time since the four of them had all been together. Sara wanted the night to be special so she paid extra attention to the little details. She decided the dining room was the only place to hold what promised to be a memorable friends' dinner. It was an elegant room with a crystal chandelier that glowed and sparkled with light.

Digging through the antique mahogany hutch, she pulled out Aunt Lil's good china, white table linens with matching napkins, and elegantly etched wine glasses. Dusty from not being used, Sara quickly but carefully washed each piece. She lit candles and set up her MP3 player. The room filled with soft music.

To honor Aunt Lil, Sara tore apart several of the flower arrangements sent by well-wishers earlier in the week. She made a fresh arrangement of flowers that still had life. Pink roses, white mums, and star lilies filled a crystal vase and that she found in the hutch. She placed this at the head of the table—Aunt Lil's spot.

Sara ditched the cardboard containers for glass bowls. The food would taste the same, but look better. And there was so much food. She had remembered to order everyone's favorite dishes. Beef with Broccoli for Ellyn, Shrimp with Lobster Sauce for Beth, Shrimp with Chinese Vegetables for Rachel and Sweet and Sour Chicken for herself. Add to that egg rolls, fried rice, crab rangoon and almond cookies and you had a feast for kings—for best friends.

"Sara, you've outdone yourself," said Ellyn when she entered the dining room.

"How did you get this done so fast? We were barely upstairs five minutes," said Beth as she surveyed the table. Rachel, who was the last down the stairs, just stopped at the doorway. Making eye contact with Sara, there was really no need for words. Her smile beamed her appreciation for all of Sara's efforts.

"Everyone sit," said Sara as she poured white wine into the glasses. "Raise your glasses, please. I propose a toast to our hostess, Rachel, and her beloved Aunt Lil. May she rest in peace."

"L'chaim. Let's eat!"

"So Ellyn, what's with Mark? What did he have done?" Rachel asked plopping some fried rice on her plate.

"Dare I say colonoscopy at the dinner table."

"Did they find anything?" asked Rachel who sensed that the others already knew the answer.

"Two polyps which they took care of. Said he was good to go for five years. His uncle had colon cancer so he was really nervous before it. Over now. All clean," said Ellyn as she raised her glass. "To Mark's colon staying clean."

"I'll drink to that," said Sara. "Pass the egg rolls."

"Beth, how's Adam doing?" asked Rachel.

"Good. He's in Afghanistan now. We Skype with him every few days."

"Be sure to give him my love."

"Will do."

"How's Williamsburg? Miss us? You know you can move back here anytime," offered Ellyn.

"Yes, I miss all of you and no, I'm not moving back. I'm done here. I really like it where I am. Summer was really hot, and humid, but it's been a beautiful fall so far. And just think, I can do my daily five mile walk around Colonial Williamsburg now, not the track at the health club. How cool is that?"

"Do you really do that?" asked Ellyn.

"No, but I can," laughed Rachel.

One topic led to the next. Everyone got filled in on the comings and goings, good times and heartaches each one was experiencing.

"I can't eat another bite," said Beth. "And we still have so much food."

Beth pushed away from the table, grabbed her plate and headed for the kitchen. Everyone followed, hands full of bowls and plates.

"Sara, this is the good china, right?"

"Yep, not dishwasher safe. Hand washing only," reminded Sara. "And that is why none of us use our good china. Since I made the decision to use it, I'll wash it. I just felt the occasion warranted it. Ellyn, you dry. We can get this all washed and dried in no time. Then we play."

"My set's upstairs," said Beth. "I'll get it. I need to go upstairs anyway and let the girls out. This bra is killing me."

"Go get comfortable, but no need for your set. We can use Aunt Lil's set. It's right here," said Rachel as she retraced her steps back into the dining room.

Rachel opened the center doors on the lower portion of the hutch and pulled out a beautifully engraved rosewood box. There were intricate carvings on all four sides with a brass handle centered on the top. She undid the latch and opened the door panels to reveal 3 drawers holding the tiles, dice and racks.

"Wow. This is gorgeous," said Ellyn.

Rachel started to dump the tiles onto the table. "I used to watch my aunt play all the time. Always wanted to learn and she did try to teach me, but things got in the way back then," said Rachel.

"Is it a complete set? The older sets didn't have jokers," asked Beth.

"Aunt Lil has these really pretty geisha images hand painted on blank tiles for jokers. I think a friend of hers did it." said Rachel. Everyone started to lift tiles searching for those wonderful little jokers. "See? Aren't they pretty? And here is the one bam."

"Who needs a refill?" asked Sara as she emerged from the kitchen with regular juice glasses and two bottles of wine. "Just in case I thought we'd switch to these. No sense using stemmed wine glasses that could go flying as we're picking and throwing tiles.

"Good thinking," said Beth, returning dressed in a Hofstra sweatshirt and matching sweatpants. "I'd hate to break one of these beautiful glasses when we're pushing out a wall. We always spill something when we play and drink."

"I just stuck the leftovers in the refrigerator and took care of the plates and wine glasses. The rest can wait. We ready?"

The four of them took their places around the table. Building the walls and pulling out their mah jongg cards, Rachel realized how much she missed her friends. She wondered whether she would ever find new friends that she could become this close to in her new home—the way women get close. Someone to confide in, to laugh with, to cry with.

"Ready? Roll for east. Usual five dollar pot?" asked Beth.

"Yeah," said Ellyn. "Such big gamblers!"

"Here are the almond cookies." said Rachel. "Something to munch on while we play."

Hours later, Rachel stepped out onto the front porch with a steaming cup of tea, wrapped in a blanket to ward off the night chill. The house was finally quiet. Everyone had gone to bed. She was alone. Her normal state these days.

An evening of mah jongg with her oldest friends was so

much fun. She missed them terribly. Everyone won a few hands and as usual Sara walked away the big winner. They continued to catch up on one another's lives as they picked, racked and discarded tiles. Conversations picked up where they had left off five months ago. No time had really passed between these friends. Isn't that what mah jongg was all about? To catch up, be with friends you love and who love you unconditionally.

Her eagerness to go home and get on with her new life conflicted with the pleasure of the past few hours with her friends. But she knew she had to go—and the sooner the better. She engaged her planning brain even at this late hour. There was so much to do. And if truth be told, she wanted it all to be done, over.

How selfish is that? Why am I rushing?

Rachel knew the answer to that question. Because she wanted to—needed to—get on with her new life. The old was important, held memories. But the new held the promise of what could be. And she still had a lot of living to do.

She ticked off planning steps in her mind. Work on clothes and smaller items first. Pull out what she wanted to keep and donate the rest to Amvets, Goodwill and St. Vincent de Paul. Find an estate buyer to take the furniture. Next, contact a cleaning service to really give what would be an empty house some spit and polish. Contact a real estate agent and put the house up for sale at a price that would guarantee it sold fast. Sign the papers and be gone. She wondered if Ben Collins knew a good real estate agent or an estate buyer. She'd call him and ask. And she wouldn't mind seeing him again.

What was that all about?

The idea of having a man in her life after David's death hadn't crossed her mind until now. In the last week she'd flirted and had lunch with a perfect stranger on the road and felt a strangely enjoyable flutter in her heart while sitting on the porch with her aunt's lawyer.

What was going on? What had triggered these feelings— these thoughts—these actions?

Thinking about it, she realized it wasn't about Beemer guy or Ben Collins. They had simply awakened a desire she believed long dead. There was no point denying the emptiness in her heart. She deserved to be happy.

What if finding someone to love and share her life with was the key to that happiness? That could present some interesting new possibilities. And problems.

Sitting in the silent darkness, Rachel found herself reflecting on how fast life changes. In one short week, her life had changed big time and there was no turning back. Was all of this another part of the new Rachel bursting forth?

A lone siren pierced the night. The flashing red and blue lights of a police car whizzed by with an ambulance close behind. *Hope they make it* thought Rachel as she followed the ambulance's path down the street until it was out of sight.

In the blink of an eye, what was can be gone. Aunt Lil had died alone. Well, not alone. Jimmy had been there. As Rachel mulled this over she found herself stuck on his presence at Aunt Lil's so early on a Sunday morning. She got the call from the doctor around eleven. Bureaucracy does not work that fast. Considering all the things that had to happen to initiate that call, Aunt Lil had to have died at least two hours earlier. There was some niggling thought trying to get a foothold in her mind.

What the heck had Jimmy Raconti been doing in Aunt Lil's house so early on a Sunday morning?

And then there were the diamonds. They were safe for the moment and would remain so. Out of sight, but not far from her mind. One stone would ensure that she and her loved ones wanted for nothing for the rest of their lives. Figuring out what to do with the remaining stones to honor Aunt Lil's memory by putting them to good use would take some time.

Chapter 7

Saturday, October 5

"Where do we start?" asked Sara as Rachel walked into the kitchen.

"Coffee," answered Rachel, heading for the pot, clearly a woman on a mission. "Did you sleep well?"

"Yeah. Being wrapped in that quilt is to die for. I felt snug and safe as if nothing could touch me. Your aunt made that quilt, didn't she?"

"Yes. She'd be pleased that you like it so much. Would you like the quilt, Sara? Consider it yours."

"Wow, thanks, Rachel," said Sara, embracing Rachel in one of her signature hugs. "That means a lot to me."

"I'm glad. There are a few things that I want to keep— things of Aunt Lil's that I remember from my childhood. I can't wait to display her mah jongg set. I have the perfect little table in a corner in my living room. The set is so beautiful. It's a shame to keep it hidden away. Now, if I could only find some people to play with." sighed Rachel. "Any sounds from Beth or Ellyn? Do I need to go wake them?" asked Rachel.

"Nope. They're up and out. Went down the street to get fresh bagels. Should be back—"

"We got bagels," said Ellyn bursting into the kitchen, the smell of fresh bagels filling the room. Beth had the rest of the goodies.

"The only thing better than the smell of fresh bagels is eating fresh bagels. Gets your day off to a perfect start, I always say. We got cream cheese too and belly lox, Rachel, your favorite," said Beth.

"Belly lox. Like I've died and gone to heaven. Way to go, Brooklyn. I love old Jewish neighborhoods. Fresh bagels and good deli," cried Rachel. "Can't beat it."

The four friends proceeded to grab the necessities— plates, knives, forks, and spoons. Coffee all around had Sara making another pot. Once everyone had had her fill, the talk turned to the task at hand.

"Like I said before, Rachel, where do we start?" asked Sara. "What's your plan?"

"I'm thinking we start with things like clothes that we can give to Goodwill or Amvets. On Monday, I'm going to call around and see if I can get a few people who buy estates to give me a feel for what's here and make me an offer. That should take care of most of the furniture."

"Rachel, there are boxes everywhere. No matter what closet you open, it's stacked with boxes. What's in them?" asked Ellyn.

"Got me. My aunt saved everything. Probably had something to do with when she grew up, during the war, and before that, the depression. She was in Germany then but what we call the great depression hit Europe too. She was the ultimate pack rat."

"And I think my mother is the ultimate pack rat," Beth chimed in. "Every time she complains about how cold it gets here, my Dad suggests moving to Florida. She tells him to go alone, she's not going. There's too much to pack."

"Keep your eyes out for a ceramic cat in a curled up sleep position. It's black and white. I remember it having a blue collar around the neck. Need to find that. And somewhere is my aunt's dreidel collection."

"Rachel, I thought you were the only person I knew who collected dreidels," said Ellyn.

"And who do you think got me started? Aunt Lil. She collected dreidels from all over the world. Whenever she and Uncle Abe traveled she would go into the Jewish section and buy a dreidel for me and one for herself. Never the same one, she would tell me. That way, when she died and I got her collection, I'd have all different ones."

"Okay. Got it. Black and white ceramic cat and dreidels. Anything else?" asked Sara.

"There are a few pieces of jewelry, brooches mostly. And to all of you—if you see something that you would enjoy having, please help yourself. I know Aunt Lil would be pleased."

"Ellyn and I brought enough clothes to stay for a few days so we can help," said Beth. "What about you Sara?"

"I'm here for as long as Rachel needs me. We can work by day and play mahj at night. Throw in some wine and good Chinese, and I'm a happy camper."

They spent the rest of the morning tackling Aunt Lil's clothes. At one point, a game of dress up got out of hand as each tried to out do the other. Giggles and silliness overtook the sadness. Vintage dresses from days gone by, hats, gloves and shawls wound up strewn across the beds in at least two of the second floor bedrooms. Aunt Lil had spared no expense when she shopped. Clearly, Uncle Abe had been a very successful pediatrician in his time. And back then, doctors made house calls and people paid in cash. Rachel always thought the children he helped get well actually helped him more. He and Aunt Lil had not been given the gift of children.

"Look at this shawl," said Ellyn. "It's stunning."

"I remember that one. Aunt Lil brought it back from Spain. The different colored roses on the black background just pop. Do you think you would wear it, Ellyn?"

"Are you kidding me! I'd wear it all the time."

"Then it's yours. Wear it well. And think of Aunt Lil's loving arms wrapped around you when you do."

"Thank you so much." Ellyn wrapped the shawl and her arms around Rachel and squeezed tightly.

"Daniel, got a minute?" asked Dr. Grayson Mitchell, Medical Examiner rapping lightly on the door frame of Detective Daniel Berger's third floor office. There were files everywhere. Mitchell always marveled that Daniel could find anything or get any work done surrounded by this mess.

"Hey, Gray, nice to see you. What's got you here on a Saturday morning?" asked Daniel as he raised his head from the file he was reading.

Daniel was usually at his best in the morning, but not this morning. Last night's series of shootings had resulted in two officers down. As they waited for news of how their brothers in blue were doing, he and his partner, Brad Cooper, were playing the "what if" game with their current open cases, hoping it would take the edge off the waiting. You could tell by Daniel's tight grasp around his morning coffee cup that it wasn't working.

"Rough night? You two look like shit," said Gray as he threw a nod to Cooper.

"We've had better," said Daniel.

"I'm sure. Heard about the shootings. Any word on how they're doing?"

"Nothing yet. They were still in surgery last I checked. What's up, Gray?"

"I just saw this paperwork," said Gray holding up a folder. "You know those deaths you asked me to keep an eye out for? Looks like we had another one. Last week, Sunday. White female. Age ninety. Cause of death listed as myocardial infarction. Doctor signed off on it at the ER. No autopsy. Jewish—so the twenty-four hour burial thing kicked in. Buried last Monday. Surviving kin shows to be a niece in Virginia."

Gray crossed from the doorway and plopped the folder on Daniel's desk.

"Could be nothing, just what it says, the natural death of an old lady. You said you wanted to know when these things came across my desk. So I'm letting you know."

Gray stopped talking, poured himself a cup of coffee while Daniel skimmed the file. Another seemingly innocent passing of an elderly woman in the middle of a community of many elderly people. Nothing out of the ordinary about it. Old people died all the time. And yet, for some reason Daniel's detective gut was telling him otherwise. He just couldn't put his finger on what was making it do flip-flops or why he had asked Gray to alert him to elderly deaths. But he had learned over the years to pay attention to his gut. What he was feeling was definitely not gas.

"Does sort of fit your pattern, doesn't it?" asked Gray. "And I did what you asked. I left a standing order for a vial of blood to be drawn on all deaths of people over ninety where no autopsy was ordered or required. Didn't get permission so that could be sticky down the road. But we have blood to test if you want to."

"What are you guys talking about?" asked Cooper. "Are you going to let me in on it?"

"Relax. No biggie. Remember that string of home invasions we were having last year? Led to that meeting downtown last winter?"

"Yeah, I remember. The more we talked, the more it became obvious that we weren't the only borough being hit. Queens got its share. Staten Island too. But no one could get a handle on any pattern. And if I remember correctly, they just stopped."

"That's the part that started to bother me, that they just stopped," said Daniel. "We didn't have a clue about what was going on. Talked to our usual suspects and snitches and got zilch. And then they stopped. Or did they?"

"As I remember it, the thefts were small time. Little stuff that wouldn't be immediately missed," added Cooper. "Always on weekends, when people were out and about so strangers might not be as obvious. Family always seemed to be away for the day so the place was empty, which means we know they were scouting their targets."

"Quiet communities, but not overtly wealthy ones. So we thought kids. Kids on drugs, gang initiations, doing break-ins, grabbing what they can easily sell and getting out," said Daniel. Even now, Daniel seemed to be lost in his own head, reviewing his theory as he spoke it out loud.

"In one of my less than successful attempts to sleep through the night, I started to replay some of the more recent burglaries and it kind of hit me. Maybe the MO just shifted. Maybe they hadn't stopped at all, just changed targets.

"So I pulled all the burglaries reported since June and started reviewing details looking for patterns, anything that linked them. Two things popped. The age of the victims and the sex. Old and female. Mostly old ladies living alone. And in this newer grouping, a few of the victims died. And I quietly asked our esteemed colleague here to give me a heads up to any deaths that fit this pattern: female, elderly, lives alone, outwardly healthy, uninvolved immediate family or no immediate family—and to pull some blood before the body was released for burial."

"And yes," said Gray interrupting, "there's that one other interesting item you asked me to watch for on the paperwork. The lawyer for this deceased is someone you know—Ben Collins."

"Interesting. Thanks Gray. Let's keep this between us still. Keep me in the loop. Pull the door closed on your way out"

"So what are you thinking, Danny boy?" asked Cooper barely waiting to hear the door click shut. His mind was on full charge. They had something new to think about to replace worrying about the two officers in surgery.

"Don't know exactly. Just some loose ends that don't fit for me."

And that was the problem. Daniel didn't exactly know what he was thinking. Bits and pieces of disconnected information was all he had right now. The biggest common denominator was the lawyer—Ben Collins. He knew the name. Their paths had crossed early in both of their careers when Collins had been a PD. Daniel knew that Collins had opened his own practice years ago. Had some big time clients and did well. Then things went to shit. Rumors circulated—about Collins blowing easy cases—about a gambling problem. His current clients were small time criminals. Why his name was showing up as the lawyer of record on elderly deaths definitely needed an answer. He didn't do estate law. Could be nothing. Probably nothing. Then again, another death, similar details. Maybe something—maybe everything.

Chapter 8

At noon, Rachel and Sara made their first trip to Goodwill. When they returned to load up the car again, they found Jimmy seated at the kitchen table having coffee with Beth. There were times, Rachel thought, when the light hit him just right—he was one good looking guy. That rugged Mediterranean appearance—muscles in a t-shirt, the beginning of a beer belly, nice, tight butt—could be very attractive. Then, there were other times when his features would take on a chilling, more ominous cast.

"Ma and I were talking. We made a list of all the things we remembered Lil saying needed fixing around here," said Jimmy, lifting the yellow pad he had in front of him. It looked like there were about ten items. "Nothing I can't handle. And, I promised your aunt that I would do it. They probably need to be fixed before you put the house up for sale. That's what you're going to do, right? Sell it?"

"Yep, that's the plan. So if you know anyone interested in living in this part of town, let them know this house is for sale. I'll need a week or so to get everything done," said Rachel as she poured coffee for herself and Sara.

"Let me see your list, Jimmy," said Sara as she pulled the

pad out of his hands. "You said something about the furnace the other night, when you scared Rachel and me half to death. And we got the back door lock fixed the next morning so we can check that one off right away," said Sara as she scribbled through that item on his list.

"What else? Loose stair treads on the basement steps, cracked window on the landing, peeling wallpaper in the hall bathroom, leak in the upstairs shower, corroded pipe by the water heater."

Ellyn appeared at the door, her arms loaded with clothes. "Since I was the last person to shower this morning you may want to add a new hot water heater to your list. My Uncle Sam's in the business. He can get you a good deal."

"And the place definitely could use fresh paint, inside and out. I'm sure it would help with any sale," added Beth.

"I agree about the paint part. The house is the same as I have always remembered it," Rachel said as she looked around the sunlit kitchen. "I see these walls in shades of blue with white curtains, and the cabinets painted white. Then again, it's not my kitchen, so maybe basic beige would be best.

"Or really, just price it in line with how it is now," said Ellyn. "Tell prospective buyers the price includes a ten thousand dollar decorating allowance. Let them do the painting they want."

"I like that idea, Ellyn. Good thinking. I won't have to be here after we get the house cleaned out and the real estate agent can take care of showing it without me around. I can go home sooner."

"Okay people, coffee break's over. Back to work," said Sara, clapping her hands together and taking the clothes out of Ellyn's arms. "Rachel and I have at least three more loads of clothes to bring to Goodwill. What if you two tackle the kitchen. Leave enough plates and silverware for two and some pots and a fry pan or two. Unless you know someone who is setting up housekeeping and could use dishes and things, the rest of this stuff can get boxed up and given away. Anything you're not sure about, put on the dining room table."

"And, as I said before, if you see something you like, take it. I'd rather have Aunt Lil's things enjoyed by friends," added Rachel.

Jimmy was giving no indication that he was in any hurry to leave. Rachel thought she'd help him along. "Jimmy, is your mom home?"

"Yeah, sure. I think she just got back from the market."

"Great. I'll walk over with you. There are some jewelry pieces that I think she might like. You two have been so kind. I'm sure Aunt Lil would want your mom to have some of these. I'll be right back with them."

Before she left the room, Rachel said, "And ladies, tonight's dinner is on me. Think about where you want to go. My vote is Little Italy but I'm open to other suggestions." With that Rachel headed upstairs to retrieve the pieces she planned to offer Mrs. Raconti.

Knock. Knock. Knock. Opportunity knocking. Like music to his ears, Jimmy knew that's what he had just been handed—an opportunity. They would be out for an evening on the town. The house would be empty. He'd have time to search.

"I'm just going to go into the basement and check on the size wrench I need to fix that pipe," said Jimmy once Rachel was out of sight. He knew his time was short. He immediately headed down the stairs before anyone could say a word, let alone object. Thinking on his feet was definitely one of his stronger talents.

Walking over to the small window above the washing

machine, he quickly unlatched the locking mechanism. His size did not preclude him from squeezing through. After all, he'd come in this way before. He added some tool type noise for effect and was back in the kitchen before Rachel returned.

Jimmy opened the back door and he and Rachel walked into a dingy looking kitchen. Millie Raconti appeared from a back room holding a wire shopping cart. Dressed in black stretch pants and a loose-fitting purple sweater, her hair and make-up ready to face the world.

"Here, I'll take that," offered Jimmy. "Look who's here with me—Rachel. They're working hard next door. You should see the place."

"Come in, Rachel. Can I get you coffee?"

"No, Mrs. Raconti. Thank you. I want to thank you again for all of your help. As I was cleaning out Aunt Lil's things, I came across several brooches," said Rachel as she pulled a velvet covered crimson box from her sweater pocket. Opening it, she displayed its contents on the kitchen table. "I think these are the prettiest and I want you to take your pick. I know this will make Aunt Lil happy."

The four pieces sitting on the table before her were indeed beautiful and Millie Raconti could not hide her excitement. The cameo caught her eye first.

"This is beautiful, Rachel. Look at the face. How soft and delicate. And these red stones and the little pearls around the edge. Rubies, yes? I've always wanted a cameo. And the gold."

With that, Millie Raconti took the brooch, working to pin it to her sweater as she headed to the hall bathroom to admire it.

"Eeeeeh. This is gorgeous."

Jimmy and Rachel exchanged smiles at the screams of

delight emanating from the bathroom. Reappearing, pure joy shone on Millie's face.

"Ya' think she likes it?" Jimmy had picked up a flowered brooch and examining it more closely asked, "These are fake stones, right?"

"I think they are semi-precious stones. Citrine, garnet, tourmaline, peridot. My aunt loved Jewelry TV. I think she was their best customer. She loved wearing rings and pins and pendants with all sorts of colored stones. She loved how the colors sparkled."

"Rachel, every time I wear this cameo I will remember what a kind, loving woman Lil was. Thank you so much."

"You're welcome. Is there another that catches your eye? Funny, I remembered a starburst pin being her favorite. She loved the amethyst center and all the delicate white sapphires spreading out like tendrils. Uncle Abe had it made special for her. I was really looking forward to wearing it to remember her. But I didn't see that one in her jewelry box."

"I remember that one," said Millie as she shot Jimmy a sharp look. "I'm sure you'll find it. Probably just tucked away somewhere or pinned on a sweater or coat. Her hand reached for the flowered brooch Jimmy had been looking at.

"This is also very pretty. All the colors. You could wear it on so many things."

"Keep it too, Mille. I know Aunt Lil would be pleased." Replacing the garnet eyed cat and tourmaline tulip back in the case, Rachel headed for the door.

"Back to work. There is so much left to do. And we're going into the city tonight for a girl's night on the town."

"Girl's night out. That sounds like fun," said Millie. She cast a sideways glance at Jimmy.

"Thanks again for all of your help," Rachel closed the door behind her, not waiting for any reply.

"Feel better now?" Jimmy's belligerent tone cautioned Millie that any response needed to be offered with care. "You got something. Fake jewelry. Whoopee." Scorned oozed from every pore.

His eyes flashed. *If looks could kill,* thought Millie. She knew Jimmy's moods all too well. He could go from kind to cruel in a heartbeat. And she had learned that it didn't take much to set him off. As much as she wanted to ask him about the missing starburst brooch, silence now was definitely the smarter choice. He'd get his soon enough. Karma's a bitch.

Befriending the old woman had been easy. Lil had been a kind soul, someone she had come to love and admire. Who knows? Had her own life taken a different path, others might remember her as a kind soul. Maybe someone still will. Then again, you can't outrun your fate. But can you change it?

Jimmy's cell phone broke the silence.

"A progress report," demanded the voice on the other end.

Goose bumps rose on Jimmy's arms. Cold, calculating, detached, the mechanized voice gave no hint as to its owner.

"What is the status of your assignment?"

"We've had a minor set back. Nothing I can't handle. The old woman, she died last week and…and…the place has been crawling with people."

"This is not what I want to hear. You do realize what's at stake here, don't you?"

"Yeah, yeah. The niece caught me sneaking in the other night so I've had to be more careful."

"Your excuses are not impressing me. You were hired to do a job. You need to deliver or suffer the consequences. And, if you fail, you will suffer, I assure you."

"I have a plan. They're going out tonight so I'm going in. I'll have a good four hours of undisturbed time."

"Good. Keep me informed. We'll speak again soon."

With that the line went dead.

All color drained from Jimmy's face. His eyes bulged. She could see the vein at his hairline pulsing and twitching.

"Who was that?" asked Millie.

"No one. Forget it."

Not good, thought Millie. *Whoever the caller was definitely got Jimmy's attention. She'd have to report this new turn of events.*

"I'm going out for awhile. Watch the house. If I'm not back by the time they leave, call me," said Jimmy as he headed for the back door.

Shit. He was screwed. Fucked this job up big time by agreeing to do it for two people. Different people, with vastly different styles, both wanting him to steal the same prize. Raw diamonds. *How fucked is that,* he thought walking down the street to his favorite bar. Since no one really knew how many diamonds Lil had, his plan had been to split the diamonds between them, keeping at least one or two for himself.

A few beers with the guys would settle his nerves. He needed to be clear-headed tonight. Keep his eyes on the prize. Once the diamonds were in his hot little hands, he'd figure out how to deal with both bosses.

Millie placed a call. A man answered on the first ring.

"What's up? I didn't think I'd hear from you today."

"We may have a problem. Jimmy just got a call. Don't know from who, but it scared the shit out of him."

"Interesting."

"Maybe we should stop. Walk away. We've done well—got more than enough for all of us."

"But they're diamonds—uncut stones. Do you know what they could be worth?"

"Doesn't matter what they're worth if we can't get them, or if Lil's stories are just that—stories. We aren't even sure she had them. We're risking a lot for something that might not be real."

"Hang in a bit longer. Has he got a plan yet?"

"I think he's going in tonight. The girls are going out for dinner so the house will be empty."

"Okay. Keep me posted."

"Will do."

Chapter 9

He was ready. Dressed in his work clothes—tight fitting black t-shirt and pants—high on the adrenalin rush pulsing through his body. His multi-pocket tactical vest held the tools of his trade—his trusty Leatherman, a small LED flashlight with a red lens cover, extra gloves, a tactical knife and a Walther 380 pistol should he encounter any unexpected company. Whoever had invented these vests was a genius. Once zipped, the vest hugged his frame so tightly there was little fear it would get snagged or caught on anything. And, there were so many zippered pockets. Not only were the tools required to do the job close at hand, there were enough pockets to stash any small prizes he happened to find.

The space between his house and Lil's was very narrow. A wrought iron fence demarcated the boundaries between the properties. He hugged the house—went from shadow to shadow—and then along the fence to minimize any chance of being seen by the wayward glance of a neighbor.

His pulse quickened with each step. He was truly a legend in his own mind—considered himself born to do this type of work. Every fiber of his being alert to every sensation, acutely aware of every sound. He drew in a sharp breath to steady his nerves. His heart was racing—like it always did—at the start of a job. No mistakes. Ah, this is living.

The crowbar Jimmy had stashed behind the bushes easily lifted the unlocked basement window from its sash. Like a snake, Jimmy slithered inside, feet first. Once his toes touched the top of the washing machine, he had the footing he needed to complete his entrance. Using the window frame for leverage, he pushed himself through, the lower sill scraping along his back. He squatted on top of the washer.

Previous visits and methodical searching of the basement had turned up nothing. Millie had kept Lil occupied to give him both time and freedom of movement under the guise of repairing things to do a cursory search of the rooms on the first and second floors.

The attic was tonight's target. It was the only place he had yet to venture because he could never think of an excuse to go up there. After all, what needed fixing in an attic other than a leaky roof? Lil told him the roof had been replaced last year. He got a quick peek around the attic when he went to get Rachel for the will reading. It was filled with old stuff, furniture and boxes—more boxes. The diamonds had to be up there.

He waited thirty minutes after seeing the girls leave. Women had a way of forgetting things. They also changed their minds at the drop of a hat. Going into the city for dinner was their plan. He just couldn't count on it being what they actually did. He figured thirty minutes would be enough time to make sure they were gone.

Not knowing how much actual time he would have for his search concerned him a bit. The last thing he wanted was to get caught in the house when they got back. He set the timer on his watch for two hours. He would reassess his progress when it beeped.

Allowing his eyes to adjust to the dim light in the basement, he eased into a sitting position atop the washer with his legs dangling in front of him. He did a quick scan of the space thankful for the blue glow of the night light plugged in by the stairs. Like his basement next door, the dankness of the air made his nose hairs itch. He took a few deep breaths and then pushed off the washer to the floor. Making his way slowly to the stairs he still managed to trip over a basket filled with clothes, dumping its contents on the floor.

Shit!

He scooped up the clothes and dropped them back into the basket. That had not been there earlier today when he had snuck down to unlock the window. He wondered what else might get in his way.

Climbing the steps to the landing off the kitchen he stood still for a minute to get his bearings. There was no need for the flashlight at this point. The hall light on the main and second floors had been left on. He rounded the corner and made his way down the hall to the main stairs. The place looked like a tornado hit it. Stuff was everywhere.

He easily reached the second floor and headed for the attic door. It was closed tightly. He would have to make sure he left it that way. Turning the knob, he opened the door. The musty smell of dead air hit him hard. He pulled the attic door almost closed behind him, allowing the hall light to cast a glow on the lower stairs.

Fifteen steps. He'd counted them the other morning when he climbed them to get Rachel before the will reading. Now, he recounted them—thirteen…fourteen…fifteen. Dammit. Total darkness. He could hear the sounds of the street below, but not even a sliver of light came through the heavy shade on the lone dormer window. Leaving the attic door slightly ajar did not shed much light up here. He could pull up the shade but decided not to take a chance that someone outside might notice his flashlight beam. Circumstances being what they were, Jimmy knew the darkness would slow down his search. His clock was ticking.

His pulled his flashlight out of his vest pocket and turned it on. *Where to begin?* Using the mental image of a clock to create an artificial grid like he'd seen on a TV episode of Real Crimes, he did a quick circle of the space with the flashlight. Directly in front of him, at twelve o'clock, he saw a pile of open cartons that appeared to be filled with books and magazines and knick-knacks wrapped in old newspapers. Unwrapping and rewrapping these would take time. Moving the light to his right—three o'clock—it cast its glow on a man's bicycle, a small treadmill and a pink tricycle.

Must have been hell dragging the treadmill up the stairs, he thought. *Treadmills and bikes go in basements. Every fool knows that.*

More boxes were behind those items, pushed against the attic wall. He could see the names of people and names of rooms printed on some of these. An old table, armoire, a huge steamer trunk, a bed frame, mattress and box springs were also leaning against the back wall, at the six o'clock position. There were two shadeless lamps on the table and more boxes. *The steamer trunk might hold treasures and be a good place to start,* he thought. Off to his left, at nine o'clock, he saw an old doll house, a brown rocking chair, and an assortment of suitcases. And more boxes.

He walked forward and started with all the boxes directly in front of him. Ignoring the boxes of books and magazines, he focused on the ones with stuff wrapped in newspaper—slowly unwrapping and rewrapping each item. A long, frustrating hour into his work revealed the challenge before him. It was like searching for a needle in a haystack. He knew what diamonds looked like.

What did uncut diamonds look like? The unknown voice on the phone who hired him for the job had said rocks. They looked like dull rocks.

What slowed down his search even more was the fact that he had to search neatly. Theft was a craft to him and he considered himself the ultimate craftsman. The layers of dust clued him into the fact that Rachel and her friends had not yet started looking at the stuff in the attic. The last thing he wanted to do was leave any trace behind to show that someone had recently been rifling through the old lady's stuff—that her home had been violated. To Jimmy's way of thinking, other than Rachel on the day the will had been read, no one had been up in the attic for years.

Time was ticking away. Looking at his watch he could see that he had less than five minutes left before the beeper denoting two hours went off. All he had to show for his time so far was a mouth full of dust. Pulling a black flask from one of his vest pockets, he took a swig. Water—his beverage of choice when working. His buddy, Jack Daniels, would have tasted better, but it would have dulled his senses. The Jack would flow when the job was done. Jimmy reset the alarm giving himself another hour. Back to work.

He looked around the room hoping for divine guidance. He needed direction. Then he remembered. The day he came up to get Rachel, she'd been over by the doll house, bent over one of the old suitcases so immersed in what she was looking at that she jumped when he spoke. Maybe that area would prove more fruitful. He returned the flask to his pocket and moved toward the doll house. Car doors slamming and peals of laughter stopped him cold.

Shit! What were they doing back so soon?

Too late. The front door opened just as he reached the bottom of the attic stairs.

Fuck!

There was nowhere for him to go. He retreated back up the attic stairs—quickly and quietly. New plan. Stay in the attic until everyone falls asleep and then sneak out of the house. He could tell by the laughter reaching his ears that they had been drinking. He just needed to be patient. A smile crossed his face. *Patience. Not one of his stronger qualities,* he admitted to himself.

Music from the sixties blasted and laughter bounced off the walls. The girls were whooping it up, having a party. They clearly were not yet ready to call it a night. He heard them singing and guessed they were dancing. Hmm, ladies moving and grooving to music, undulating, swaying hips, uninhibited by drink. He moistened his lips fantasizing about how he would fit in the center of their dance circle. *A little dirty dancing anyone?*

He needed to find someplace comfortable to settle in for a few hours. They'd get tired soon enough. As he assessed his surroundings he realized that getting comfortable would be easier said than done. No sofas or cushy chairs.

A bare slither of light entered the space from the staircase to guide his movements. He didn't want to make noise and call attention to the attic. Even with the music blaring so loud it could wake the dead, he had to be very careful. Every step became perilous. Jimmy knew from experience that the more effort he put into being quiet, the harder quiet was to achieve. Slowly he made his way around the staircase opening to the right. He tucked himself into a corner in the darkest part of the attic, the space that appeared to offer the most cover should anyone feel the need to visit the attic in their exuberant revelry.

He couldn't let sleep claim him. Staying alert would be his only salvation should one of the girls venture up here. Why they would do that was anybody's guess, but he had given up trying to figure broads out years ago. He considered his options and quickly realized that there was no way to win any encounter with them. He was the trespasser hiding in the attic. He couldn't kill them all. Besides, murder was not his game. Finding the damn diamonds, if they even existed, was the prize, not some dead sixty year olds.

Rachel awoke in a cold sweat. Well past menopause when this was a nightly occurrence, she ripped off the covers and lay still in the dark.

What time is it?

Her heart was racing. Peering at the clock she realized she had only been in bed for about an hour. She'd had a weird dream—the kind she'd heard people had after drinking too much.

She'd been walking a dog down a dark, unfamiliar street and felt a presence. It was all around her. No matter which way she turned the feeling someone was watching her overtook her. There had been a noise, a loud clunk, like someone kicked a can and it hit a garbage can or something. The dog she was walking had not reacted, but she was sure she heard something.

That sound. It was so loud. Did I really hear something or did I dream it?

An incessant pounding drummed all around her. Her hands went to her ears attempting to block it out. It would not stop. Her entire body felt like it was pounding. Swirls of colored, flashing lights stung her eyes.

Ugh. Migraine.

She'd had red wine last night. A lot of red wine with dinner and more when they got home, which led to their impromptu dance party—fun she was now paying for. She needed aspirin, but moving intensified the pain between her eyes. Trying to lie still, she hoped it would pass. Not happening. Years of having migraines had cemented the familiar pattern. Wake up to the pain, take the aspirin, cold sweats begin, salivate, throw up, cold towel on forehead, back to bed, fall asleep. She knew the routine. Sharp knives stabbed at her eyes as she pressed her fingers along her brow line working to reduce the tension.

Slowly, Rachel got out of bed. Sliding her feet into her fuzzy slippers and tying her robe, she made her way down the hall heading for the bathroom leaning against the wall for support. She was surprised when the attic door clicked closed under her weight.

I've got to get this latch fixed.

The familiar pre-heave saliva secretion started inside her mouth.

Move!

Shallow gasps for air replaced normal breathing. Steadying herself with one hand on the toilet rim and one holding back her hair, Rachel hung over the bowl. Convulsive retching seized her stomach. Remnants of what had been a good dinner spewed out. Tears mixed with saliva dripped from her mouth. Tearing off a few sheets of toilet paper to wipe her eyes and blow her nose, she knelt with one knee hugging each side of the toilet. When there was no more left inside of her, wave upon wave of dry heaves rolled through her body. Her stomach muscles ached. A vise-like pain shot behind her eyes. Flashes of colored light pierced her sight.

That'll teach me, No more red wine!

Turning around on the cold floor, she leaned her back against the wall for support. Wobbly elbows dug into her knees as she held her throbbing head in her hands. Pressing her thumbs into the corners of her eyes and along her brow line, she worked to massage away the pounding pressure.

After a few moments of concentrated deep breathing, she regained control of herself. Sliding her back up the bathroom wall Rachel leaned forward grabbing hold of the sink and opened the medicine cabinet.

Shit! No aspirin.

Soaking a wash cloth in cold water, and holding it up to her forehead, Rachel headed downstairs to retrieve aspirin from her purse. The house was deadly quiet. Everyone was asleep.

What the—?

Something went flying. Her feet went out from under her. She went down. A soft whimper left her lips. One of Sara's shoes was now closer to the front door than it had been a second ago. She had a memory of Sara putting her shoes on the bottom step. Said she would move them later so no one tripped. That was before the dancing and more wine. She must have forgotten.

Slowly, Rachel pushed herself off the floor. She took a moment to regain her balance and make sure her feet were stable underneath her. With one hand holding the cold wash cloth to her head and the other sliding along the wall, she padded to the kitchen for water. She continued making the circle into the dining room for her purse and her beloved Bayer. Swallowing two aspirin, and praying they would stay down, Rachel headed through the living room back to the hallway to the stairs and her bed.

Ouch! Shit!

Reaching out, Rachel grabbed for the banister to keep from winding up on the floor a second time. If she went down again, she was going to stay down the rest of the night.

Looking around, Rachel realized that she had again tripped over one of Sara's shoes.

The pounding in her head intensified when she bent over to retrieve both shoes. She tucked them next to a chair in the living room, out of the path of any foot traffic. She'd have to remember to ask Sara about the shoes in the morning. After her head stops pounding. For now, only sleep will stop the throbbing.

Jimmy's skull was on fire, pounding, throbbing. Replaying the events of the previous few hours only exacerbated the pain in his head. He'd gotten shit-faced drunk after his late night escapade. Now, he was paying the price. The smallest movement magnified the pain tenfold. Looking around he realized that he was lying on the cold, hard floor of the back parlor. Eventually, he'd have to get up for aspirin or something stronger.

One point crystalized for Jimmy. Almost getting caught in Lil's house was too close for comfort. He was amazed he got out. He was rushing, not being careful so he had kicked something coming down the stairs. Damn broads! One of them had left her shoes on the bottom step. The sound of a shoe hitting the wall could have awakened the dead.

Just as he reached the basement door he heard a door creak open and footsteps above his head. He froze.

Shit! Someone was up. Probably got to piss.

He remained still while he listened for clues. The telltale flush should signal that she finished her business and was heading back to bed. A second flush—then a third.

Fuck!

He heard soft, slow footsteps on the stairs. Then a crash and a muffled cry. Whoever it was must have kicked the remaining shoe on the bottom step and fallen. *Too bad. So much for chivalry. Can't go help her. Gotta get out of here.*

Cautiously, he inched his way down the dark, basement steps. He heard footsteps above him in the kitchen—water running—and the footsteps retreating. Another sound—mumbled curses—then nothing.

He waited, hidden in the basement, squeezed behind the furnace until he was doubly sure he heard no sounds coming from above. When he was confident everyone was back in bed, he eased himself out of his hiding place and retraced his entry steps. Pushing himself up onto the washing machine, he turned to lift the window. Placing one foot on the washer control panel he pushed off and slithered out, at first allowing the window to ride along his back and then turning to use the sill for leverage to complete his exit. He pushed the window closed. He'd still have to find a legitimate reason to get back into the basement to latch it securely before anyone found it not completely closed and locked.

Once outside, he lay still in the grass until his rapidly beating heart slowed. Then he hugged the wall, staying in the shadow of the house until he could duck behind the garage of his house and get inside.

What had gone wrong? His watch never beeped—not at two hours—not after he reset it. Was it broken? Did he screw up when he set the timer? Was the battery dead? Had he badly miscalculated how long four friends would spend on their night out in the big city? These questions raced through his mind, aggravating his headache.

Mille had been waiting for him. When he returned empty handed, her facial expression conveyed her anger at his failure. Ignoring her, he grabbed the bottle of Jack Daniels from the kitchen counter and headed to the grimy old brown chair in the back parlor to do the only thing he could do at this point—get blind, stinking, rotten drunk.

The raw facts were hard to ignore. Failure, again. And the bigger question—what now? How would he explain away this latest failure and save his ass?

Unbeknown to Jimmy who was deep into his drunken stupor, Millie had quietly gathered her purse and walked out the back door, opening and closing it as carefully as she could to minimize any sound. It was time for Millie Raconti to disappear.

Chapter 10

Sunday, October 6

Ben Collins' elbow found the button for the bell as his hands held tightly to the cardboard tray holding overly full cups of liquid brown gold and the bag of bagels he carried. A professional juggler couldn't have done better.

"What a nice surprise!" said Sara. "Rachel, Ben Collins is here. Come on in. We're all in the kitchen."

"Hi ladies. I've brought nourishment. I wasn't sure what you all liked or had in stock so I got two decaf coffees. That other cup has cream in it and here are sugar packets." Seeing the other two women around the table, he added, "I didn't know you had company or I would have brought more."

Placing the tray of coffees and the bags on the table, Ben beamed his best pearly white smile around the room. He could see that returning early from Atlantic City to woo Rachel with his charm had been a good idea. He was smooth. He knew how to treat women. Four very sleepy, appreciative faces met his smile.

"Thanks, Ben. Late night or should I say, we all had a tad

101

too much to drink. These are my friends, Ellyn Markam and Beth Ingram. They're heading home today. Husbands can't survive any longer without them. Something about needing clean boxers and food. Since you brought it, can I get you some coffee?"

"No thanks, Rachel, I can't stay. And I hope you don't mind me dropping by without calling."

"No, not at all. Anyone who brings coffee and bagels is always welcome. Anything specific you need from me?"

"Not really. Just thought I'd check in and see how you were doing." Glancing around the kitchen, he saw empty cabinets and boxes. "Looks like you've made great progress. Anything I can do to help?"

"Now that you mention it, do you know a good real estate agent? Or a reputable company that buys estates? I'd love to be able to dispose of my aunt's furniture without running all over town."

Rachel stopped. "Oh…I didn't mean for that to sound as cold and calculating as it came out." *Is this what it all comes down to,* Rachel wondered. *Stuff and more stuff. What would Jenny and Scott do with her stuff when she was gone?*

"No need to apologize. Times like these can be overwhelming." Ben's warm smile reassured her that he understood where she was coming from.

"I have two agents—ReMax and Century 21—and an estate guy I got out of the Yellow Pages coming over tomorrow afternoon to look around and give me quotes, but if you know someone—a referral might be a better way to go."

"I think I can help on both counts. The crazy workaholic agents I know will be in their offices today—or at the very least—reachable by cell. Let me make a few calls."

"Thanks. I'll walk out with you." She led him down the hallway and onto the front porch. "I really want to thank you for taking care of so many of the details when my aunt died. It all happened so fast."

"Rachel, your aunt didn't want to be a burden to you. She had done so much to be ready prior to her death. The technology these days simplifies everything. She was in the hospital's system. She had left instructions about what to do if she was ever brought into the ER unconscious. She had a DNR order on file. When they accessed her records, it was all set in motion. The staff just followed her requests. Sadly, in this instance, she was already gone when the paramedics reached her."

"It was just so fast." Leaning against the porch column, Rachel remembered she and Ben had first met at this same place less then a week ago. Hesitatingly she continued, "I got the call around eleven. It…I…how did—"

"What's bothering you?" His soft, gentle tone warmed her heart. This was a man she could talk to, confide in. Resisting the urge to reach out and touch his arm, she continued.

"It was so early. I've been playing the timing of everything around in my mind. I guess I don't understand what the neighbor guy was doing at my aunt's house so early in the morning—and on a Sunday. I mean, I'm glad he was here to call nine-one-one or she could have laid there for hours. I'm just wondering…I can't get it out of my mind…what was my aunt doing up so early? She liked to sleep late. We talked almost every day around noontime simply because she liked her beauty sleep. What was he doing in her kitchen so early in the morning? It had to be—what—seven or eight o'clock?"

The question lingered on the air between them.

"Did you ask him?"

"No, I don't want to hurt his feelings or have him think I'm not grateful that he was here and helped. I just—. Never mind. Forget I said anything. You've got to go. Thanks for the coffee and bagels. Let me know if you have any contacts that can help with selling the house and finding the furniture new homes."

Rachel's words clearly signaled that the conversation was over. Ben hesitated for another minute before turning to leave.

"I'll call you later today with those names. If there is anything else I can do for you or if you just want to talk…Rachel, your aunt was a special client. You're special. And I want you to know, I'm here for you."

Another smile and he turned away and headed for his car.

"He screwed up," said Millie when she heard his sleepy hello come through the earpiece.

"What now?"

"Got stuck in the house last night. Girls came home and he was still in there."

"Schmuck!" A long silence followed. She could picture his movements. He was rubbing the sleep out of his eyes and looking at the clock. "Okay, anything connected to you left in the house?"

"No. Wiped the place clean just in case while I was waiting for him."

"Smart. Come home. We'll figure it out when you get here."

Keeping a go-bag stashed with everything she needed for a clean get-away in a locker at the twenty-four hour UPS store down the block from the house had also been smart. Hours earlier, when she walked out of the house, leaving Jimmy to clean up the mess he'd made, she only needed to go one block to retrieve her things. There was nothing at the

Studio 8 motel that connected to her. It would be a day or so before anyone realized the guest occupying room twelve was gone and they wouldn't care. The bill had been paid in full with cash for another week. With everything she needed in hand, she had hailed a cab to JFK and off she went.

Emerging from the ladies room, Marissa, aka Millie Raconti, felt a thousand pounds lighter. And she was lighter, just maybe not a thousand pounds. The heavy fat suit was gone, buried deep in a black plastic bag in the trash bin, never to be found. Gone too were the brown contact lenses, revealing once again her sparkling, violet blue eyes. And the theatrical prosthetic pieces that served her well these past few months were cut up into tiny bits and flushed into the New York City sewer system. These had worked perfectly, just as advertised. The broader nose and double chin neck prothesis had added years to her appearance.

Her frumpy pilled sweater, black stretch pants and sensible shoes had been replaced with a soft, silk floral print outfit and flaming red, Manolo Blahnik stilettos. With fresh make-up and the addition of some bangles and beads, the image that looked back at her from the bathroom mirror was not the same shapeless person that had entered the bathroom a half hour ago. If anyone was following her, which she doubted, they would wait a long time for Millie Raconti to emerge from the restroom.

Thankfully, this was one of those rare times when she was the only person in the ladies room. The handicapped stall provided her space and privacy—her change completed without prying eyes or arousing too much curiosity. Marissa never got over her transformations. Make-up and assorted prosthetic accouterments truly did the job. They allowed her to dramatically alter her appearance.

As she walked down the American Airlines concourse toward her gate, she could feel her natural sway return to her hips. Always conscious of her appearance, the way she could turn heads when she walked down the street or into a room, these last few months had done a number on her self-esteem. Millie Raconti was not a look she coveted. It fit the role she was playing nothing more. And in a con, details were important. You had to be thorough with what you could control because there was so much totally out of your control. And now that role was over. Millie Raconti was gone—a ghost or a figment of someone's over active imagination, never to be seen or heard from again.

Settling into her seat, Marissa was grateful for her first class accommodations. Not a good flyer, the drink in her hand and those to follow, would ease her flight back home. She knew the limo would be waiting for her when the plane landed. Details, details, details—all the small details taken care of by others so she could start to decompress.

Marissa bolted awake as the plane lurched.

What time is it? How long have I been asleep? Did I just scream?

Disoriented, she felt her heart pounding in her chest. The plane rattled and jolted. Her fingers tightened around the arm rest.

"Everything okay, ma'am?" asked a concerned looking flight attendant, who was now at her side.

"Yes, I'm sorry. Guess I dozed off a bit. Can I get a glass of water?"

"Of course, my pleasure."

Resting her head against the seat back, she closed her eyes and took some deep, cleansing breaths, working to steady and calm herself.

Returning with the water, the flight attendant smiled reassuringly.

"It's been a bumpy flight. We are so sorry. The captain is

trying to go around an approaching weather system. It should be a little smoother from here on. Can I get you anything else?"

"No...Yes. Another vodka on the rocks please." Marissa popped the two aspirins she was holding in her hand and emptied the glass. If the aspirin didn't work to relieve the throbbing, the vodka would at least dull the pain.

Marissa turned her gaze to the sky outside her window. Wispy white clouds threaded their way through an otherwise clear blue sky. The ocean below was a carpet of blue hues. Sky meeting sea as far as the eye could see.

Marco had told her to come home earlier this morning after they talked. She remained calm, business like, as she relayed the details of Jimmy's escapade the night before. The schmuck! He had gotten himself trapped in the damn house. She was watching from an upstairs window. She knew Jimmy was still in the house when she saw the girls return home. She knew Marco had to be called. That was what burn phones were for, emergencies. And this con was going down the toilet fast. From first class plan to fiasco in a New York minute. Total failure eminent. Abort!

Everything Marco did was precisely orchestrated to minimize the possibility of failure, of anyone getting caught or worse, killed. What had gone wrong here would be finely detailed and examined in an after-action meeting. She knew that he didn't really need a meeting to know he screwed up. He should have never inserted himself that day at the bar when he overheard a young hot-shot kid boasting about a job and uncut diamonds. He knew better than to get involved with an outsider, but the lure of uncut diamonds was irresistible. And the after-glow of the con they had just successfully completed had him riding high, feeling invincible. Damn the male ego. Right now, it was time for plan E, extraction. She was being extracted. What would become of Jimmy was not her concern.

She took another sip of vodka. Using a petty thief like Jimmy had not been her choice or her call. Jimmy had fast become a liability. Schmuck! Too stuck on himself for his own good. He took chances, too many chances. Continuing to replay the events of the last twenty-four hours in her head helped her sort things out. The vodka refill, the flight attendant had just brought her, helped too.

People really can be scared to death. Who knew! That's how the old lady died. Marissa had not been invited for tea that night. Jimmy decided to go over anyway, sneak in, take the chance that even without the small dose of crushed sleeping meds in her tea, she would sleep soundly. Wrong! Aunt Lil woke up saw a shadow moving in the darkness of her bedroom, screamed from fright, had a heart attack and died.

Jimmy's panicked call changed everything. She told him to get Lil's body into the kitchen immediately so it would be easier to explain how he found her when he came over to do some early morning repair work. She warned him to be careful because any bruise could show up later should there be an autopsy.

She called Marco to alert him to the new situation. Improvisation time. Fortunately, he was in D.C., not Florida. He had a few hours to plan his next moves. The niece, Rachel, was the key. Lil had talked a lot about her niece giving Marco time to do his homework. He knew where she lived and what kind of car she drove, had even successfully planted a tracking device on it. He now planned to casually meet Rachel on the road while she was driving to Brooklyn for the funeral. One thing was crystal clear. Rachel stood to inherit Aunt Lil's estate. The diamonds would belong to her.

❖

Five miles after crossing the bridge over the inter-coastal waterway, the limousine turned right off the highway and headed down a rugged, gravel road. Private property and no trespassing signs were nailed to trees every ten feet. The gravel crunched under the tires while the late afternoon sunlight twinkled through the canopy of tree branches that lined the roadway. The road ended abruptly with the appearance of a twelve foot high pinkish stone wall that enclosed the property and hid the splendor and beauty of what lay beyond from prying eyes. Huge, black, wrought iron gates topped with gold tipped fleur-de-lis secured the entrance. At the center of each gate, embedded in the iron overthrow was a familiar symbol—Le Maschere—the masks of comedy and tragedy. Marco held this image as a fitting symbol for the lives he and his compatriots had all led for so long—a testament to the masks they were forced to wear. Years ago, he adopted it as the family crest.

Marissa thought it was always inspiring to watch the gates open, welcoming you home. Home was safe. Home was peace. Home was sanctuary. Once through the gates, everything changed. What had been a poorly cared for road became a smooth, elegant avenue. All the land at this end of the island belonged to the family.

On each side were well manicured lawns, flowers bursting with color, ponds and waterfalls that galvanized your senses. A half-mile down, the avenue fed into a rotary. Taking the first spur brought you to the side of the island where several small, Florida style homes had been built for staff. There was a private clinic, a school, maintenance buildings and ten acres of land yet to be developed. Continuing around the rotary and heading off at the second spur, due east, a Mediterranean style estate began to reveal itself. And beyond that lay the Atlantic Ocean.

The last spur took you to the north end of the island,

Marissa's destination. Hers was the first of three homes, each with its own distinct architecture. She modeled her home after the Nantucket beach cottage used in the movie *Something's Gotta Give*. She dug up photos online and sent the architect a DVD of the film so he could draw the plans. Then he added the modifications needed to pass the new hurricane code restrictions put in place after Hurricane Andrew.

Marissa closed the front door, pressed her back against it, shut her eyes, and inhaled deeply.

Home. Dorothy was right. There's no place like home.

After a long moment she opened her eyes and looked around the room. Everything in its place and all is right with the world. Nothing could touch her here. Marco saw to that.

She crossed the room and threw open the french doors. The Atlantic Ocean rose before her. Marissa kicked off her high heels and stepped out onto the lanai. Moving quickly around the pool, she headed down the stairs, practically leaped off the slate stone patio, onto to the sand and ran to the ocean's edge. Salt air—a magic potion if ever there was one to calm the soul.

"Here, Miss Marissa, put this on. Welcome home."

Turning, Marissa saw Rosa coming up behind her with a broad brimmed, white straw sun hat in one hand and her favorite drink, a frozen strawberry daiquiri topped with whipped cream, in the other.

"Thank you, Rosa. You always know just what I need." Marissa placed the hat on her head and reached out for the drink. Taking a long, refreshing sip, Marissa embraced Rosa warmly.

"It is so good to see you. How have you been? The kids?"

"Fine. Everyone's fine. We are so glad you are home. You've been away too long this time. Everything okay?"

Rosa had worked for the family for almost as long as the

compound had been on the island. And she had taken care of Marissa for the last five years. She knew better than to ask where Marissa had been or what she had been doing. Fine was the operative word—and the accepted answer.

"Yes. Thank you so much for getting the house ready. The flowers are beautiful." *Thank God for Rosa,* Marissa thought. She had done a great job airing the place out. The hurricane shutters were up. All the vases had fresh flowers.

"Will you want dinner this evening? The refrigerator is fully stocked and I can make you whatever you like."

"Not just yet. I just want to stand here—get my bearings. You go on home. I'll take care of myself tonight."

"Yes, ma'am. Mr. Marco left a message. He said to take all the time you need. He's set a family meeting for Tuesday morning. He's hoping you'll join him for a late breakfast tomorrow. Just text him with a time. Do you want me to do that for you?"

"No, Rosa, I'll take care of it. You go on. Kiss that handsome husband of yours and your kids for me."

"Okay. See you in the morning. Sleep well."

Marissa plopped herself down in the sand. Losing herself to the ocean's sound, the salt air, and the warm, late afternoon breeze was the perfect way to decompress. The slowly setting sun danced off the water. The tide was coming in, row upon row of white-capped waves flowed towards shore, ending in lace and foam on the sand. Mesmerizing. Soon she would have to move or get wet.

Always choices to make, she thought. *Move or get wet. Quit and get out or get caught.*

As she got older, each con seemed to take more out of her. Maybe it was time to stop, to pack it in, to call it a day and be done. Marco would understand, the family would understand. As Marissa lost herself in the rolling waves and surf's roar, distant memories flooded back like they always did when left to her own mental wanderings. Tears found their way to her cheeks.

Shit! Hers had been no life for a young person. She had been used and abused for so long. Love? What was love? The only love she really could count on was here, on this narrow strip of sand with her invented, chosen family.

The family, if you could call it that, was really four people brought together by circumstance—Marco, Sophia, Dom, and herself. Cast aside, unloved, thrown to the wolves to fend for themselves at an age when most children were nestled in the protective arms of loving parents. Turning to the streets, they did what they needed to do to survive. Street entertainers, petty thieves, fortune tellers, prostitutes and magicians once upon a time, working Atlantic City, Key West, New Orleans, Ft. Lauderdale, Miami, places where happy, vacationing tourists let their guard down and could be easily separated from their hard earned money.

The desire for a better life, a midnight meal with cheap wine flowing, and an off-the-cuff comment had bonded them for all eternity. Each had sworn a blood oath to one another, to the family they created over three decades ago. Each had one vote. Marco, as the eldest, was chosen the leader. He had two votes and made the final decisions on how the games would play out. That was what they called their cons—games.

It was all getting old, very old, especially after this last one with that stupid shit, Jimmy. *What was Marco thinking?* It was only a matter of time before she got caught—any one of them got caught. Their luck had been really good to this point. No one had landed in jail. And, as a quick look around this little strip of paradise could attest, it was clear they were all very successful at what they did.

"I thought that was you," shouted Marco startling Marissa who turned in the direction of the voice to watch him approach. He came prepared.

Only a few steps away now, Marissa never ceased to be enamored by his good looks. Graying at the temples, tall and strong, his unbuttoned white shirt billowing open by the afternoon breeze, revealing his honey tanned chest. Blue seersucker shorts completed the look. *Right off the pages of GQ,* Marissa thought, a bottle of wine in one hand and his sandals and two wine glasses in the other.

"Glad you're back. Don't get up," he said as he sat down next to her on the sand. "I saw you from my deck and thought I'd join you. Now toss the silly kiddie drink and enjoy some of this."

"With pleasure," smiled Marissa setting aside the strawberry daiquiri she had barely touched and reaching to accept the glass of wine he offered her. "Got your message about meeting for breakfast. Okay if we wait till then for any shop talk?"

"Of course. Not why I came down here. I just want to be with you right now. Share the moment." And with that, the two of them fell into a comfortable silence broken only by the sound of squawking sea gulls and crashing waves.

"It never gets old, does it?"

She and Marco locked eyes for a moment, the electricity of the connection reaching to the depths of each one's soul. They broke at the same time, turning their eyes seaward, back to the ocean, listening to the rhythmic crashing of the waves rolling ashore, savoring the salty air.

"No. It never gets old," Marissa sighed. "Keeps me sane. Fills me. Restores me."

Chapter 11

Jimmy wobbled to the kitchen, retrieved another beer and held the cold bottle up to his forehead in a feeble attempt to quell the throbbing in his head. He'd been drinking all night. Jack Daniels first and after he emptied the bottle, he turned to beer.

What a shit storm. Everything was falling apart. He had to regain control.

Think, man!

He couldn't see a way to get back in the house. Rachel was making good progress. With her friends' help, most of the closets on the first two floors were empty. Doomed! He'd failed and failure had consequences. And that bitch, Millie, was nowhere to be found. Talk about dead weight. Good riddance.

His cell phone blast seared through his brain. He answered it without thinking.

"Yeah?"

"Status report now."

Jimmy dropped the cell phone.

Fuck!

Should have looked before he answered it. *What was he*

supposed to say? That he fucked up? He didn't know who this guy was—only a menacing voice on the other end of the line. Saying nothing, he pressed the end button. His only job now was to stay alive. He had to disappear. And he better act fast.

Get it together, man! First, get out of this house. Get back to the apartment, grab some stuff—get gone.

He'd done it before. Not that hard really. A huge shadow economy supported hundreds of thousands, if not millions, of illegals. It had supported him in the past when he needed to disappear. It would do so again now.

He didn't own anything worth a damn. Thief wasn't exactly the type of occupation that required a social security number. Retirement? If he wanted a retirement plan, he would have been a plumber like his old man. Hell, he'd be lucky to make it to forty alive.

Saying goodbye to Jimmy Raconti would be easy. He kind of liked the muscle-man, greaser look. It was a total attraction magnet with the ladies. He'd keep the look, change the name. Maybe hitch to Atlantic City first for a few days. The ladies there were an easy mark. Someone would take him in, let him crash at her place, feed him, soothe his aching soul with her sweet embrace. It never ceased to amaze him how easy it was to get in bed with some pretty smelling bimbo who only needed a few kind words to give up her goods.

He opened the back door and smashed the phone into the cement stoop. Then he took it apart like he'd seen countless operatives do in the spy movies he watched. The SIM card was heading for the bottom of the Hudson River and he'd scatter the rest of the pieces on his way out of town. He grabbed his jacket from the porch hook and his back pack, closed the back door and headed out.

This job is so over, he thought, as he rounded the corner on his way to being gone—very, very gone.

116

"I'm home," shouted Beth, as she walked into her kitchen. "Rachel sends her love."

Silence greeted her.

That's odd, thought Beth who knew Jacob's car was in the garage which meant he was here, somewhere.

"Honey, you here?"

Only silence.

"Jacob?"

Dropping her keys and purse on the small desk, she walked into the den. Jacob sat in his favorite chair staring into space—catatonic. As she approached she could see raw, red swollen eyes, tear stained cheeks.

Beth bent down in front of the chair and grabbed both her husband's arms, shaking him.

"Jacob? What happened? Jacob, talk to me! Is it Adam?" He raised his eyes to hers—his grief palpable.

In a flash of motherly knowing, "Oh, God. How bad? Is he dead?" Their only son, Adam, served as a lieutenant colonel in the Army and was currently on his third tour of duty in Afghanistan.

"Is he alive?" she screamed. "Answer me. Say something!"

"IED. They said he was alive…Medi-vaced to Kandahar…something like that. I don't know. I didn't hear the rest."

"Oh God…Oh God…what do we do? Who do we call?"

Beth slumped to the floor, wrapped her arms around her knees and started to rock back and forth. Jacob pushed himself out of the chair and wrapped his arms around her. They swayed together, a somber motion of loving unknowing.

They had felt the pain of losing a child before. Their little girl, Hannah, the apple of her daddy's eyes, had been lost to Tay-Sachs at the tender age of four. It never crossed their minds to get tested. They were both Ashkenazi Jews, sure, but what were the chances that they both carried the gene? They decided no more children. All that remained for them was Adam, their first-born.

It seemed like hours before either one let go. They needed to get there, wherever there was. Forever practical, Beth sprung into action. She needed more information.

"Jacob, who called? Did they say where to call for more information? Who can we call?"

"It was some commander or colonel. I don't remember. Oh God, Beth…Adam, our Adam. What are we going to do?"

"We're going to be strong for him—get there—be there—do whatever it takes to bring our baby home. That's what we're going to do."

Walking back from the kitchen where she retrieved her cell phone Beth was frantically scrolling through her contacts.

"Got it. Adam left this number for me. He said if anything ever happened to call it and they would tell us what to do—where to go."

Chapter 12

Monday, October 7

Sitting at the kitchen table, with another cup of coffee, picking at a bagel, Rachel was grateful for the time alone. It was a blessed reprieve from the hustle of the last few days. Beth and Ellyn had gone home yesterday to take care of their husbands. Grown men and they still couldn't boil water. Sara was on her way downtown to see her Uncle Stan who had spent his entire life working on Forty-seventh Street, the Diamond District. She carried one small treasure in her pocket, carefully tucked next to what she considered her own crown jewel. Her task was simple. Talk to her Uncle Stan and glean some insight as to how Rachel can best handle this surprising, life changing aspect of her aunt's death and legacy.

Saturday night had been fun. Deciding against going into New York City, Sara took them to a small French bistro that had gotten rave reviews. Staying local gave them more quality time together without fighting Saturday night traffic. Although it was not spoken aloud, they all knew that it would be a long time before the four would be together again. Hours after they swapped memories in the living room pierced by more giggles and dancing to oldies, they had climbed the stairs leaning on one another for support as they headed off to bed. She'd really rather forget the getting sick and throwing up parts of Saturday night. She'd barely eaten anything since.

Ben had not called yesterday with any recommendations. It was Sunday. Probably off having fun with someone special. Not important. She had a real estate agent and an estate guy coming by later today to see the house. If he called her today with other names, she could contact them and set up appointments for later in the week.

She was actually enjoying the solitude. She needed this time alone to think—to really begin her private grieving for her aunt. By the end of this week she planned to be on her way home. Many of her aunt's things would be coming with her. Each time she wrapped herself in one of the handmade quilts, warm fuzzy memories of her aunt, a woman who loved her more than anyone else, comforted her. She took a sip of coffee.

Cold.

Spitting it back into her cup, Rachel got up, poured it down the drain and rinsed out the carafe to make a fresh pot. What was bothering her? Like a mosquito bite she couldn't reach to scratch, a few things about her aunt's death nagged at her—details that did not feel right. At the moment, a new thought had started noodling around in her head. That attic door thing. She remembered that her weight closed it when she leaned on it on her way to the bathroom to throw up. She was sure she'd closed it tightly earlier in the day. *Why was the door open?* She was sure no one had gone up to the attic yet. She and Sara were cleaning it out tomorrow. Getting the latch looked at was just another item on a long list of things that needed doing before the house sold.

Maybe she'd talk to Sara tonight about the door thing.

The doorbell rang, announcing the arrival of either a realtor or the estate guy. Looking out the sidelight she was pleased to see a very handsome man looking back. Tall, with short, wavy gray hair, dressed in a tweed sport jacket with a pale yellow shirt and a tie that screamed fall. What really got her attention was the badge he flashed.

"Yes?" said Rachel through the sidelight glass as she stared at her visitor.

"I'm Detective Daniel Berger. May I have a moment of your time, please?"

Opening the door, Rachel stepped onto the porch. Detective Daniel Berger reintroduced himself and offered her his credentials for closer inspection but she kept her arms crossed and her hands tucked under them.

"What can I do for you, Detective?"

"I'm not really sure. I've been looking into the deaths of some of our elderly citizens and I came across a Mrs. Lillian Steinmetz at this address. I have a police report that a nine-one-one call was made and an ambulance sent here. I've got a name, a Jimmy Raconti, as the person who made the nine-one-one call. Is he here?"

"No, he doesn't live here. He lives next door," she said, pointing at his house. "He found her. She was my aunt. She died a week ago, Sunday. Is there a problem?"

"No." A long pause, then, "at least I don't think so. What can you tell me about her death?"

"Not much really."

"Had she been sick?"

"Not really. She told me her doctor said she'd live to one hundred." A tiny smile crossed Rachel's face. "Guess they like to tell older patients that. Anyway, we talked every day around noon because she liked to sleep late. My aunt loved her beauty sleep. And Jimmy found her in the kitchen on the floor the morning she died."

"About what time was that? The report shows the nine-one-one call coming in at nine o'clock and the ambulance arriving within five minutes of that."

"I'm not really sure. I got the call late Sunday morning. I called my daughter, Jenny, who lives in New Jersey to get things rolling. We're Jewish so we bury within twenty-four hours. And then I left. I drove up from Williamsburg, Virginia." Rachel drifted for a moment, seemingly lost in her own thoughts.

"My aunt had already made all her own arrangements, years ago really. She was very particular. She wrote instructions about what she wanted done. When the ER pulled up her records, everything was right there. She had a DNR on file which they didn't need because she was already dead, and a list of who to call. And then, it just went like clockwork. There's not much more I can add. By the time I got here, it was all done."

Detective Berger had taken a few notes during Rachel's review of events.

"Do you know she still walked a mile almost every day?"

"That's pretty good."

"She hadn't been complaining about anything out of the ordinary aches and pains of someone in her nineties. In her mind, she was the picture of health." That last comment brought another smile to Rachel's face that slowly morphed to sadness. After a few moments staring into space, Rachel sighed, "I'm going to miss her a lot."

"I'm sorry. I don't mean to upset you. One or two more questions, if I may."

"Would you like some coffee, Detective? I've just put on a fresh pot and I could use another cup."

"Yes, that would be nice. Thanks."

He followed Rachel inside and down the hallway into the kitchen. Pulling another mug from the drain board, Rachel poured the steaming hot coffee.

"Sugar? Cream?"

"Both please." Seeing all the boxes, empty cabinets and packing materials, he added, "Looks like you've been busy. What are your plans for the house?"

"Well, my Aunt Lil left everything to me. Since I don't live here and my children are grown, married and already have homes, I'm selling the house. I've got a real estate agent coming over today to talk about listing it. In fact, that's who I thought you were—until I saw your badge, that is. Anyway, most of my aunt's clothes and things have gone to Goodwill and I'm hoping an estate buyer will handle the larger pieces of furniture. The smaller things like her Toby Mug and Lladro collections," said Rachel pointing to the dining room table. "She loved those pieces. I'll pack those and take them home with me."

"Williamsburg, you said? Now that's a pretty town. I was there years ago. I'm a history buff and the town reeks of it. What made you pick Williamsburg, and not say, Florida?"

"I just fell in love with the town when Jenny, my daughter, was considering going to William & Mary. She picked Penn State, but Williamsburg was always in the back of my mind. And then, well, my life—my husband died a few years ago—."

"Sorry."

"Thanks. It was very sudden. One minute he was there—then he was gone. Just like that." Rachel's voice choked a bit and she could feel her heart tighten.

"Aunt Lil, well, she was my rock. She kept telling me to live out loud, not to fade into the background. Not to settle. That I'd done the mother thing, the wife thing—the settling thing. That I needed to do what she called the Rachel thing."

"What's that?"

"I'm not really sure. She was like that. Strong. She'd been alone so many years and it never stopped her. She was so alive in every sense of the word. And that was what she wanted for me. I guess that's what she meant by the Rachel thing. She pushed me and pushed me to start over, turn a page, strike out. She said that each of our lives is like a great story and we get to tell it through how we live it. We're the directors. You just keep inventing new chapters and characters for yourself. You should have heard her go on and on."

"I am hearing her—right now—through you. You know, I think I would have liked your Aunt Lil, especially her attitude about life and living it fully. The closer I get to retirement, the more I think about what I want to do next. Heck, I could have retired years ago, but just couldn't get a picture in my head of a next chapter. I'm alone. Sons grown and off on their own. Lost my wife years ago. So I keep doing this detective thing—over and over and over again. Wonder if she would have told me to go do the Daniel thing."

How is it, thought Rachel, as she sat in her aunt's kitchen sharing coffee and tidbits of her life with this stranger, *that it feels like I've known him for years.* There had been a few other people in her life who had affected her this way, most notably Sara. And here was another person, a man, who was as comfortable as old socks and had a stick to your ribs warmth like mac and cheese on a cold winter's night. Maybe they had met in another life.

"I hear you. Last New Year's Eve my friend Sara asked me what my resolutions were for this year and I just started to cry. I couldn't stop. I couldn't catch my breath. I told her I didn't want to live like I was already dead, bored out of my mind, going through the motions, waiting around for nothing. That I wanted to feel alive, be alive. The more I thought about it, the only way I could think of to set myself on a different path was to be someplace different so that I would be forced out of my comfort zone—forced to do things differently. So I moved."

"Did it work?"

"Too soon to say. I'd like to think so. That's why I'm moving so fast here. Because I want to get back to my new home, my new life. You should come visit," blurted out Rachel before she could self-censor.

Where did that come from? Looking at the man seated across the table from her, she realized that she'd turned a corner in her life. There was no going back, and now, with Aunt Lil's death, there wasn't anything to go back to. This man appealed to her. His warm brown eyes crinkled at the corners when he smiled. Extending the invitation to visit might have been out of character for the old Rachel; it was totally in line with who she was working hard to become—a self-assured woman who went after what she wanted.

"Maybe I'll just do that. But for now, I've taken up too much of your time."

Standing, Detective Berger, took his coffee cup to the sink. Before she knew it, he washed it out and replaced it in the drain board.

Housebroken.

"You didn't need to do that," said Rachel.

"Thanks for the coffee." He reviewed his notes.

"Just one more thing. Does the name Ben Collins mean anything to you?"

"Yes. He's…" Hesitating, Rachel took a long breath, "he was my aunt's lawyer. He told me that she became his client after his father died—when he took over his father's practice. He took care of her will and other affairs. In fact,

I'm waiting for a call from him. He said he could recommend a real estate agent and an estate guy for all this furniture. Is there a problem?"

"Don't think so. His name has come up in several of the other cases I've been reviewing. Taking over his dad's practice would explain how he had so many elderly clients." He jotted down that tidbit of information and flipped through a page or two from his notepad.

"One other question. You mentioned your aunt usually slept late—liked her beauty sleep I think you said. Do you have any idea why she was up so early the day she died?"

"No. Maybe she had someplace to be. I know it wasn't church. We're Jewish," laughed Rachel. "Practical people. We do Friday nights, and if you're really into it, which my aunt was not, Saturday mornings. And even then services rarely start before ten o'clock. Nothing much on Sundays. That particular Sunday—I don't know. She didn't say she had any plans when we spoke on Saturday."

"Okay, and you also said that your neighbor, Jimmy, found her. Any idea what he might have been doing in her home so early?"

"No, I don't. And since you brought it up, I've been thinking a lot about that too. Jimmy is…I don't know…he keeps showing up here at the strangest times. The other night I found him in the back alcove heading down to the basement. Said he was checking on the furnace. I was sure I locked the back door so I don't know how he got in. Aunt Lil always talked about him and his mother being helpful and kind neighbors. The mother used to come over for tea at night and keep my aunt company. I don't want to be mean, but Jimmy makes me uncomfortable. I'm not sure what more I can add."

"How long have they lived here?"

"I don't really know. I moved away in June and I never

remember seeing them when I visited my aunt. But they could have been here. This is a very stable neighborhood."

"That's true. Maybe I'll just stop next door before I go."

His slow saunter towards the door surprised Rachel. Was she imagining his pace? For someone with such an important job, he didn't seem to be in a hurry to leave. Through the glass she saw a well dressed woman reaching out to ring the bell just as the theme from the old Dragnet TV show blasted from his phone.

"Excuse me. Berger."

He listened intently then sharply declared "On my way." Replacing the phone he said, "Rachel, it has been a pleasure. I can't remember when I've enjoyed a cup of coffee so much. Here is my card in case you think of anything else."

Detective Berger put out his hand. Rachel's hand met his. Another first touch flutter tickled her.

He seemed to be stalling. *Was there more,* she wondered.

With a slight hesitation in his voice, he asked somewhat shyly, "When are you planning to go home? What I mean is, if you're going to be around for a few days, maybe we could grab dinner one night?"

"I'd like that. I'll be here at least through the weekend." Holding up her finger signaling him to wait, she walked to the small table by the phone and scribbled on a post-it note. "Here's my cell."

Rachel heard the voice in her head.

I like this man. Daniel—nice name—has a warm ring to it. He's different somehow. What is it about him that feels like home? Maybe he'll call. Maybe I'll call him.

They walked out to the porch and Rachel turned her attention to the woman now standing next to her.

"Hi, I'm Janice Stone, ReMax. Are you Rachel?" asked the peppy young woman whose smile seemed to go from ear to ear.

Clearly dressed to showcase her success—very tailored emerald green toned St. John knit suit, fall colored Hermes scarf stylishly tied to her leather brief case, and enough gold jewelry to choke a horse. Impressive to anyone who might question her sales talents.

"Yes. I've been expecting you. Come on in," said Rachel, her eyes turning back to the street, following Detective Berger to his car. Not at all what she expected as an outcome from a visit with a police detective. But, then again, expectations are highly overrated. Surprise. Surprise!

Chapter 13

Sara loved the diamond district. When she was a little girl she used to walk down Forty-seventh Street, humming the then popular tune, *Diamonds Are A Girl's Best Friend*, and dreaming of her diamond, the one her knight in shining armor would give her after which they would live happily ever after. It would be big—two carats—blue white—pear shaped—in a platinum setting. She had seen it in her dreams and in the store windows and booths that crowded the street. The only place it had never appeared was on her finger. Then again, the knight never showed up either.

When Sara arrived at the door she saw no one in the showroom save Uncle Stan leaning over the counter looking at a small piece of jewelry through his loupe. *Good,* she thought, *he's alone.* Sara gently knocked on the bullet proof glass door to get his attention.

A smile that could easily light up the world spread across his face when he saw her. He quickly buzzed her in and came around the showcase with his arms outstretched. Sara made a beeline for him. He was her favorite uncle and the warm hug they exchanged reaffirmed for her that the feelings were mutual.

JANE FLAGELLO

"Sara, I loved getting your call that you'd be coming to see me today. How are you? The family?"

"Everyone is fine, Uncle Stan. And you, how are you? Aunt Belle?"

"Good. Her arthritis is acting up now that the weather is getting cooler. But, hey, that's what Florida is for. We're leaving right after Thanksgiving. She'll stay down there for the winter and I'll go back and forth. Not ideal, but you do what you've gotta do. Can I get you something to drink? Coke? Pepsi?

"No, thanks. I'm fine."

The showroom never changed. Shades of cream and beige covered the furniture. Mirrors and impressionist paintings adorned the walls. Soft lighting and comfortable seating made the room elegant—inviting. Each item on display was an originally designed piece of jewelry. That was Uncle Stan's specialty and his skills were legendary. You would not see your ring, earrings or necklace on anyone else. Each piece was an inspiration. Customers loved his talents.

Customers also loved Uncle Stan. Standing close to six feet tall, balding and built like a bulldog, when his arms went around you in a hug, they went all the way around you. He was soft and warm and cuddly. Uncle Stan had a heart of gold and would give you the shirt off his back if he thought it would help you. No need to ask. In the Yiddish vernacular, Uncle Stan was a mensch.

"So, Sara, what brings you downtown?"

"I need your help. Some information really. I have a friend…" Sara paused mid-sentence and decided to take a different tack. "I need to learn a bit about uncut diamonds."

"Interesting topic, uncut diamonds. They are not as rare as you might think. In this building alone, there are easily a hundred dealers that trade uncut diamonds. Look on the internet and you'll find all sorts of companies that deal in diamonds."

"That's the confusing part. I did look on the internet. There is so much information out there. It's overwhelming."

"Confusion helps people like me. We become the experts and once we get a customer comfortable and seeing us as just that, an expert, someone they can trust, more than half our sales job is done. Then we just have to listen to what they want and make it appear." A quick snap of his fingers accentuated the point.

"Okay, but what if you had an uncut diamond. How would you go about finding out how much it was worth…or getting it cut…or selling it?" Direct and to the point. Small talk was not exactly Sara's style.

"Well, that's easy. You'd come to me."

Uncle Stan's jovial response did not elicit the smile he expected to see on his niece's face. Her eyes were tight. He could tell Sara was on a serious mission and needed more from him.

"Okay, Sara, down to business. What's really going on here?"

"I just need some information for a friend."

"What you're asking about takes a lifetime of learning. Come, let's sit," he said gesturing toward one of the sofas along the window looking out on Forty-seventh Street. He sat. Sara paced.

"Here's a quick and dirty version. Stop me with any questions. There are different classes of diamonds— investment diamonds, industrial diamonds and gem quality diamonds. And they all start as uncut stones. There are major cutting centers in places like Antwerp, Tel Aviv, Bombay, and of course, here. And yes, there are differences in the quality of the rough. Beyond that, it's what happens next that really determines their value. The cutting. And here is where you want an expert, a great cutter, someone who can see into the heart of the stone, feel what it wants to become and imagine its possibilities."

Uncle Stan watched his niece, looking for clues—trying to see what direction he needed to take. She had not been making eye contact with him as he talked, appeared almost jumpy as she paced from case to case. Was he imagining her sideways glances out into the hallway? Sara simply was not acting like his Sara. Her whole body seemed tense, out of kilter.

"Sara, why all the questions? What do you need, honey?" he asked in a voice that oozed love. "What's wrong? How can I help you?"

Sara's left hand had been in her pocket the entire time she walked around Uncle Stan's showroom. Stopping, she turned to look at him straight on and approached the sofa where he sat. Taking her hand out of her pocket she opened it to reveal her prize.

"What about this stone?"

Stan's eyes looked from the stone to Sara and back to the stone. To the untrained eye, there wasn't much to see. Stan lifted the stone and moved it between his fingers. Getting up, he walked to the counter and picked up the loupe he had been using when Sara arrived.

With the loupe pressed against his eye, he carefully examined the stone, slowly turning it this way and that way. Pressing a hidden release latch behind the counter, he opened the gating that kept him somewhat safe from visitors and motioned for Sara to follow him.

Once in his private office, he switched to a more powerful loupe, silently continuing to examine the stone.

"Where did you get this?"

"From a friend. Is that important?"

"It looks like a very high quality stone, a very rare stone from what I can tell. I only say that because of how few inclusions I can see using the high powered loupe. Cutting it well will be the key. And I know one or two really good cutters I can introduce you and your friend to. So, when do I get to meet your friend?"

It had been a long day all around. Chinese take-out containers covered the small kitchen table. Sara and Rachel filled their plates.

"Why shop for food when there are so many places within walking distance to get good take-out." Sara bit into an egg roll. "Too bad Beth and Ellyn aren't here. Guess we can't play mah jongg with just two of us." Sara knew Rachel could use the distraction.

Sara repeated what Uncle Stan told her about the one diamond she had shown him.

"Have you heard anything I've said?" asked Sara who sensed that Rachel was not listening because she wasn't asking any questions.

"Yes. Okay no. Not really," said Rachel putting down her fork. "The strangest thing—when the ReMax lady was here this afternoon, she said that it was very rare for two houses next door to each other to be for sale at the same time in this neighborhood. She didn't think I'd have much trouble selling Aunt Lil's house, since it was a corner property. But that means the house next door—the other house for sale—is the one the Raconti's own."

"So?"

Pausing for a moment to consider what she just said, Rachel continued, "Doesn't that strike you as odd?"

"What—that they didn't tell you their house was for sale?" asked Sara, shoveling another chopstick full of General Tso's chicken into her mouth.

"Yeah. They know I'm selling Aunt Lil's house. You would think they would have offered to have their agent come by, or call me. Or—I don't know. Something about them, about Jimmy more than her, just doesn't sit right for me."

Again, Rachel seemed lost in her own thoughts. She couldn't shake the feeling that something was not right. She couldn't let it go—the agent's comment about the two homes being for sale. The woman had droned on and on. Loved Aunt Lil's house, blah, blah, blah. She knew several estate people and she'd make sure at least the two, who were in her opinion the easiest to deal with, called the next day. Blah, blah, blah. Ms. Stone left saying she would call tomorrow to see if Rachel had any questions.

Rachel had nothing but questions. None were about selling her aunt's house. All were about the Racontis—the house next door. They kept popping into her head the more she thought about it. Why no For Sale sign? That was the first thing Ms. Stone had asked Rachel about. She couldn't wait to stick a For Sale sign in the front lawn.

"Is this your gypsy blood working overtime?"

"Probably. Shit. Never mind, ignore me. Eat." Rachel took a bite of her egg roll. "Tell me again what Uncle Stan said."

"Bottom line, he said he could help you. With selling or cutting. That he had a close friend who was an expert cutter and to come see him when you're ready."

Rachel put down her fork. "Let's go next door. I'll take one of the smaller Lladro pieces as a gift."

"What? What's gotten into you? You already gave her some jewelry? Why another gift? What's the point?"

"I don't know. I just know I want to get inside that house. That's all. You coming?" Rachel was up and heading for the dining room table where all of the Lladro had been laid out.

She picked up the small ballerina piece, wrapped it in some colored tissue paper and was almost to the front door before Sara could catch up.

"Do you know what you're going to say?"

"How hard can it be to say here's another gift from my dead aunt?" Rachel saw Sara wince and realized her tone was a tad too sharp. She quickly apologized and they walked to the Raconti's house and climbed the front steps. Rachel rang the bell.

Sara wandered across the front porch. "This can't be good," said Sara as she peered into the front room through the window. "Rachel, you better come see this."

"What?"

"Nothing, that's what. There's nothing in there. No furniture, no nothing. They do live here, right? This house is occupied?"

"Yeah. Millie and Jimmy live here. I haven't seen them today, but they live here."

"But there's no furniture. How can they have no furniture?"

Rachel joined Sara at the window. "Wow. You're right. I was only in the kitchen and I went in through the back door. Never really got a look into the rest of the house. Barely made it to the kitchen table the other day when I brought over the brooches for Millie. Maybe they moved their furniture out, thinking it would sell faster and they'd have less to move later."

"Then they're only living back there, because as you can see there's not a stick of furniture in the living room."

"No one's home. Let's go look around back."

Rachel headed off the front porch, across the small front lawn and around the back with Sara at her heels. Seeing inside the house was a bit harder from here.

"Rachel, put the Lladro down. Come hold me steady so I

don't lose my balance and fall." Sara grabbed an old metal milk crate and stood on it. The crate gave Sara the height she needed to see inside the back room window.

"Okay, we've got a chair, a lamp and a TV. That's it in this room. Can't see into any others. And you know from when you were here that there's a kitchen table."

"This is weird. Something's up. Let's go before anyone comes or sees us."

Back in Aunt Lil's house, Rachel poured more wine into both of their glasses. She had switched to white trying to avoid another whopper wine headache.

"You know, not having any furniture fits that creepy feeling I get around those two. With all that's happened over the last few days, I sometimes feel like I am losing my mind. Did I tell you about the detective I met today?"

"What detective?" asked Sara who was now way more interested in hearing about a new man than zapping the plate of cold Chinese food in her hands.

Rachel dug in her pocket and produced his card. "This detective," she answered, passing the card to Sara. "He came by this afternoon, just before the realtor got here. He was asking about Aunt Lil's death, talking about other elderly deaths and even mentioned the lawyer, Ben Collins. He was going to stop next door to talk to Jimmy since he was the one that found her body and called nine-one-one, but he got a call and had to go."

Working for two bosses sucked, thought Jimmy. *Not my smartest move.*

The guy he'd met at the bar a few months back didn't worry him too much. The voice on the phone scared the shit out of him. He was sure the person behind the voice, the guy telling him where to go and who to rob, had a very long reach. After Saturday night's screw up, he ran. Unfortunately, he didn't know who he was running from.

He'd spent the last twenty-four hours on the streets, moving from place to place. The bus stop, Penn Station, Times Square, anywhere with crowds of people. Constantly watching over his shoulder to see if anyone was tailing him, looking too interested in him.

There was stuff he needed at the apartment he shared with Jolene, a friend with benefits. He made his way downtown on the subway. When he reached the apartment, he found her still in bed. Thankfully, alone.

"Ooooooooo," she cooed as he softly touched her arm to wake her, brushing back a stray curl of her auburn tresses that had fallen across her eyes. Jolene slid the sheets away to reveal bronze-tanned legs, bent at the knees. Patting the space beside her, she invited him in.

"Not now, babe. I gotta go."

"Why so stressed? Relax. Come here," she whispered expecting a different response then his rejection. "I know how to help you relax." While not the brightest person he had ever met, Jolene did have other talents that Jimmy appreciated.

She wrapped her arms lightly around his neck, pulling him close. The smell of sweat filled his nostrils. Cigarette breath. She'd had company. She only smoked after sex. This bed had been used recently. He felt no inclination to be its next occupant.

"No!" he hissed defiantly glaring down at her as he broke free from her embrace. "You need a shower and I gotta go." Jimmy went to the closet, grabbed a black duffle bag and began stuffing it with his clothes.

"What's up? You leaving?" Puzzled, Jolene sat up and tucked the sheet under her arms covering her well endowed assets. Playing her role, she asked, "Can I come too?"

"This isn't a vacation. I've got some business that needs to be taken care of." He could see her pouting reflection in the mirror above the dresser. "Look, babe, I'm kind of pressed for time right now. I need to travel light, move fast. Tell you what, I'll call for you when I get settled."

Walking back to the bed, he took a deep breath and held it as he kissed her. Turning to leave, he said, "Take care of yourself. If anyone comes around asking about me, tell them I went out to the Hamptons to see my Cousin Phil. Jolene, can you remember that?"

Jimmy locked eyes with her and seethed, "This is important. Pay attention."

Pouting, Jolene answered in a voice reminiscent of a disappointed two year old. "Yeah, sure. Hamptons, Cousin Phil. I got it."

"Gotta go."

Jimmy walked out, knowing that he would not be returning.

Jolene listened to Jimmy's footsteps pounding down the stairs. When she was sure he was gone she reached for her cell phone. She didn't expect anyone to answer the number she called. Her voice message was short and direct.

"Uncle Al, it's Jolene. Jimmy just left. Gave me some line about going out to the Hamptons. Took most of his stuff. Looked scared. I'll see what more I can find out when I see Ben Thursday night."

Jimmy headed for the Battery. He'd miss Jolene. They had developed a special relationship—fun with no strings attached. And Jolene was totally built for fun. He accepted that she was a working girl—had other men.

What the fuck. Doesn't matter anyway. Not like I'm

planning to marry her. There are thousands of Jolene's out there. And the Hamptons? Shit. They can look long and hard, but they won't find me out there.

The Staten Island ferry was as good a way as any to get out of the city and the next boat was leaving in a few minutes. Whenever he needed to clear his head after a tough job, he'd ride the ferry. In less than an hour he could get his shit back together and the scenery was some of the best on earth—the Statue of Liberty, Ellis Island, the New York City skyline.

This time was different. There would be no return trip tonight, or for a long time. Let things cool down. Hide out in Atlantic City. Fun place. Love the action. But more action meant more eyes watching. What were his chances of getting lost there? Philly, or someplace further south, would be a better choice.

Jimmy planned to hip hop across Staten Island. He figured between hitching rides and local buses he'd be across the Goethals Bridge by morning. Maybe he'd get lucky and some trucker would pick him up and take him all the way. *All the way where?* He'd figure that out when he needed to.

Hell, right now all he wanted was a beer and some food. When the ferry docked he headed out to the street. Looking one way then the other, all he saw were deserted streets. Staten Island was not exactly a swinging town late at night. He'd been walking a few blocks when he saw a flickering neon green bar sign down one of the side streets to his right. Crossing the street he headed for the flashing green sign. At least he'd get his beer.

Rattling chain sounds got his attention. A street-wise guy with good instincts, he felt them before he saw them. He moved closer to the storefronts. Maybe he'd catch a reflection in a store window showing him what was behind him. Nothing. He could feel them. Two blocks to go. The bar was getting closer with each step.

Two guys suddenly popped out of the alley in front of him. One leaned against the brick walled building at the edge of the alley. The other took a position at the curb, leaning against the street lamp post.

This can't be good thought Jimmy. *Stay cool. I'm one of them, not a cop or a dude in a suit.*

"Got a match?" asked the one by the curb. He was big and black, dressed in black from head to toe. Jimmy could see a gold chain with a huge cross dangling around his neck. A large diamond stud glistened from each ear and a matching diamond stud pierced one eyebrow.

"No, man." Jimmy kept walking. The two fell in behind him. He sensed there were more than these two guys following him.

"Guessin' you're heading for Moe's. How 'bout we join you?"

It sounded like the same guy's voice, but Jimmy wasn't about to stop, turn around and look—or invite them to join him. Just keep walking. Less than half a block now.

Sharp pain! He felt the cold metal of the knife plunge into his lower back. Its force propelled him forward. A guy now in front of him caught him before he could fall. Pushing him back a bit, they made eye contact. Another sharp pain. This time in the front yanked upward. He looked into empty, cold lifeless eyes. Breath left his body. Jimmy faded to black.

Chapter 14

Tuesday, October 8

Sara introduced Rachel to Uncle Stan as her best friend in the world. And the hug Rachel received confirmed that Uncle Stan understood the intention behind Sara's words. As they settled in, getting as comfortable as they possibly could in Stan's cramped office, Rachel felt as though the stones she now carried, hidden for so long in a dusty attic, were burning a hole in her pocket. *What would Aunt Lil want her to do with them?*

"So, Sara tells me that you need my help. She showed me your problem. An interesting problem to have."

"Yes. Definitely a nice problem to have. Wouldn't mind having that kind of problem myself," laughed Sara. Catching the glance she got from Rachel, Sara said, "What? I'm just saying you've got a really nice problem and I wouldn't mind having something like it. That's all."

"So, how can I help you?" asked Uncle Stan.

"Well, Sara showed you only a small part of my problem." Hesitating a bit Rachel moved her eyes from

Uncle Stan to Sara and back again. "I need someone I can trust, and well—you're Sara's family which, in my mind, makes you my family."

With that, Rachel stood up and pulled out the money pouch she was wearing under her jeans around her waist. She unzipped it and removed a purple leather pouch. Untying it, she pulled each of the eight stones out one by one and placed them onto the white pad Uncle Stan had resting in front of him on top of his desk.

"Here's the full problem. I don't know where to begin with these," said Rachel as she sat down again.

No one spoke. All you could hear was Uncle Stan's labored breathing. For what seemed like an eternity, Stan stared at the stones resting on the pad before him. His mouth gaped open and he licked his lips. He looked up at Rachel, then to Sara and back to Rachel. *Are those tears forming in his eyes,* wondered Rachel.

"First, Rachel, thank you for your trust." From the warmth in Uncle Stan's voice and the softness of his tone Rachel knew she had made the right decision coming to him. He would take care of her and her precious cargo.

"This is a delicate matter and I am deeply honored that you have come to me for help." With a simple hand gesture toward the stones, he said, "May I?"

"Of course."

One by one Stan lifted each stone. He rolled each one around between his knowing fingers, held each one up to the light, and then examined each one through the powerful loupe that sat on the side counter by his desk. He said nothing.

"May I ask, with all due respect, where did you get these? Are they yours?"

"Yes, my Aunt Lil," tears formed in Rachel's eyes at the thought of Aunt Lil and the tremendous meaning these stones had once held for her. "They were hers. She died last week—left all of her belongings to me. I found these in an old trunk in her attic. She told me stories about how they were given to her by her father when she came to America. She called them her life diamonds because they would guarantee her life in America. They're mine now."

Uncle Stan continued his examination of the stones. His movements were slow, methodical and reverent, picking each stone up, inspecting it and returning it to the pad with a gentleness one would use with a newborn baby. He sat quietly for a few minutes, seemingly lost in his own thoughts before speaking.

"Okay then," Uncle Stan said finally. "If I may, can I call a dear friend? If he is available we can go see him. He's just down the block."

The call was made. The friend available. They were off.

Emerging onto the street, the sunlight and fresh air felt rejuvenating. Uncle Stan's office was cramped and the hallways of the building were dank and stale. Forty-seventh Street was vibrant and alive with activity. Even the street lights looked like diamonds. He gestured to the right and took the outside position as the three of them began their walk.

Uncle Stan warmly greeted so many of the people they passed. He seemed to know everyone. As Rachel watched, small groups of Hassidim, very religious Jewish men, dressed in black with wide brimmed hats, would stop to talk. With barely any obvious movement, parcels and envelopes exchanged hands, a *mazel* and a handshake sealed their deals. Rachel knew this was how the diamond district worked. You were only as good as your word here among the Hassidim, who controlled a significant portion of the local diamond trade.

"Excuse me," said the stranger who bumped into Rachel

practically throwing her to the ground as he rushed past her.

"Sure," said Rachel as she regained her balance. Her eyes followed the man down the street watching him disappear into the crowd.

"Who was that?" asked Sara.

"Don't know. But I've seen him before—several times—on my aunt's street, walking past her house."

"No way."

"I'm sure I've seen him there. I'm not crazy. I remember because he was pushing a baby carriage and he looked so out of place doing it."

"What's wrong," asked Uncle Stan who rejoined them after finishing one of his many conversations.

"Nothing. Someone ran into Rachel and she thought she recognized him."

"Forget about it. Let's go. Your friend is waiting for us," said Rachel. "Lead on."

Crossing Forty-seventh Street, they entered a building about halfway down the block. They merged with others standing in front of three sets of gleaming brass elevator doors. No one spoke. Their eyes were watching the old fashioned floor indicators. One elevator was heading up as the brass arrow moved to the right past the five, then the six, then the seven. The other two were descending. When the doors to the middle elevator opened, they got in and Uncle Stan pressed eight.

The eighth floor's hallway lights cast a yellow glow. Door after door revealed little about the business or the people beyond. Stopping at Suite 812, Uncle Stan pressed the buzzer. Looking through the thick beveled glass, Rachel could see a young girl with spiked, jet black hair with neon blue highlights sitting behind the desk. When she looked up, black framed raccoon eyes nodded recognition. A buzzer sounded and the door unlocked.

The girl's nose ring, black sparkling nail polish, a tight white t-shirt over a black bra stood in stark contrast to her surroundings. The room epitomized older times. Understated elegance. Tall windows flooded the room with light. Oak stained wainscoting rose halfway up the walls. Cream paint continued up to intricately carved moldings that hugged the high ceilings. They didn't build them like this anymore.

The girl came around and gave Stan a warm embrace.

"How are you, Dolores?" asked Stan.

"Didi, Uncle Stan. My name is Didi. Remember?"

"Right. Didi. These are my nieces, Sara and Rachel." Uncle Stan cocked his head toward a closed door on the right. "He's expecting us."

Rachel was surprised at her new niece status.

"Yeah, you know the way. See if you can get him to eat something while you're up there. He forgets to eat."

Stan headed toward the closed door to the right of the entrance. Another buzz and the door unlatched. To Rachel's surprise, beyond the door was a staircase going up.

"You can't be too careful," laughed Uncle Stan as he ascended the stairs with Rachel and Sara close behind. Didi watched their progress from the bottom of the staircase. When they all reached the landing another buzz unlatched another door. Stan smiled, opened the door and held it as Sara and Rachel entered another world.

Marissa's days had fallen back into their natural routine. Today was typical. She arose just before dawn, poured her coffee into a thermal mug to keep it warm, wrapped a blanket around her shoulders to shield her from the early morning chill and headed out. Staying on her patio wouldn't do. She needed to feel more connected, more grounded to earth, sea and sky. Walking down the steps, cold sand greeted her bare feet. Her hands tightened around the warm mug as she made her way to the shoreline.

Soft magenta hues were beginning to kiss the eastern sky. Marissa stood still, watching the sun grow larger and larger on the horizon, mesmerized by the dance of color greeting her eyes. And then, the sky burst to life, a brilliant orange, with yellow tentacles of color spreading out from its fiery center. Another beautiful sunrise heralded the birth of a new day.

It never failed to amaze Marissa how alive she felt at the ocean's door. Astrological Cancers were truly water people. Her birth sign fit her. Her morning walks on the beach were doing the job—restoring her soul. She would lunch on her patio and then head back to the beach. She had been home for a few days and each day brought her deeper to that nirvana state of inner peace and contentment she missed while on assignment.

From watching a glorious sunrise this morning, she had gone to a not-so-glorious debrief meeting. Marco was not happy. She feared he was not going to let this go. Like a terrier chomping on a meaty bone, Marco was tenacious when it came to completing cons.

The original plan—find the diamonds—replace them with fake stones—disappear—had been a good one. Lil had begun to trust Marissa's alter ego, Millie—actually telling her a story which included the diamonds. As Millie, she hinted that she had never really seen an uncut, rough diamond, hoping that would get Lil to show her one. That would both confirm their existence and give Millie a much needed idea as to where Lil kept them.

The loose cannon, Jimmy, proved to be a wild card, getting wilder with each passing day. He must have done or said something to spook Lil. She'd changed a few days before she died—acted differently—more cautiously—the last evening they had tea together. Then she didn't have time for tea the next evening, or the evening after that. What had happened was the unanswerable question. They'd never know. Had Lil not suddenly died, it might have all worked. In cons, as in life, there are no guarantees.

The diamonds were still out there only now the niece, Rachel, had them. Whether she knew she had them or not was the interesting new twist in the mix. *What if she didn't know? What if she had yet to find them? Would she even know they were diamonds? She cleared out the house really fast. Jesus, what if she threw them out or gave them away?* Getting to her was going to be a tad more problematic though Marco had already made an initial contact as the handsome Mark Rogers.

Marco…Marco…Marco. She loved this man. Had loved him since they first met. Unrequited love. He had been her savior, her knight and protector. No man could hold a candle to him which was clearly why she had never married. Affairs, yes. She wasn't a nun and did have needs. Marriage, no. Maybe when they were both old and gray they would decide that in many ways they were already a married couple. Consummating it would be the final acknowledgment of the trust each one had placed in the other.

Shit, could they ever become so old they couldn't do it?

As Marissa walked the beach to clear her head, she wondered what Marco would do next. The epitome of the astrological Gemini twins, he could be a formidable adversary when challenged. The magical twinkle in his eyes turned stone cold. Ice ran in his veins. And then there was the other Marco, the Marco of her heart. Soft, loving, incredibly kind. The pain of his upbringing may have hardened his heart to those he perceived as his enemies. It also warmed it beyond belief to anyone he held in the cocoon of his love.

Her pocket vibrated indicating an incoming text. It was addressed to her and Marco from Dom. Short and to the point.

47th street. Lost them in elevator. Advise.

Dom's text answered Marissa's question. Rachel showing up on Forty-seventh Street meant only one thing—she had the diamonds. Marissa headed back up to her house to change. She knew Marco would want to talk.

In the corner of the small, cramped room, a frail looking man was hunched over a wooden workbench on which sat a grinding wheel, a computer, several loupes and microscopes. Dust floated in the air and coated every surface. It sparkled when the light hit it just right. Carbon dust. Diamond dust. For that was what diamonds were, carbon touched by the hand of God—transformed.

Slipping off his stool, this gentle man walked to them with arms outstretched.

"Stan, how good to see you."

"And you, old friend. It's been too long." Their arms wrapped around each other. There was love there. "Leo, you remember Sara, my niece. Davie's daughter. And this is Rachel. Rachel, meet Leo Schwartz."

With a full head of gray hair and black framed, thick lensed glasses that magnified his hazel green eyes, Leo Schwartz stood barely five feet tall. Dressed in a button down, white shirt and pale blue Perry Como style sweater, Rachel had a flash back to her own dad who loved those sweaters and had one in every color. Though Leo's sweater was buttoned, she could see that his brown pants were hiked up higher than where a natural waist would be. His appearance screamed grandfather, not master diamond cutter.

And yet, according to Uncle Stan, Leo Schwartz was the best in the business, one of the last of a dying breed of skilled craftsmen. He had emigrated from Germany in 1939, a young man in his twenties. Now in his nineties, his eyesight failing—his heart strong, Leo came to work every day, to do the only thing he knew how to do. It kept him alive.

"Sit, sit," said Leo, as he fumbled to move the piles of papers and magazines, to clear the few chairs in the room so his guests could actually do what he was inviting them to do, sit.

"So, to what do I owe this visit? Not a social call, I suspect."

"Rachel has something to show you. She came to me. I have brought her to you. Leo, she needs our help."

There was something about this man, this small cramped room, which made Rachel feel at ease, safer than she had in days. As she had done before, she pulled out the money belt, unzipped it and pulled out the purple pouch.

"My aunt recently died and left me these," said Rachel as she handed Leo the pouch.

Leo took the pouch into his aged, but steady hands. He could feel the stones it held even before he saw them. He cleared a space on his workbench and pulled a clean white pad off the shelf. With reverence, he spread the pouch ties and opened it. Pouring the stones into his left hand, he placed them ceremoniously—one by one—on the pad.

Time seemed to stand still. Rachel watched as Leo repeated the same process Uncle Stan had done an hour ago. Slowly and methodically, he examined each stone. One by one, he swabbed each stone with alcohol to remove any surface dirt. He lifted each one to the light, looked at each one through his loupe, examined each one under a microscope and then used a computer to establish a pattern and a more detailed, albeit preliminary, appraisal of how each one might be cut and its possible yield.

Then he was done. He sat for a moment just staring at the stones.

"Ah, Lily" he murmured. Tears formed at the corners of his eyes and he sat very still with his eyes closed. Rachel watched him closely. And then he turned to her—took her hands in his, looked deeply into her eyes and spoke softly.

"I am so sorry for your loss."

"You knew my aunt." It was more of a statement than a question.

"Lily, dear Lily. It was a long time ago…a very long time. A lifetime. We crossed together… so many years ago. There was even a foolish thought…the kind only young lovers can conjure…that we could be together. But it was not to be. The demands and commitments of different lives got in the way. My benefactor…he had three unmarried daughters and no son to leave his business to. What can I say? You met my granddaughter on the way in."

"You're the Leo in the letters I found. I'm so sorry. I invaded your privacy. I read a few of them." *Was life about to come full circle?*

"To business," said Leo, slapping his palms on his thighs. "To be honest, Rachel, I've seen these stones before, many years ago. Lily brought them here to me. That was the last time I saw her. I am so sad and so sorry that she is gone. May she rest in peace." He bowed his head and stopped talking aloud, though Rachel could see his lips moving. He was whispering Kaddish. After a few moments, he looked up at her.

"Rachel, you are about to become a very wealthy woman."

Chapter 15

Wednesday, October 9

Ben Collins greeted Detectives Berger and Cooper with a warm handshake at the door to his office.

"Detectives, nice to meet you. It's a beautiful day out there. I love fall. We won't get too many more days like this. Please have a seat." *Wonder what these guys want? Keep it smooth,* thought Ben, *smile, be cordial, be helpful.*

"Thanks for seeing us. I'm Detective Daniel Berger and this is Detective Brad Cooper. We are looking into some recent deaths of elderly women and your name has come up in our investigation."

"Really?" asked Ben, looking from one to the other.

"You're shown as the lawyer of record in several cases. Just a week ago, a Mrs. Lillian Steinmetz passed away. Does that name sound familiar?"

"Yes, of course. Mrs. Steinmetz. Such a sweet lady. I was so saddened to hear about her passing. What does this have to do with me?"

"She was your client?" asked Cooper.

"Yes. Well, she was really my father's client. He died two years ago and I took over his older clients as a favor to him." Ben felt the need to continue explaining. "It was one of those last request things my dad made of me. You know how it is. There was a group of clients who had been with him for years. He didn't want any of them, all of whom were elderly, to have to try and find another lawyer. When he died I took over for him."

"Makes sense," said Cooper, nodding his head. Neither detective made any move to get up.

Moments passed and the silence in the room was deafening.

There's more, thought Ben. *Stay calm.*

"Anything else, detectives?"

"We were just wondering about cause of death. Were you privy to any of the death certificates?" asked Daniel. "The most recent deaths, two in the last three weeks in fact, were all said to be healthy people, at least according to their doctors and the family members we spoke to."

"Yes, I did see the death certificates." Ben stopped for a moment, thinking it a good idea to add some drama to his telling. "It's always sad when someone passes away." Pausing for effect, he asked, "What was Mrs. Steinmetz, ninety? And the others?"

Not waiting for any response, he continued, "They may have been healthy, but they were healthy for their ages. Living to ninety is a gift these days. I'm really not sure what else I can tell you."

Still no movement from either detective.

"Gentlemen, if there is nothing else, I've got a client meeting at two o'clock and I need to pull a few things together for it." Ben stood up hoping the detectives would follow his lead. They didn't move.

"Not to get too philosophical," continued Ben, walking

around his desk to join both detectives, "but when your number's up, when it's your time to go, well I just hope I go peacefully in my sleep, if you know what I mean."

With that, the detectives finally stood. This meeting was clearly over. As Ben shepherded them towards the door, he added the usual, "If I can be of any help, please don't hesitate to call." He remained in his doorway as both men left.

Ben knew he'd pay for his sins. Heaven wasn't in the cards. He was heading straight to hell—guilty of three of the seven deadly sins that doomed you there—pride, greed and envy.

His achilles heel was envy. He wanted what they had— the rich and famous—with their fancy cars, expensive suits, beautiful women, bling, and fat rolls of cash. Raised in an upper middle class home, he never wanted for anything. His problem—he always wanted more. His never ending quest for the good life had doomed his marriage to Brenda.

He could still hear his dad admonishing him. "Benny, keep it simple. Keep it real. Be content with what you earn. Don't chase the sparkle."

And then Atlantic City was reborn in the late 1970s as a gambling mecca. Harmless fun at first. Easy drive for a weekend get-a-way, sucking in the glitz and glamour. Drop in a few bucks, pull the lever and out comes more. Repeat as desired.

Baccarat was his ultimate undoing. That's the game of the beautiful people, and Ben so wanted to belong. He'd seen the movies. Richly appointed rooms, lavishly adorned with gold leaf filigree atop graceful columns, Persian rugs, and splendid art. Elegant women in flowing gowns, jewels and furs, men in tuxedos. Cannes. Monte Carlo. He was smart. He could read people.

How hard could it be?

And therein was its curse. Lady luck dug her teeth into him big time and she was a cruel mistress. She let him win big to hook him, dangled the promise of more and then kicked him when he was down. Just when he won enough to walk away, she tempted him. Her perfume was intoxicating. The lights, the glitter, the bells and whistles consumed him.

At first, he took funds from different trust accounts his dad's older clients had established to help with final arrangements. He'd been careful to spread it out. A little from Mrs. Gold, a few thousand from Dr. Moran and so on. When he won, he'd keep some of the money and return the rest to the accounts. If he was ever asked, he'd chalk it up to sloppy accounting. During his check-in visits to see how these clients were doing, he'd excuse himself to the bathroom. He'd take his time and help himself to any jewelry he saw laying around. One piece, a starburst amethyst and white sapphire pin he lifted from the Steinmetz woman a few weeks ago had brought in several thousand dollars from a pawn shop in Atlantic City. Those proceeds were again split. Some for his troubles. Some back to the accounts.

He rationalized. What was taken would not be missed by those from whom it had been secured. They would be gone. Ashes to ashes, dust to dust. They'd come into the world with nothing. Why not go out the same way? And besides none of the old timers felt any hardship. Their families would get plenty and be none the wiser.

Lately, he was down on his luck—very, very down. Taking from the accounts couldn't cover his losses. Foolishly, he borrowed from Big Al, confident that his luck would turn around. It didn't. He borrowed more.

He'd even made a special trip to Atlantic City yesterday to see Big Al. Better for Ben to seek out Al than the other way around. His mind went into replay mode, revisiting the details of his meeting and the conversation he had with Big Al.

"I want to settle up with you," Ben had said when the two sat down for a drink in a large and very empty ballroom. "I have the money I owe you—three hundred and fifty thousand dollars." As Ben started to reach inside his coat jacket, he felt movement behind him. Sensing more than seeing Big Al's bodyguards presence, Ben stopped moving.

Al waved them off. "Certainly. How nice. I always knew you were a man of your word, that you would take care of our business. That's three hundred and fifty thousand dollars—plus interest—which brings it to four hundred thousand dollars. Is that what you have, what you're offering me today, four hundred thousand dollars?"

"Four hundred thousand dollars?" questioned Ben, his voice catching in his throat. He could never figure out how Big Al actually calculated the interest and was too scared to ask. "I thought it was just three hundred and fifty grand. That's what I've got—three hundred and fifty grand. I'm fifty thousand dollars short."

"Good. That's fine, Ben, really." Al's tone was gentle and falsely kind. It unnerved Ben. He could feel a tight knot forming in the pit of his stomach.

"I'll take the three hundred and fifty grand as a show of good faith. You can pay me the remainder—say, Sunday night—before you leave. I'm assuming you're planning one of your usual weekend visits to our fair city. Unless, of course, you think you might need a bit more time.

"No, Sunday sounds good. I didn't want you to think I was running out on you."

"I wouldn't think that about you, Ben. This is just business—and we're both business men. So, Sunday then—we'll settle up on Sunday—and with the additional interest for this extension, that will be a hundred grand. Right?"

Breath caught in Ben's throat. "Yeah, right—a hundred grand—right—Sunday."

Ben sat motionless as Al took the envelope Ben offered him and led his small entourage out of the ballroom. It had become all too clear to him that he would never be done with Al. There was always more interest, on top of the interest, on top of the principal amount he originally borrowed.

Ben pulled the vodka out of the credenza and poured himself a drink. His hand shook as he raised the glass to his lips. Replaying events like the previous day's meeting with Big Al only made things worse. It showed him his mistakes in vivid technicolor. Doing business with Al ranked right up there as a colossal blunder.

He emptied the glass and poured another. Right now, he had bigger problems than two detectives snooping into elderly deaths. Jimmy Raconti was missing. He should have dumped him years ago. Big mistake. The kid was a perpetual thief. Got high on the danger. Once told Ben it was better than cocaine. Had been doing small jobs for Ben for years. Until now, Jimmy had proven to be extremely good at what he did.

Lillian Steinmetz was supposed to be the big score, the one that would help him finally end his business dealings with Big Al, pay off his debts and have money to spare to disappear to some exotic island in the sun. He'd listened to her stories about Jews coming to America with life diamonds. She never specifically said she had them, but there was something in the way Lil spoke. Ben always suspected her stories were more truth than fiction.

Or was it hope?

Shit, Ben thought. The plan was so simple. Get in, find the stones, get out. Easy! He had handed the job to Jimmy on a silver platter. Jimmy just didn't know it was Ben doing the handing. Since Jimmy's mouth was way bigger than his brain, all of their transactions were done over the phone. Ben had even used a voice modulator every time he called him. And the schmuck screwed it up.

Ben's string of bad luck seemed endless. Murphy, as in Murphy's Law, had showed up yet again, and events were now spiraling out of control. And he still owed Big Al a hundred grand. At his point, compound interest sounded better to Ben than a compound fracture—or worse.

Chapter 16

"Got another one," said the voice on the other end of the phone.

Daniel immediately recognized the heavy Brooklyn accent as belonging to Dr. Grayson Mitchell, the ME.

"Good morning to you too, Gray." Daniel snapped his fingers to get Cooper's attention as he hit the speaker phone button. "You're on speaker. Cooper's here too. Where and when?"

"The ME from Queens just called. She saw the informal information bulletin I sent out asking to be notified about any elderly deaths that don't seem right somehow."

"You mean she didn't just come out with the standard, 'old people die all the time' line? She actually stopped and questioned a death?"

"Yeah. Megan is one of the good ones. Very detail oriented and thorough. It seems the woman's son was screaming holy hell that his mother had not been sick a day. He demanded an autopsy. Even got himself a lawyer already."

"A lawyer different from his mother's lawyer?" asked Daniel.

"Yep."

"Let me guess. The mother's lawyer's name is Ben Collins, right?"

"You got it," chuckled Gray.

"Send me a copy of the autopsy report when you get it, Gray. Thanks for the heads up."

Disconnecting the call, Daniel mused more to himself then Cooper who was the only other occupant of the room, "There is something going on. I can feel it."

"Really? Come on, Daniel. Old people die every day. It's just that the odds aren't in your favor after a certain age. When your time is up, you go," said Cooper, refilling his coffee cup. "Do you really think there is some deep conspiracy lurking here, someone out to rid New York City of the elderly?"

"No, not a deep conspiracy. But my gut is telling me that a few—not all—but a few of these routine deaths may not be so routine. You know how I feel about coincidences. And Ben Collins name is popping up too often. I suspect if we push a little more, look for some common denominators other than old and alone, we may find that what was first accepted as the normal death of elderly people, will start to look like these deaths aren't so normal. Know what I mean?"

"Yeah. Your gut's got you hooked," said Cooper as he put down his coffee cup, grabbed his jacket and headed for the door. "And since there is no official case here, we gotta do some extracurricular digging to make it a case. On my way. I'll let you know what turns up."

Never a dull moment in the city that never sleeps, thought Daniel now alone in his office with only his own thoughts for company. He pushed back from his desk, leaned back and looked out the window of his third floor office. What is it about beautiful fall days—for that matter, any day—that makes people want to kill each other? Of the thousands of deaths that took place in New York City each year most were through normal circumstances—diseases, accidents and old age.

Then there were the ones he got involved with—the murders. These ran the gamut from drive-bys, hit and run, beatings, to stabbings. The reasons? Jealousy, rage, greed, gang initiation—you name it. Some people were just in the wrong place at the wrong time. One crass line of thought was that the nightly drive-bys were God's way to thin the herds.

There were murders designed to send a message, like a gruesome body that got fished out of the East River a few days ago. Double tap to the back of the head. Hands and feet cut off. Symbolic. The message, unequivocal. The penalty for failure clear. You can run but you can't hide. Screw up and you wind up dead. The people the killing was done to motivate understood immediately. Maybe they'd catch the perp, maybe not.

Finally, there were those murders that didn't really look like murder. Murders that were elaborately planned and carefully choreographed down to the last detail. Daniel was convinced that some of the elderly deaths would fall into this category. Most times the murderer slips up and they get the guy. Sometimes these turned into cold cases that haunted good detectives for years.

During his rise from beat cop to detective he had successfully thwarted a few bank heists and prevented a murder or three. He did a stint with the special victims unit and worked hard closing down a major Eastern European sex crime ring. These cases always unnerved him. The girls were so young. He'd been instrumental in uncovering an Islamic cell's plans to unleash sarin gas during a Saturday matinee of the Lion King. That one sent shivers down his spine. All the children that would have been in the theater. A total mitzvah. Thank God!

Daniel had made his reputation working the streets and he was good at what he did. People naturally trusted him, told him things, confided in him. As a kid, he loved working one thousand piece puzzles and as a detective that was what he saw himself doing, solving puzzles. Only these pieces were not cardboard. They were living, breathing people.

What was wrong with this picture?

Within a six month period, old women, living alone, were dying in numbers that seemed higher than normal. And the one glaring commonality was their lawyer, Ben Collins. He was the lawyer of record for at least ten deaths in the last month. His father had been their lawyer and since his death, Ben had taken over. And the deaths escalated. But these elderly…he couldn't shake the feeling something wasn't quite right about some of these deaths. True, old people died every day. His gut was telling him something else was going on here. It was a death cluster, if there even was such a thing.

He needed answers and he was not going to get any sitting in his office. His instincts were telling him Collins was up to his neck in something and innocent people were dying. It was time to hit the streets. He needed to directly connect the dots.

Exiting the building he made his customary stop under the blue and yellow umbrella of the Sabretts cart. Gus, who had seen him come out the door, was popping the kraut on top of his dog. Gus was an institution on this corner, had been there for as long as Daniel could remember. And the hot dogs? Street meat at its best. Even if you weren't hungry, you could always eat a hot dog. Grab and go. May the fools at city hall never ban food carts—gems of gastronomic gluttony.

Chapter 17

Sunday, October 13

"Rachel…Rachel"

Hearing her name, Rachel spun around in the direction of the voice, careful not to drop the ice cream cone she was enjoying. Seeing Daniel, her enjoyment ratcheted up a notch.

"Hey, Detective Berger, what a nice surprise. Didn't expect to meet anyone I knew here. How are you?"

"I thought that was you. And please, I'm off duty. Call me Daniel. How are you doing?" asked Daniel hoping his demeanor expressed just the right mix of professionalism and friendly interest. "That looks great" he said pointing to her ice cream cone.

"It is. Got it from that stand over there. The line took forever but it's worth it. Ice cream is a major food group in my world and nothing beats chocolate with dark chocolate bits in it."

Now this is a pleasant surprise. Wonder if he's alone.

"How are you doing? I know this is a really difficult time for you."

"I'm fine—well, not really fine. I was better when my friends were here. We were so busy, had so much to do. It's amazing how much stuff my aunt collected over the years. I don't know where it all came from. There were boxes and boxes of stuff. It's all settling in now. Sara left Friday. And the estate guys came to take away my aunt's furniture, except for a few pieces I still need to stay there. The house is so quiet…and empty…and lonely."

Shouldn't have said that. I sound so weak—feeling sorry for myself. He must see that. He's being so quiet and letting me ramble. Got to perk it up.

"That's why I came down here this morning. The guy at the pizza place told me they had a food festival here on Sundays." She looked out at the sea of food stands. "I'll admit it. I've been doing a lot of take out," she laughed. "Way too much take-out!"

"My goal is to eat my way through Smorgasburg," laughed Daniel. "That's what this food fest is called. I've been coming down since they started this thing last year. The guy who set all this up is a genius."

"I've always loved this park. The food is an added bonus. Aunt Lil and I would walk along the path and enjoy the view and talk. I mean, my God, look at this view. This place became sort of special."

As Rachel swept her hand toward the skyline of New York, she took another lick of her ice cream. Daniel's eyes followed her hand briefly, but quickly came back to her.

"I agree. It's a great view."

But you're looking at me, not the view, thought Rachel.

"We even tried to walk across the bridge one of the times we came down here. Can you imagine? Walking across the Brooklyn Bridge?" Her eyes were bright as she stared at the majestic old bridge, the memories of good times filling her voice with love.

"Well, we got halfway across before Aunt Lil suggested we turn around." Rachel smiled at Daniel as she came back to face him. What are you doing down here?" she asked, eager to lighten things up and change the subject.

"Can you think of a better way to spend a beautiful fall Sunday? Look at all these people. Everyone having a good time, eating and drinking, playing with their dogs and their kids."

"Nope. My sentiments exactly." Rachel's gaze went back to the New York skyline. Leaning on the railing, her thoughts took an unexpected turn to the man standing beside her.

This is good. We can be quiet, enjoy the view. Wonder what else we could enjoy?

"When are you planning on heading home?" Daniel asked after a few more minutes passed.

"Maybe tomorrow afternoon or more likely, Tuesday morning. A few more things to clean out. I have a final walk through meeting with the real estate agent tomorrow. The estate guy has to get back to me about when he can come by and pick up the rest of Aunt Lil's furniture. I needed a bed and a few things so I didn't have to sleep on the floor."

"Well, then I guess we have to do our dinner tonight. Italian okay? I know a nice little place, family owned, food's great. Much better than take-out. That is—if you're free tonight."

"Wow—sure. It's not like I've got a huge social life here."

Ugh, shouldn't have said that.

"I'm sorry. That didn't come out right. Yes, having some company would be really nice. And you're right, I can't continue the take-out routine. A nice dinner would be a refreshing change for me."

"Great. I'll pick you up around seven."

"Works for me." Rachel hesitated a bit. "Look, in case you get busy—you know, something comes up and you can't make it. You still have my cell number, right?"

"I'll make it." Daniel backed away from her.

Did she imagine it or was his smile bigger now.

Flowers! He brought me flowers.

"Daniel, thank you so much. These are beautiful. Come on in. I think I still have something under the sink that I can use to put these in water."

Rachel found an old glass pitcher under the sink that had not been tossed yet. She took a moment to breathe in the scent of the bouquet. Cutting off the ends of the stems, she couldn't remember the last time she had been given flowers. David had stopped bringing her flowers years before he died.

If this is how the evening is starting I can't imagine how much better it will get.

"I'm ready," Picking up her purse and shawl. "Where are we going?"

"To get great food and creamy Tiramisu. I hope you're hungry."

"Starved!"

Hours later as they lingered over coffee, Rachel thought back to the start of their evening and tried to replay every detail in her mind.

Dinner was great. Daniel had definitely not oversold the food or the restaurant. The Flounder Francese was scrumptious. They talked like old friends. No long silences, no awkward moments. Rachel found herself not wanting the evening to end. Finally, she felt like her old self.

Boy, it has been a rough two weeks.

"You know, I was going to call you before I left to go home. Something happened that was unsettling, to say the least."

"Then our meeting this morning was meant to be," he chuckled giving her a warm smile. "What happened?"

"This probably will sound foolish. Remember the woman at the door the other day, just as you were leaving? She was from ReMax.

"Vaguely."

"Anyway...it's just that... well...when we were talking, she mentioned how rare it was to have two homes on Aunt Lil's street for sale at the same time."

"Makes sense. Your aunt lived in a popular section of Brooklyn. Old neighborhood, safe, low crime, everything you need in walking distance."

"But that's the point. She was talking about the house next door to Aunt Lil's. The one the Racontis live in—those helpful neighbors I told you about—the guy, Jimmy, who found my Aunt Lil—or at least I thought they lived in."

"I'm sorry. I'm not following you."

She could see Daniel lean in and sit up a little straighter. Whatever she just said got his attention.

"Well, when Sara got back from the city Monday afternoon, I told her what the real estate agent said. She and I went snooping. I'd always gone to the back door so we went up to the front door and rang the bell. No one answered. There was no lock box. If the house was for sale, wouldn't there be a lock box?"

"Not always, but that's a good question."

"Anyway, Sara peeked in the front window and there was no furniture in that house. We went around back and Sara stood on a milk carton. There was only an old chair, an old TV and the kitchen table stuff. How's that for strange?"

Rachel had been avoiding eye contact until this moment. Her pleading eyes locked into Daniel's.

"And then there was the attic door left open...that I was sure I closed...and...the back door that I was sure I

167

locked…but we heard a sound…and Jimmy was there in the kitchen…and the man who ran into me on Forty-seventh Street that I'm sure I saw in front of Aunt Lil's house." Rachel stopped talking sensing how silly she must sound.

"Oh, God. I sound insane. My mind is working overtime. I'm sorry to spoil our evening."

"You are not spoiling our evening. I can see you're concerned and you have every right to be. I'm sure there's an explanation though right now I can't think of one. Too much wine. Clouds the brain," he grinned as he twirled his finger next to his ear.

He reached out and placed his hand on top of hers as it lay on the table.

Warm. Strong. There's that tingle. And did his expression just change—his eyes seem more sharply focused on me. Like I hit a nerve with my words. He's hearing me.

"What you're saying does sound odd. And I've got this thing—Cooper calls it my detective gut. I can see you're upset. And I do want to help you. Let me look into this for you. See where it goes—if anywhere. Okay?"

"That would be great. But I don't want to impose. I'm sure you're busy with real cases."

"Not too busy to check this out. Were you ever in their house?"

"Just the back. In the kitchen. Didn't really pay much attention. Wasn't there more than maybe fifteen minutes."

"Tell me about the attic thing. What's that about?"

"That was last Saturday night. We all went out to dinner. We were supposed to go into the city but we stayed in Brooklyn and went to this really nice French restaurant Sara knew about. I know I pushed the attic door shut but when we got home it was open. So I closed it before I went to bed. I'm sure I did. Then I had to get up in the middle of the night. Had a bit too much wine and needed aspirin. When I leaned on it, it moved. I heard the latch click. But I remember closing it. I'm sure it caught."

"Okay. Interesting. And the thing about Jimmy in the kitchen?"

"Sara and I heard a noise. I found him in the kitchen alcove heading down to the basement the night after the funeral. Really scared me. I know I locked the back door but he said there was a problem with the lock—that it didn't always catch. We called the locksmith the next day. Had the lock changed."

"This guy—Jimmy. Sounds like he was around a lot. Any idea why? Why he would take such an interest in your aunt?"

"Not really. My aunt just said he and his mother would come by. He would do odd jobs around the house and his mother and my aunt would have tea at night. I've only been gone five months, but I don't ever remember meeting them before I moved."

"Do you remember when your aunt first started talking about them—like when she first met them?"

"No, not really. Maybe a few months. It wasn't that I wasn't paying attention when my aunt and I would talk. I was just happy that she had caring neighbors, people who checked up on her. Really stupid of me now that I think back on it."

"Don't beat yourself up. Guilt is a wasted emotion."

"That's what I always say."

"Then we agree. Let me take over. Do what I do best— my detective thing—see what I can find out. Okay?"

"Thank you. It would really mean a lot to me—put my mind at rest."

Tiramisu topped off the eating part of the evening. As they got up to leave, Daniel took Rachel's hand and escorted her away from the front door. Her surprise changed to delight as Daniel pulled her through a curtained alcove and led her down a narrow hallway into another world.

"Care to dance?" asked Daniel as they emerged into a cozy piano bar. Rachel couldn't believe it. Warm light flickered from amber glass wall sconces creating a very intimate space. The scents of rose, jasmine and sandalwood surrounded her. Couples seemed to float on the small dance floor. Others, seated in overly stuffed cushioned booths were drinking champagne out of fluted glasses. Rose petals were scattered everywhere. Had she found wonderland? Gone down a rabbit hole and into her dreams?

The piano player fingered the first notes of *As Time Goes By*, one of her favorite songs. Before she could even respond, Daniel slowly lifted his arm and twirled her around. He took her purse and shawl out of her other hand and placed them on a small table at the side of the dance floor.

She was in his arms.

"He's really good," said Daniel, nodding in the direction of the piano player. "Plays music we know. Music we can dance to."

Rachel barely heard the music playing in the room. She was listening to the music playing in her heart. There were powerful arms holding her and tenderly guiding her steps. Her chin came to rest on his shoulder. They fit together. They moved as one. Every breath she took was of Daniel. An inner warmth she had not experienced in a long time filled her. She could feel his heart beat aligning with her own.

Is this really happening? How is this possible?

Rachel couldn't remember a time when she had felt so at ease in a man's arms. One tune meshed into the next. Music she remembered. Music he softly hummed in her ear as he held her tightly pressed against him.

Hours later, as they walked up the front steps of Aunt Lil's home, her mind was racing with thoughts of what may come next and what to do about it.

Wow. It's been way too long since I've been in this position. Feels good.

"I had a great time tonight," said Rachel as she turned to face him.

"Me too. And I have a favor to ask."

"Okay. What can I do for you?"

"You can let me do a walk through in the house right now. Considering what we talked about tonight, I'd feel a lot better. It'll take me five—ten minutes tops. Okay?"

"Yes. That would really be great. I was going to move to a hotel after Sara left but then I thought that was silly. I've always felt safe here. Come on in."

He stood behind her on the porch as she unlocked the door and stepped inside. The space was empty of most things that made a house a home. A lone chair, table, lamp and small TV was all that remained in the living room.

"Okay, got a flashlight?"

"Yep. In the kitchen. Let me get it. Want to follow me or stay here?"

"Following."

Together they made their way through what was once the loving, warm home of Aunt Lil. Daniel did a quick look in all the rooms starting in the attic and working his way down to the basement. Rachel followed along beside him, glad she had agreed to grant him this favor. He checked window locks and closets, anywhere anyone wishing to do her harm might hide. Other than a basement window over the washing machine, everything was locked up tightly. He reached up and locked that window. They returned to the front hallway and faced each other.

Daniel took the lead before it could get awkward. "I had a great time tonight."

He gently took her hands in his, squeezed softly, leaned in and lovingly kissed her forehead.

Sweet! thought Rachel.

"I'll be in touch. Lock the door. Let me hear that click."

Through the now locked door he called, "Sleep well. Sweet dreams."

She watched him turn, walk down the steps and back to his car. He was gone.

She couldn't sleep. The red digital read-out slowly ticked by endless minutes. Tossing and turning and fluffing her pillows, Rachel replayed her evening with Daniel—replayed her life. For the last two weeks, she had felt so vulnerable, filled with grief, sadness and the obligation to carry out the final wishes of her beloved aunt. And yet somehow, three men had appeared and ignited a different feeling Rachel had not experienced for many years. *Was this a sign? Was God sending her a signal?*

Her mantra—alone but not lonely—worked for her. Until tonight. Tonight was different. An interesting wrinkle just entered her life and the wrinkle had a name—Daniel. He was strong, competent, confident—someone who by the very nature of his job protects, serves, and saves the day. And he was…well…comfortable. Alone but not lonely might have to change. Could she see herself as part of a new couple? What would that mean for her?

Her marriage had fallen into a rather predictable pattern of interaction. Any tingle—any spark—lost in the daily have-to-do's of life. Intimately, non-intimate. An emotionless sense of duty and obligation based on vows made in the presence of God. If David was looking down from heaven, he might not even recognize her. A lot had happened to her since his death.

She'd learned a lot in these last two years—learned how to survive—rely on herself—make decisions for herself—by herself. She could now fix a toilet, swing a hammer, check the oil in her car and the air pressure in her tires. She wasn't some helplessly weak, incompetent woman. That Rachel was gone and she wasn't coming back. Striking out on her own, moving, learning how to stand on her own two feet created a new person. And this new person that had appeared from inside her—an independent, capable woman—was someone she really liked—a lot.

Is it tempting fate to say that David's death led to my rebirth. Probably. But God forgive me, I am happier than I can remember being for years. I love my kids and I'm here for them, but they don't really need me. David and I had a good life together and I'll always be grateful for that. But things are different now. I'm different now. No, there is no going back. Knowing what I know now, feeling like I feel now—I want more. If Daniel wants to be with me—if we are to become a we, it has to be on my terms.

They could be friends. That was it—friends. No judgments, just listen and nod supportively. More than friends required her to deal with all of him—his past, his junk, his needs—yes, his baggage more directly. She wasn't totally sure what all that entailed, but everyone has stuff. And she would have to share her stuff. Friends was definitely the way to go. He could come visit for a few days and she could see him when she came up to visit her family. Yes, that felt right—friends.

But when they danced—when he held her—something more than friendship shot through her.

Did friends make your toes tingle? Did he feel it too?

Her heart, craving love, exploded and won the evening. A knight with a detective's badge as his shining armor had appeared. Magical was the only word that fit. Rachel closed her eyes and relived Daniel's soft lips touching her forehead. A whispered plea escaped her lips.

Dear God, this is what I truly want. Help me keep the magic going.

Chapter 18

Ben Collins paced back and forth, stopping occasionally to look out of his office window at the New York skyline. Another clear blue sky…another beautiful fall day…just like…. He stopped himself cold. The love of his life had died that day…his life had died that day…and the hell he was in now had been born.

Suck it up, man! You aren't the only one who lost someone on 9/11.

Easier said than done. Ben had been an up and coming lawyer then, strong, productive, a pillar of the legal community. Okay, his first marriage failed but first marriages are like that. You're young, dumb, thinking the magic, or at least the great sex, will last forever. Then come kids and bills and forever turns out to be about five years. He never had the kids and his marriage to Brenda didn't even make it to a fourth year anniversary.

After the divorce from Brenda, he reinvented himself and dived head first into building an impressive law practice. He was on top of the world. It was going great, more clients than he could handle. He met Elena. She was smart, beautiful, and they had plans. They were to be married. His world crashed when the North Tower crumbled. Elena had been in the North Tower of the World Trade Center on that fateful morning. She called him…crying…speaking of a life together that would never be…and there was nothing he could do about it.

Impotent then…impotent now.

His law practice went to hell right after Elena died. He couldn't concentrate. Word got out about a few cases that should have been slam dunk wins for him. He lost over technicalities that any first year law student would have caught. The local media had a field day at his expense. No one hires a lawyer on a publicly broadcasted losing streak.

Gambling re-emerged—became his fall back lover—demanding his time and attention, just like a woman in heat. More evil, she twisted him this way and that. Just when he thought he had the upper hand, that he had won and could walk away, she arched her eyebrow, flipped him a sly smile and reeled him back in—to the dice—to the tables—to baccarat.

Shit, I should have started drinking.

His plan to extricate himself from the grips of the accumulating debt he owed Big Al took shape when his father died and he took on some of his father's elderly clients. Ben started using their trust accounts as his own personal slush fund—as a way out of his mess.

That's how he met Lillian Steinmetz. Dear lady—sweet—trusting. The stories she used to tell when he stopped by to check on her galvanized his scheming to new heights. It had been a perfect scheme. Find the diamonds he was convinced she had in the house. There was no mention of a safe deposit box in the will, so if they existed, and he was hoping they did, they had to be somewhere in the house. Don't take all the stones, just two or three to solve his immediate problem and pay for his new life on an idyllic sunny island, preferably somewhere without a U.S. extradition treaty. He would survive greed and walk away a free man. Why did she have to die suddenly?

Who knew that Jimmy would screw it all up. His internal compass about theft should have been Ben's first clue. When Ben was a PD he first defended Jimmy. Got him off. They went for a quick beer to celebrate. Jimmy shared his opinion about his chosen career path as a thief. He never saw what he did as stealing, just relocating. He used to say, "I'm relocating it from you to me."

Ben was nothing if not the ultimate optimist. In his mind, all was not lost. He knew what he had to do and felt confident he could pull it off. He would get back in touch with Rachel. He could play on her vulnerability. He felt it the day they first met on the porch. He'd offer his continued service as her lawyer, gain her trust and get her to reveal where the diamonds were. Then he would simply make one or two disappear.

Piece of cake!

He pulled out his cell and punched in her number. Voice mail. *Crap!*

Murders in the five boroughs of New York were down, but not totally eliminated. Unfortunately, Daniel's mind was not on the bodies or the cases piling up on his desk. It was on Rachel. Her intoxicating scent, the way her hips moved as she walked, the sound of her laugh, the way she flipped back her hair when it fell across her face and tucked it behind her ear. And her dazzling smile revealing dimples as deep as the Grand Canyon. Okay, he was smitten, infatuated, totally hooked on this woman he had just met.

He had no idea where this would lead. He didn't even

really know what this was. And he didn't care. What he did know was that Rachel Resnick stirred something inside him that he thought had died years ago. He liked the feeling. Made him feel young again. And he was very willing to let it all play out.

At sixty-two, his options were shrinking fast. When he looked in the mirror, a man getting older and older every day was starting to look back. When he leaned in close, he could see crow's feet etching into the outer corners of his eyes, staying in place long after he stopped smiling or laughing. He was still in good shape, worked out every day, but how long would that continue? Even though he'd never taken a bullet, the aches and pains of all the years on the job, the bumps and bruises, were taking their toll. Getting old sucked! The alternative sucked more.

He could easily retire. But why? What would he do if he wasn't Detective Daniel Berger? Who would he be? Just another graying, has been detective. Too many of his colleagues had retired to lonely lives. They seemed to age faster once they left the job. No purpose. No reason to get out of bed in the morning their most common lament. Rather than sitting in silence with their wives watching TV at night, if they still had a wife, they'd mosey down to Sullivan's and get lost with a bottle of Jack Daniels for company, swapping war stories about the good old days to anyone who would listen. Clearly, retirement did not paint a pretty picture in his mind.

Meeting Rachel changed the picture. He noticed a new bounce in his step. Retirement, having time to do as he pleased, perhaps a lovely woman to share new adventures with, conjured up totally new possibilities for a next chapter of life. And he liked what he was imagining. He had no real ties to New York anymore. Both sons were married. One in California and one in Texas. He could leave any time he wanted to.

Yeah. That's it. He could move to Virginia. Always liked the south. Slower pace. Good food—great people—better weather. But first, he had to help her with whatever was going on. And with his ties and connections, he could be helpful. He would be helpful. Even now, he had some answers for her.

His BOLO on Jimmy Raconti produced results. A dumpster diver on Staten Island had found a body. On a hunch, Daniel got his buddy from the CSU to do a print sweep of the Raconti house. What are friends for if not to help you out when you need a favor? The prints from the dumpster body matched the prints the techs lifted from the house next door to Lil's—matched prints on file for one James Roger Calhoun. Jimmy Raconti and James Roger Calhoun were the same person.

No surprise to Daniel that there were other names associated with this particular set of fingerprints. Jimmy's rap sheet told the story, a host of B&E's, thefts and random crimes, some jail time. No big mystery about what happened to him either. Looked to be a street killing so the Staten Island PD chalked it up to a gang initiation.

A more interesting fact, in Daniel's mind, was the name of Jimmy's lawyer, Ben Collins. That man keeps popping up. Just popped up again during a call from the record's clerk who told him that the person handling the sales transaction on the house next door to Rachel's aunt was none other than Ben Collins. He was one versatile lawyer—criminal law, estate law and now real estate law. Interesting!

His gut told him that the concerns Rachel shared Sunday night at dinner were real. Her comments ignited his detective gut. Or was that another part of his anatomy? No matter. After listening to Rachel, he knew he had to investigate.

On the way into work today, he'd stopped at the Raconti's house. There was a lock box on the front door. He rang the bell twice. And waited. When no one answered the door, he did the same thing Rachel told him Sara had done. Looked in the front window. No furniture. How could someone be living there without any furniture? The heavy downpour had him forgo the walk around to the back of the house.

When he got back to his office, he called Rachel's real estate agent, Janice Stone. She confirmed what Rachel told him. The house was back on the market. Someone pulled the house off the active list for about a three month period. The reason given was odd, she remembered. Something about a relative coming to town and needing a place to stay. Anyway, she got another call a few days ago. The caller said it was okay to show the house as an active listing again.

Curious timing. Slowly the puzzle that was the Racontis was taking shape. Daniel knew that the people inhabiting the house next door to Rachel's aunt were not who they claimed to be. And one of the pair, Jimmy, was now dead. Where was the woman? Who was the woman?

His friend at CSU had mentioned that a second partial print had been found in the house. Though it could easily be from a potential buyer, the only place the partial print showed up was on the left doorjamb of the back door. Not the door knob—the doorjamb, as if someone had placed his or her hand on the jamb for leverage as he or she pulled open the door. Why only there? A buyer would touch many surfaces, but no other prints were found. However, if someone was trying to open the back door without making a sound, that person might place a hand on the doorjamb.

So far there was no hit on the partial. Someone, he was guessing the woman Rachel told him about, had clearly taken the time to wipe the place clean. Not a normal action if you had nothing to hide. Daniel didn't expect there ever to be a hit on that partial print. He could only hope that something else would soon turn up to help him connect the pieces and give him a name and perhaps a face to go along with mystery print.

Chapter 19

Wednesday, October 16

Walking out of his room at the Williamsburg Inn, Marco checked his watch. Once on the street, he had about a twenty minute walk ahead of him to get to Merchant's Square. And he needed to do more of a saunter than a walk, set a pace that would not create a sweat.

Leaving the Inn's property he crossed Francis Street heading into Colonial Williamsburg. Dom had just texted that Rachel was leaving her home. Her destination was the Cheese Shop in Merchant's Square. Next to bugs—which he had yet to install—parabolic mics were the best invention for short-term, unauthorized snooping. Dom had been eavesdropping when he overheard Rachel tell her daughter, Jenny, that she was planning to visit the Cheese Shop to do some people watching from a table on the outside patio.

The weather would be an asset. It was one of those crisp fall days that Marco truly loved. The leaves were brilliant—red, gold and orange hues had fully replaced the greens of summer. The air was fragrant with the scent of burning wood from any number of fireplaces and hearths that warmed the historic buildings in Colonial Williamsburg. Interpreters walked along DOG Street alone or in pairs. There were few tourists to interact with at this time of year so the interpreters just talked to one another.

Arriving at the William & Mary bookstore, Marco had a clear view of the outdoor patio at the Cheese Shop. Rachel was nowhere in sight. He texted Dom to get an update. Dom reported that she was coming down Jamestown Road—had her blinker on to make the turn on South Henry Street. He would text again when he saw her park her car.

Marco sat down on one of the benches outside the bookstore to watch and to wait. He had learned early in his life that cons were all about how you processed waiting. Some people were antsy when they waited, rushing events causing the con to fail. Successful con artists allowed the act of waiting to be its own reward. *Patience was a virtue,* he thought. Waiting was the calm before the storm of action.

Short wait. The text alert from Dom coincided with his own Rachel sighting. She emerged from the parking lot onto DOG Street, crossed South Henry and headed over to the Cheese Shop patio. He watched her choose a table and settle in. A server approached and he could tell from their body language that she placed her order. From his perch at the bookstore, Marco took note of the server's appearance as he would be instrumental in his forthcoming plan.

He needed to make sure she did not see him until the right time. Slipping across DOG Street he walked up South Henry turning into the parking lot behind the Craft House. He turned down the alley and entered the Cheese Shop through the side door. Looking out, he watched the server place a cheese tray in front of Rachel and what looked to be a glass of iced tea.

Game on!

It had been a long two weeks, a stress filled two weeks, a sad two weeks. Sitting at the outside patio at the Cheese Shop, Rachel picked at her cheese plate. She hadn't been hungry but ordered it to placate the waiter at whose table she was sitting.

Williamsburg was enchanting in the fall. The leaves took their slow, sweet time turning color. In New Jersey all the leaves had fallen already. The pace of life was slower here. And the warmer weather was an added bonus. She could still sit outside and enjoy some people watching. Just the thing to take your mind off yourself.

The waiter set a glass of red wine in front of her.

"I didn't order that."

"No, you didn't," said a voice from behind her. "I did."

Rachel turned in the direction of the voice and found herself staring into familiar eyes—Beemer guy.

"Well, fancy meeting you here," Rachel responded as she stood up. "This is quite a surprise."

"A pleasant one, I hope. I was walking by and I saw you sitting here alone. May I join you?"

"Yes, of course. Come sit down. Have some cheese. I never expected to see you again, let alone here in Williamsburg," said Rachel. "What brings you to town?"

"I'm doing some security work for a small local company. I've got a meeting in the morning so I decided to drive in today rather than chance the tunnel traffic tomorrow. Coming from Virginia Beach, the tunnel can be down right nasty during the early morning rush hour."

"I remember you saying that you lived in Virginia Beach. And the tunnel can be God awful almost any time of day. It's good to see you again." With that, Rachel raised her wine glass to meet his and said, "Cheers."

"To chance encounters," he responded smiling. Sipping

his wine, he said, "I wasn't sure whether you liked red or white. I thought a Pinot Noir would be a safe bet. Heck, didn't they make a film a few years ago about Pinot Noir? And besides, it goes well with cheese."

Slicing off a sliver of what looked to be gruyere, he placed it on a cracker, topped it with a small piece of apple and handed it across to Rachel. He took a sliver for himself and popped it into his mouth, following it with a piece of apple as well.

"Good stuff," he said. "All the times I've been down here and I've never really stopped to eat here. I just usually walk around to relax."

"I find it peaceful to walk here, too. All the tourists make for interesting people watching. They're sort of gone now, but everyone says they'll be back in full force from Thanksgiving through New Years."

They fell into idle chit chat about this and that. The usual topics. No religion, no politics, nothing outside the boundaries of safety. He told her more about his work, the ins and outs of software security. She told him tidbits of her life in Williamsburg. What seemed like minutes turned into hours.

"Look. It's five o'clock," said Mark Rogers looking at his watch. "Have dinner with me. That is unless you have plans."

"No, no real plans. I just got back so—"

"Good, then it's settled," he said cutting Rachel off before she could even finish her thought. "I'm staying at the Inn. The restaurant there is really lovely. And the food is pretty good too. Unless you have some place you really like to eat?"

"No, the Inn sounds fine. I've never eaten there so it will be a new experience for me." Pausing as she felt a wave of sadness rush over her, she added, "It's just that I've had a rough two weeks. I'm not sure I'll be great company."

"Let me be the judge of that," he answered with his beaming smile. "And beside you've got to eat. So why eat alone—or settle for this cheese tray that we've barely touched."

She looked across the table. Leaning in and placing her closed hand on her chin, she said with a bit of coy hesitation, "There's just this one thing."

"What's that?"

"Who are you? I mean, what's your name? I remember you gave me your business card, but as I said, it's been a rough few weeks. It's hard to accept a dinner invitation from someone when I don't even know his name." Rachel broke into a broad smile and laughed. Extending her hand, she said, "My name is Rachel."

"I'm Mark—Mark Rogers. Nice to finally be formally introduced. All set?"

Gathering up her shawl and purse, he moved behind her to help ease out her chair. He eyed the waiter and handed him two twenty dollar bills.

"We can take a leisurely stroll to the Inn down DOG Street. I've always loved that name. DOG Street. Not sure the Duke of Gloucester ever meant for his name to be associated with man's best friend. But then again, it could be worse."

Rachel laughed as she followed his guiding arm out of the patio and onto the cobblestone walkway. There was barely anyone in Merchant's Square now.

"Mind if we ride instead? I'm parked in the lot behind the ticket booth," Rachel said as she pointed and took the lead. "It's supposedly a two hour lot. They usually don't ticket you this late in the day. But I don't want to push my luck."

There was a crisp coolness to the air now that the sun was setting. Rachel wrapped her shawl around her shoulders to ward off the chill. As she positioned the shawl's end over her shoulder she fastened it loosely with a peacock brooch.

"That is a beautiful pin."

"Thank you. It was one of my Aunt Lil's favorite pieces. I'm sure it's just costume jewelry, but she wore it all the time. She loved all the brightly colored stones on the tail. Makes me feel like she is still with me." Rachel paused as her fingers touched the brooch.

"She died a few weeks ago. That was why I was on the road that Sunday when we first met. I was heading up to her funeral. Now when I wear it, I feel like I'm closer to her. Silly, I know."

"Not silly at all. Our family, people we love, are important to us," said Mark, playing his part. Sensing a deepening vulnerability emerging from the woman walking at his side, he saw his opening. He might be able to take advantage of her current vulnerable state. It might prove to be a way to get close to her. His thoughts momentarily diverted to the special people in his own life—Marissa, Dom and Sophia—and how much they meant to him. He couldn't imagine losing any one of them.

"Anything we can do to keep loved ones in our hearts when they pass is never silly. It's a beautiful brooch. The colors on the tail stones are brilliant. And I am sure your aunt is looking down now with a big smile on her face seeing you wearing it." Mark said, looking at the stones glistening as they caught the fading daylight and wondering whether they were fake like Rachel claimed or real.

The nod from Dom was imperceptible to anyone watching as Mark and Rachel passed him and crossed the street heading for the parking lot. The micro signal Dom sent was crystal clear. He saw no one showing any unusual interest in Rachel from his vantage point. All clear. He was off to take care of the next order of business while Marco kept Rachel occupied.

"So what's it like?" asked Mark once the server retreated with their dinner order.

"What's what like?"

"Retirement. Don't suspect I'll ever really stop working. Tell me, what am I missing?"

"Well" said Rachel taking a long deep breath, "it's kind of like camp." She looked into his eyes and asked, "Have you ever been to summer camp?"

"No. Missed out on that. In fact, I can't say I even know someone who has been to summer camp. Looks like you're my first camper."

"Campers have a full schedule of activities that keeps them busy all day long. At night, there are even more things planned for them to do."

"Sounds like a great way for a kid to spend a summer. In my neighborhood only the rich kids went to camp. We weren't rich enough to afford camp."

"Retirement, at least for me, is like that. You get up in the morning, have breakfast, and then decide what you are going to do for the morning. Play tennis, golf, read, mah jongg, bocci, bridge, canasta, bowl, volunteer somewhere…" Rachel stopped and moved her finger around the lip of the water glass in front of her.

"Then you have lunch. Lunch is big around here. I think I gained ten pounds my first month down here just doing lunch with new friends. And then you start again."

"You don't sound too convinced that this camp routine is a good thing."

"I'm not. I mean, it's fun and all that…to play all day with no cares. I know how lucky I really am to be able to do that…not have to work…be living in a community that offers so much. And I am truly grateful. But…" Her voice trailed off once again as she seemed to lose herself in the recesses of her mind.

"But what? Sounds idyllic to me. No work. Just play all day. What could be so bad about that?"

"There just has to be more…more to the next twenty years of my life or I'll go bonkers. When I was a kid, camp only lasted eight weeks. Then you went home and went back to school. This…" Rachel said with a wave of her hand, "this is endless."

Marco's gift was his ability to read people. It had served him well in his younger years as he trolled Times Square. He could spot a mark a thousand yards away and seemed to know just how to time his approach. His insightfulness and analytic abilities continued to serve him well. Now, as he looked at Rachel, he saw his entry point.

"What is it? What's bothering you?"

"Nothing. Sorry to get maudlin on you. But I warned you," laughed Rachel.

"Look, I know we're strangers. Two ships passing in the night sort to speak," offered Mark, putting forth his most disarming smile. "I'm a good listener. I don't pry and I don't tell secrets out of school. And I know that sometimes talking to a stranger is relieving. Think of me as a pair of ears. That's all. No advice. No judgment. Just ears."

Rachel laughed. "Excuse me. You are way more than a pair of ears."

"That's better. Here's dinner. Looks amazing." With that he raised his glass, "To strangers traveling along the same road, slowly becoming new friends."

"Yes, friends. I like that. Has a nice ring to it."

In the end, the evening turned out to be more fun than Rachel expected. The friends toast seemed to break the ice and the rest of dinner and dessert had been marked with stories and laughter that made her cheeks burn.

Unable to escort her home like the gentlemen he claimed to be, Mark expressed concern over her safety. Rachel promised to call him when she arrived safe and sound at home. He answered his phone on the first ring.

"Consider your gentlemanly duties done. I'm in my driveway."

"Good"

"And thanks again for a really lovely evening, Mark."

"You are most welcome, Rachel. I enjoyed it too. Until our paths cross again."

"Bye."

Hanging up, Rachel sat in her car gathering her thoughts. The jumble of feelings flooding her senses had more to do with them being locked down tightly for so long than a chance meeting with Mark Rogers. This was the second time their paths had crossed unexpectedly. Definitely charming and very handsome, he knew just what to say to get her to let her guard down. Any feelings surfacing for him could easily be explained away as appreciation for a pleasant evening—nothing more.

Other, darker thoughts intruded, fighting to gain footing in her mind. Was he playing on perceived vulnerabilities? Was their meeting by chance? Of all the places in Williamsburg, he just happens to be at the Cheese Shop when she's there? Was Daniel's disbelief in coincidences rubbing off on her? Her own internal radar, Sara called it her gypsy blood, had been working overtime since her aunt's death. She'd found herself overly suspicious of the most innocent gestures like the helpfulness of Jimmy and Millie Raconti. Daniel's questioning their motives at dinner the other night had her replaying and scrutinizing all of her interactions with them. Was their kindness real? Was there more to it? Lately, she even imagined that she was being watched and followed.

Sara's going to love this. She'll want a play-by-play

recount of the evening when we talk in the morning. Laughing, Rachel pushed the button to open the garage door. Nothing—the door remained closed. She tried it again— same result—no movement.

Shit!

Walking up to her front door, she pushed her key into the lock. A wave of paranoia swept over her. Glancing back to her car and the closed garage door, a chill ran up her spine. It worked fine earlier. It hadn't given her a bit of trouble since she moved in. Why tonight?

Turning the key in the lock, Rachel opened the door slowly. She stood frozen on the threshold. Light cast out a glow from her kitchen. She hadn't left any lights on. Her breath caught in her throat. Someone had been in her house. Were they still there?

Daniel. What would Daniel say to do? He'd say to call the police. But if she called the police they would think she was crazy. Even the community's security people might question her sanity, but they get paid to respond to these types of things and residents' calls.

Backing out of the house, Rachel hit the speed dial number for security. After briefly explaining her situation, the person who answered said not to worry, that one of the officers would be there shortly and to remain in her car until they arrived.

What's happening to me? Am I watching too many spy movies? How paranoid is too paranoid?

"So, did he kiss you goodnight?" asked Sara.

"Yes."

"How was it?"

"The kiss? It was just like I thought it would be. Soft, gentle…"

"Tongue?" Sara asked breaking into Rachel's replay of the experience.

"Sara!" exclaimed Rachel.

"My bad!"

"No tongue! But his kiss was nice."

Filling in the details and answering all of Sara's questions was proving to be more fun than Rachel thought it would be. She was reliving the entire afternoon and evening.

"Does he have your number at least?"

"Yes. When we were at the car, he asked me for it. Said that maybe the next time he was in Williamsburg we could get together for a stroll or dinner again."

"The hell with the next time he's in Williamsburg. Why not make the trip on purpose. Shit, what is it, an hour? Did you ask for his number?"

"No, I didn't. It just didn't seem right. Oh, Sara. I've been alone a long time and I just don't know if I'm up for a romance right now. I've got other things on my mind."

"Like what? A handsome New York City detective perhaps?" demanded Sara. "What could be so time consuming in your carefree, retired life that you couldn't spare a few hours for dinner with yet another handsome man? When it rains it pours." Sara's tone telegraphed her opinion loud and clear.

"What about the diamonds? I need to figure out what to do about them." She had decided to keep the incident last night to herself. Security had arrived, done a sweep of her house, found nothing. She had apologized profusely for her unfounded fears and thanked them repeatedly for their trouble.

"Oh yeah, right. The diamonds. That'll definitely require lots of time and having another dinner with Beemer guy would definitely stop that in its tracks." Rachel could almost see Sara's exasperated facial expression through the phone.

"Someone who has raised two children and bounced back as well as you have after the sudden death of her husband can handle what to do with a couple of million dollars in diamonds, Mr. Detective, and Beemer Guy. Guess I should stop calling him that?"

"Ya' think! His name is Mark—Mark Rogers. And thanks for the vote of confidence on my abilities."

"Speaking of the diamonds. Have you given any more thought to what to do with them? Have you talked to Uncle Stan or Leo Schwartz again?"

"No. I'm not ready to call Uncle Stan yet. I've got to get a game plan together. Figure out what I want to do with my newfound wealth," laughed Rachel.

"You wear diamonds. That's what you do with them!"

There was an uncomfortable silence on the line after Sara's brilliant solution.

"Rachel, you there? I'm sorry—didn't mean to be so flip. You know me. No editor on my big mouth."

"Sara, I'm wondering…can you come down? What if we call Beth and Ellyn and you all come down for a girls' weekend? We could play some mahj…shop the outlet…eat…drink…be merry…together? Like old times. What do you think?"

"Sounds like a plan. We can get them on the line now. Don't hang up. It's early and neither of them are morning people so they'll both still be home. We'll probably wake Ellyn up."

Chapter 20

The news hit them like a ton of bricks. Beth wasn't home. The call got forwarded to her cell. She answered from Bethesda. Adam was there—at Walter Reed—hurt. Jacob was in with him now and they were taking him for more surgery within the hour. She'd call them back later.

Ellyn, Sara and Rachel's sobs pierced the silence. None of them knew anything was wrong. And Beth had been too overwhelmed to call. Adam hurt was no different than any of their own children hurt. In their eyes, he was theirs.

Change of plans. They'd meet at Walter Reed Medical Center in Bethesda and be with Beth for moral support. Sara would find a hotel, text them the information. They'd rendezvous there and then head to the hospital. Even if they couldn't get in because technically they weren't family, they would be there, in the lobby, in the waiting room, somewhere close for Beth and Jacob.

It had been a difficult few days waiting and praying for Adam's recovery. The human destruction coupled with the spirit of hope, care and comfort Rachel witnessed all around her literally took her breath away.

She hated politicians. They sat safe and sound in their cushy offices and sent others, our youngest and bravest to fight centuries old battles that would go on for another century or two. Let a few more of these so-called leaders have their own sons and daughters placed in harm's way and they would quickly become more careful with their words and their votes. It's easy to be brave and sound tough for the TV cameras from the comfort of a big leather arm chair in Washington.

Sitting in the sterile hospital chapel had not provided Rachel any comfort. Can't have any one religion getting the upper hand so no affiliation or symbols appeared. There were candles to light, but the pews were hard—the room stark and cold.

Stumbling onto the labyrinth as she walked outside to clear her head had been a godsend.

He does work in mysterious ways, doesn't He.

Placing one foot in front of the other on the red brick path—like she did when David died—like Beth will need to do—Rachel slowly moved through the twists and turns of the labyrinth. Walk your way in, turn around, then walk your way out. Breathe, clear your mind, focus on the work before you.

Step…step…step. She hummed the Mi Shebeirah melody, the Jewish prayer for healing and silently recited, *'Help us find the courage to make our lives a blessing.'* The meaning behind that line in the prayer always brought tears to her eyes. *Such powerful words,* thought Rachel. That you are here to make your life a blessing for others, not cause pain and heartache. She'd worked hard to help Jenny and Scott grieve and heal when David died. Now she'd be here for Beth. Her son so hurt. Her pain must be tremendous. *Do I have that courage? How can I really help?* She steeled herself for the task at hand, comforting Beth. And looking up, seeing the walking wounded around her, what could she do to help all of these men and women who answered their nation's call and paid so dearly?

And then there was Daniel...and Mark. *When it rains, it pours,* she thought, repeating the same phrase Sara had used. Two men paying attention to her now where none had dared to tread for years. Or was it that something had changed inside her, that she was now somehow more open and receptive?

Daniel had called just as she was leaving. She told him what had happened. She could hear sadness in his voice. Nice that it touched him so deeply considering he had never met Beth. Then again, isn't that what makes our lives meaningful...caring about others...moments passing in time...casual meetings...gentle touches...made all the more precious because the seeds of caring begin to take root.

Eyes focused downward. Step...step...step...winding deeper and deeper towards the labyrinth's center. A crisp fall breeze surrounded her. Stopping and looking up, it seemed somehow off that the sky should be so blue, free from clouds, the air smell of autumn. The leaves were in full color mode, decked out in their fall glory. Soon they would all be gone and the trees barren with the promise of rebirth come spring. What could be better than the cyclical beauty that is nature to offer healing to the soul, so necessary to the thousands here fighting to heal their bodies and minds.

Back to the labyrinth. Step...step...step. One foot in front of the other. Slowly navigating the course. Allowing the mind to drift and then pulling it back to the immediate task, reach the center, turn and retrace one's steps.

Mark had also called Thursday morning to say how much he enjoyed their dinner the previous evening. He suggested another dinner later that day. When she declined due to a previous commitment, deciding not to go into detail about Adam's injuries, she could hear the disappointment in his voice. They left it there. He said he was heading out of town for business and would call when he returned.

Rachel reached the labyrinth's center and stopped. Boots met her Birkenstocks. Her eyes moved upward, from shoes to legs in blue jeans, to brown leather belt with a husky dog face carved into the brass belt buckle, to a blue, red and white flannel plaid shirt, to the neckline of a white t-shirt, to a face she knew. Daniel.

"How did you find me?"

"I am a detective, remember?" he chuckled and his wide grinning smile warmed her. She literally fell into his open arms.

"How are you doing? How's Beth?"

Rachel did not move. She stayed in his embrace, took in his scent and felt safe in his arms.

"She's…well, she's…Oh, Daniel…I don't know how she is really," Rachel pulled slightly back so she could look into his eyes. "She's putting on a good front, acting strong and all that. But deep down I can see her pain…and I don't know what to do. I feel so helpless." And with that she nestled back into the space between chin and shoulder, nuzzling his neck, trying to lose herself in the safety of his arms.

"And what do we have here?" asked Sara as she approached, surprised to see Rachel in a man's arms.

"Sara, this is Detective Berger—Daniel. He's been looking into the Racontis. I told him about our suspicions and he's been kind enough to follow-up a bit."

"Nice to finally meet you. I've heard a lot about you." Eyeing the two of them, Sara quickly realized that there was a lot more investigating into each other going on here than Detective Berger investigating the Racontis. *Good,* thought Sara. *Rachel needs a distraction—and a very good looking one at that.*

Chapter 21

Thursday, October 24

"Hungry? I know a great place for burgers and seafood."

"I'm there."

"I'll drive," said Rachel. "It's about a half hour ride. You're going to love the scenery along the way. It's beautiful."

Within minutes they were cruising along Colonial Parkway on the way to Yorktown. There are very few highways like Colonial Parkway. It broadcast the beauty of every season. Fall saw the parkway decked out in autumn splendor.

There was little conversation. To Daniel, Rachel seemed lost in her own thoughts. He was also enjoying the silence— lost in his own thoughts—about her. She seemed nervous, jittery. Maybe she would open up to him about what had her so unsettled.

"WOW!"

"I thought you'd say that. That's what everyone says when the trees part and they first see the river. It's a total wow."

Rachel made a left into the first overlook facing the York River and stopped the car. The small parking lot was empty. Turning off the car, she took a deep breath and opened her door.

"Come on."

As Daniel emerged from the passenger's side, he realized she was scanning the horizon. *What's she looking for?* There wasn't a car, or anyone in sight. Daniel followed as she led him down a narrow, worn path to the river's edge. They stood there, side by side, just looking out over the water.

Even as he looked out across the river, Daniel stole sideways glances at her. She had been on edge since he met her in Bethesda. Then again, Sara and Ellyn weren't much better. All three were trying to be strong for Beth, who seemed to be the strongest of the group. When Daniel offered to follow her home and spend a few of his unused vacation days in Williamsburg she jumped at his offer.

Yesterday, enjoying an afternoon pizza at Sal's, he admitted that he had never done the Colonial Williamsburg thing. His time years ago in Williamsburg had been spent at Busch Gardens when his boys were young. They couldn't have cared less about history and he had promised them a fun vacation that summer, nothing school related.

Rachel became an instant tour guide after they finished eating. They roamed the streets of Williamsburg, arm and arm until it was too dark to see. Being a history buff, he not only asked tons of questions, but could fill in the blanks when she got her history and details twisted. It was the first time in days he had seen her so animated and happy.

Returning to her home caused that happy, carefree woman to disappear. He sensed a different type of tension as she invited him in for coffee. Cruising TV channels, he felt her tension escalate when he stopped at the Will Smith movie, *Enemy of the State*. She seemed caught up by the scene of the little girl seeing herself on TV and Jon Voight's character finding the mini camera in the smoke detector. He watched her eyes go immediately to the smoke detector in her living room. Was he imagining it or was something going on here.

"You okay?"

"Yeah, just tired. It's been a difficult few weeks."

Her words seemed empty and hollow. Why didn't he believe her?

"I should be going. I still need to find a place to stay."

"Stay here. What I mean is, it's silly for you to spend money on a hotel when I have so much space here."

Her eyes told a different story. They were beseeching him to stay. He saw a low level fear there. Engage detective gut.

And now, as they stood on the shore of the York River, watching a bald eagle's graceful flight and enjoying an awesome fall afternoon, he resisted the temptation to wrap her in his warm embrace. He could tell she was making a decision. His gut told him it was a decision about him. He had already decided. He was in love.

Eyes alert to her surroundings, Rachel said, "I think I know what they're after."

"What are you talking about? What who's after?"

"Remember when we were at dinner in New York and I told you I thought someone had been in Aunt Lil's house?"

"Yeah," he answered turning away from the river to face her. His 'yeah' had a questioning uplift as he drew out the word.

"Well, last night—the reason I invited you to stay—more than just enjoying your company, I mean," blushed Rachel. "I think someone has been in my home here, in Williamsburg."

"Hey, just because you're paranoid doesn't mean someone isn't out to get you," laughed Daniel, his crooked grin generating a tiny smile from Rachel.

"Daniel, please, it's more then being paranoid. I even called security when I got home one night and had them walk through my house to check it because a light was on in the kitchen and I was sure I didn't leave it on." Rachel buried her face in her hands. "I must sound crazy."

"No, not crazy at all," said Daniel. Turning her towards him, he looked squarely into her eyes. "What's going on? Tell me. Let me help you."

"Since Aunt Lil died I always have this feeling…like I'm being watched. Even last night, as we were walking around Colonial Williamsburg. And…I think I know what they're after…it's why we're here…where no one can hear us or watch us without being seen."

"Who's they?" asked Daniel, picking up on her serious tone and remembering what he had learned and had yet to share with her about the people occupying the house next door to her Aunt Lil's in Brooklyn.

"I don't know who *they* are. But I know what *they* might be looking for," said Rachel, emphasizing the word they both times.

Rachel unwrapped her cape and pulled her sweater up a bit. She unbuttoned the waistband of her jeans and pulled out a money belt.

"Hold out your hand." Unzipping the front section, Rachel pulled out one of the stones. She placed the stone into the palm of his hand. "This."

"It's a rock."

"It's not a rock," chided Rachel. "It's a stone. Some detective!"

"A stone?" repeated Daniel as he thought for a second, moving it around in his hand, "as in gemstone?"

"Yes, as in diamond. An uncut diamond to be precise. According to Sara's Uncle Stan, what I have," she said as she placed her hand on the outside of the money belt, "could be worth millions."

"There are more?" asked Daniel looking at her hand on top of the money belt.

"Yep. Eight all together."

"Whoa. Put this away," said Daniel, handing her the stone as his mind immediately shifted into full detective mode. "We need to talk about this more. Why aren't these in a safe deposit box? Why are you walking around with them strapped around your body? You need to tell me everything that's been going on. And you're obviously getting chilly standing out here so let's start with those burgers."

"Change of plans," Daniel said as the server placed his beer and Rachel's wine on the table. "Skipping the burger and going with the crab cakes."

"Good choice. Sides?"

"Fries and slaw."

"Me too. Crab cakes, but I'll do the half order with cole slaw. Want to share potato skins first?"

"Sounds good to me."

Daniel had cautioned about being overheard so abiding to the agreement they made at the river's edge, their initial conversation was all about the food. A glance around the restaurant assured them privacy. It was the middle of the afternoon, in the middle of the week, in the fall. For the moment, at least, they were the only ones in place.

"Okay, let's start with your home. What makes you think someone was in your home?"

"As I told you, the kitchen light was on when I got home the other night. And I didn't leave it on. I know I didn't."

"Is it on a timer?"

"No. Timers are still on my to-do list. Just haven't gotten around to buying them. But it was daylight when I left and I was only planning on being gone for an hour so it would have been daylight when I got home. That's why I'm sure I didn't leave any lights on. But I ran into someone I knew and my hour turned into dinner," said Rachel sheepishly realizing that he might ask about her dinner companion.

"And when you got home…was anything disturbed…other than a light being on?"

"Nothing that I could see," said Rachel, throwing up her hands as she leaned back against the booth. "It's a gated community. No one should be able to get in. That's why I chose it."

"Rachel, gated communities give you the perception of security. Few walls are high enough, few gates solid enough. You can't keep the bad guys out if they want to get in. When we drove into your place, I could see a dozen ways for someone to easily get in without going through the monitored security gate."

"I know. And I understand all that," said Rachel.

Daniel was in full detective mode. "Tell me more about what you were doing when you thought someone was in your home. Was that night the only time you felt someone had been there? Did you call anyone before you left that day to say you'd be out?"

"Not that I can remember. I did talk to Jenny earlier that day. She knew where I was going. And yes, that is the only time I felt someone had been in my home. But I've been gone for weeks. And that day—I was sitting on the patio at the Cheese Shop. Remember, I pointed it out to you last night. And this man I met on my way up to Brooklyn—when Aunt Lil died—showed up." Rachel heard herself, really heard what she was saying for the first time. "He was just there. Out of the blue."

"Who is he?" asked Daniel. A man she met on the road showing up didn't sit well with him on several levels.

Then again, wasn't he a man she just met?

"I don't really know." Rachel's eyes were flittering back and forth searching to connect events that, at face value, seemed so innocent. "We crossed paths a few times on the road—you know—like playing leap frog when you were a kid. Then he was there—at the McDonalds where I stopped to eat when I was going up for my aunt's funeral. And then I ran into him again here. I was sitting at the Cheese Shop, enjoying a nice afternoon and all of a sudden, there he was. God, when I say it out loud…I have his card." She fumbled in her purse to retrieve it. Handing it to Daniel, she continued almost speaking to herself more than him. "His name is Mark Rogers."

"Rachel, as I've said to you before, I don't believe in coincidences. What was he doing here—in Williamsburg? Did he say? His card says Virginia Beach."

"He said he was here doing some work for a local company. He works in security—software security. He had some great stories about companies not having good security on their computers. I never questioned what he said," exclaimed Rachel, a look of terror briefly crossing her face. "What was I thinking?"

"You were thinking that you needed some down time after a few stressful weeks," reassured Daniel as he took her hand into his. "There was no reason to question what he told you. And to me, he sounds like someone who played on that stress—on your vulnerability. But why is the question."

"We just had a nice evening. Dinner—conversation— then I drove myself home." Looking across the table at Daniel, Rachel asked, "Am I really that naive?"

Ignoring her question, Daniel continued his quasi-interrogation trying to keep his tone soft so as not to alarm her unnecessarily. "Other than companies with security issues, do you remember anything else? What else did you talk about?"

"Nothing really. Just general dinner conversation. He asked how I liked living here…about my family…what I did to keep myself busy."

"Your little secret stash?" he asked gesturing towards her waist.

"No, that never came up. We talked about nothing…his clients…my move…working…retiring. It was just talking."

Daniel could sense Rachel heading down a path that would not be productive to learning more about her interactions with this guy. Lightening up the atmosphere, he said "Okay. Enough. Eat," pointing to her food. "Your crab cakes are getting cold."

After a few bites, Daniel held up the business card. Rogers & Associates, Security Investigations. "Do you mind if I do some digging—look into this company?"

"No, please, go ahead." He noted a decided change in her tone. It was stronger, not as high pitched and thready. Sitting up straighter, her body projected a newfound toughness.

"Did he say anything more about what he did or his life that might give me more to go on?"

"Nothing that I can remember. The first time—when we met at the McDonalds—he said he traveled from Virginia Beach to New York every week. Honestly, Daniel, it was all very innocent. Two people who were alone one minute and then the next minute they were enjoying a meal together. I probably should feel stupid, but what I'm really feeling is angry."

"I can see that. Let me see what I can find out before you get too angry. It could be nothing. He could be just a nice guy looking for someone to share a meal with and talk to when he is out on the road." Daniel's mind finished the thought.

Then again, he could be something—someone—much different.

He pledged in his mind, or was it his heart, to do a little serious digging and find out more about this mystery man, Mark Rogers.

Chapter 22

Jolene was right on time. Wearing her favorite designer, Versace, always made her feel glamorous. And this little black evening dress with its cut out neckline showed off her new amethyst pendant, a well earned and well deserved birthday gift from her Uncle Al. Looking tall and slender in her new Jimmy Choo five inch stilettos with a touch of bling adorning the ankle straps and carrying a Bottega Veneta silver evening bag surely telegraphed to anyone and everyone that she was an important woman.

Jolene laughed seeing her reflection in the mirror when she got off the elevator at Ben's condo. She was the ultimate chameleon. Dress her up, like now, and she fit right in with the rich and famous. The other night when Jimmy came to collect his stuff, she was relaxing after completing a transaction from her other lifestyle. Either way, Jolene was a woman who never let morality get in her way. From skanky to swanky. A true femme fatale, she was all about taking advantage of every opportunity that came her way.

"I've missed you," said Ben as he embraced her, lifted her off the ground and pulled her into his apartment. "You look wonderful, smell wonderful, feel wonderful."

"Stop, you'll ruin my dress! We are going out? Le Cirque you said, right?"

"Yeah out, but no, not Le Cirque. Things didn't go that well, babe. Just need to finish one little thing here. Make yourself a drink," said Ben as he headed back into his bedroom.

Walking to the bar, Jolene dropped three ice cubes into a glass. After filling it with Grey Goose, she tiptoed to the bedroom door. Information was priceless in her line of work. Ben rarely closed the door. Clearly, he was doing something he did not want to share.

He was on the phone. Of that she was certain. She couldn't really hear what he was saying. No worry. She had a way with Ben. He eventually told her everything. He trusted her. And why not. She was his love kitten. One night after an exceptionally good romp between the sheets he told her about this sweet old lady who told stories about uncut diamonds. If he could just get his hands on them, his problems with Big Al would be solved.

Tonight's dinner was supposed to be a celebration. Unfortunately, nothing had gone according to plan. From the tidbits she picked up, the guy he hired to do the actual stealing, screwed up. She knew it was her friend Jimmy— Jimmy the screw up. So, what else is new?

Jolene hurried back to the sofa as she thought she heard a muffled "bye" ending Ben's conversation. Settling herself between the pillows, like she saw the glamorous stars of old time Hollywood do, she immediately made eye contact when Ben opened his door.

"Everything okay, babe?"

"Yeah. Just some loose ends to deal with. Nothing to worry about," muttered Ben. His facial expression screamed worry. "Let me just have one for the road and then we'll go. Reservations are for seven. That nice little Italian place you like by Central Park. With the awesome risotto. Okay?"

He poured some vodka into a glass and took a gulp to steady his nerves. His conversation with Big Al had not gone well. Al wanted his money—all his money and then some—a hundred and fifty grand to be totally free. Period. End of story.

The original plan had been solid—easy pickings from an old lady. No one gets hurt. *Where was that son of a bitch?* The last time he used the voice modulator to call Jimmy for a status report, the kid had answered the phone, but then the line went dead—and stayed dead. *And the diamonds—did he find them and run? Or just run because he screwed up?* Whatever, Ben needed money and he needed it fast. *Shit. Why did Lil have to die?*

"Okay, let's go," he said, after chugging his drink. "And you do look amazing. There won't be a woman not green with envy looking at you, babe. Not a man thinking that he wants to be me tonight."

Maybe it wasn't Le Cirque but it was still good food in an elegant restaurant with waiters fawning all over them. That was what Jolene loved. Doors opened. People taking notice. People waiting on her. Scrumptious dinners, expensive wine, sorbet to cleanse one's palette between courses. Happy times for a girl from nowhere Nebraska.

Laisser le bon temps rouler! Let the good times roll! she thought.

Jolene learned how to use her natural charms to her advantage early on. She was born with what would grow to become exceptional equipment. Barefoot, pregnant, and in the kitchen held no allure. No rug rats for her. And her profession of choice did not require hours of study or years of school. Her heart was set on glitter and glam any way she could get it.

She'd had some great teachers. Turn a few tricks. Perfect your skills. Work your way up. Escort service. Exclusive status, by appointment only. Her secret benefactor—her sugar daddy—was Uncle Al—Big Al. Not an uncle by birth—an uncle by choice—and a very generous uncle.

Her current assignment was simple—keep tabs on Ben and Jimmy. What appeared to be two chance meetings had been carefully choreographed by Uncle Al some years ago. First Ben, once a rich, well-connected lawyer. Gambling had sucked away his riches. But he didn't learn his lesson. He kept playing—getting deeper and deeper in debt to Big Al. Her job was to keep tabs on him and report back to Al. Ben came with a bonus—he was great in bed. Attentive to her needs, gentle, powerful. Icing on top of the cake.

Jimmy was a totally different story. He already had a connection to Ben so all she had to do was insert herself into his life to complete the loop. She reeled him in after following him to his favorite bar. She invited him to move into the apartment she kept as her work apartment a few months ago. Everything was set. Ben knew Jimmy—and Jimmy knew Ben—and they both knew Jolene—intimately. She had both of them where Big Al wanted them— whispering sweet nothings into her ear—confiding in her about all aspects of their lives.

In Jolene's line of work, sex was highly overrated. She had learned to live with sex as a means to an end. Nothing more. No fairy tales for her. No prince charming. No knights in shining armor. Just men to take you places and buy you things. Pay you for your services. Spend what you want and save some for a rainy day. Or at least for the time when parts started to sag and she would need to go under the knife or retire. She'd already made up her mind. No knife. Retirement.

"Ben, you've been quiet all night. Tell me, babe, what's wrong?" cooed Jolene, hours later, as she stroked Ben's chest and curled his few hairs with her index finger.

"Just things on my mind. I'm sorry it wasn't Le Cirque tonight. I know how much you wanted to go there." Ben kissed the top of her head as it lay on his chest. "Another time. I'll take you there. I promise."

Promises, promises. She'd heard them all before and would hear them again and again. "Is there anything I can do to help you? You know how helpful I can be."

"No. Not this time." Ben reached for his drink on the bedside table. He offered her a sip, took one for himself and laid back down. Jolene held her tongue and waited. Ben felt safe with her and safety loosened his lips.

"Remember that guy I told you about? The one I helped beat a theft charge when he was a kid? The one I try to help with odd jobs?"

"Yeah, sure. I remember you saying something about a guy you helped." She hadn't let on that she knew Jimmy when Ben mentioned his name months ago, bragging about this guy he'd helped stay out of jail when he worked as a PD. He loved taking credit, being seen as a good guy.

"Well, he was doing some work for me and I haven't heard from him. I'm worried about him. I've been putting out feelers to find him but no one has seen him for a few days."

"Oh?" Jolene's attention was aroused. Rolling off Ben's chest, Jolene rested her head on a midnight blue satin encased goose down pillow. She thought back to the night when Ben's pillow talk had aroused her more than sexually. He told her about an old lady and some diamonds. How he was going to clear up all his gambling debts so they could go away and start fresh. That he was using a guy he'd used before. The next morning she called Uncle Al and told him about the conversation.

Right now, she didn't know all the details but she knew enough. He was talking about Jimmy and she didn't like the picture being painted. He'd been scared when he stopped by her place to get his stuff last week. He didn't take her up on her offer of comfort to ease his pain. Just got his stuff, told her where he was going should someone ask about him and rushed out the door. He had lied, of course. In her world, everyone lied. She connected the dots in her mind.

Rising up onto her elbow, resting her head in her hand, she said, "That's what I love about you, Benny. You're this big powerful lawyer and yet you still care about other people. It's so sweet that you care about him…and where he is. I'm sure he'll turn up…maybe he just tied one on."

"Yeah, maybe you're right. I know he likes to drink. Maybe he's just sleeping it off somewhere."

Jimmy wasn't a bad kid—just stupid, thought Jolene. *Always after the big money, the easy score.* And she remembered him boasting that his current job was the big one, the one he had waited for all his life, the one that would make his dreams come true, the one that would put them both on easy street. Schmuck! He thought he was in control, pulling the strings. What he didn't know was that it was all a set up. Al wanted his money from Ben and Jolene's relationship with both men was the path.

Lying next to Ben, Jolene said a silent prayer for Jimmy. Yes, he was a punk. Yes, he was an egotistical ass. Yes, Uncle Al and Ben were both using him. Yes, Jolene used him too. But even egotistical asses didn't deserve to get dead.

Chapter 23

What now? That was the million dollar question. What had been a simple con had gone to shit. Marco refilled his glass with Maker's Mark and made his way to the overstuffed sofa opposite Marissa. He'd been back at the compound for a few hours and had invited Marissa to join him for dinner. Sitting down with his glass pressed to his chest, he tilted his head back and closed his eyes, conjuring up his memory of that first afternoon months ago when he met Jimmy at that bar in Soho.

Marco had stopped in for a celebratory beer after completing a con. He was still in character—dressed in jeans, a flannel shirt and the heavy work boots befitting a construction guy. Even tinted away his gray to appear younger. His nom-de-plume for the con had been Ed Bentley. That was what he loved about his work, the costumes and play-acting the different persona.

The bar was empty except for a group of guys playing pool in the back alcove. And there was this guy, the lone guy at the bar, having a Guinness and talking to the bartender about this new gig and how he was going to be rich. Nursing his own beer two stools away, Marco sat quietly, carefully listening to Jimmy's rant, absorbing the details about his upcoming big score. Marco's mind went into hyperdrive. The kid had a big mouth, was clearly an ass, but what he was talking about was enticing—too enticing to ignore.

Using an old con trick, Marco asked Jimmy to pass the peanuts. He knew the way to get a guy to let his guard down was to ask him to give you something. Jimmy complied, took it a step further, played the big shot, told the bartender to refill the bowl with fresh nuts. To thank him, Marco motioned to the bartender to refill Jimmy's glass. Jimmy made the big move, changed bar stools. Introductions came next. Marco had him. Now, to reel him in.

Just two guys at a bar, whiling away a rainy April afternoon. The addition of a few rounds of tequila was all it took. There was no shutting this kid up. He spilled his guts about his plan, even let Marco know there was another guy involved. This other guy, a faceless voice on the phone really, had pointed him to the stash. He'd get a cut, but Jimmy was in charge, a true legend in his own mind.

Diamonds. That was the lure. Diamonds owned by an old lady who lived alone. Easy mark. Marco kept the booze flowing in Jimmy's direction and soon the two of them were thick as thieves. When Jimmy provided the opening with his rambling idea about how he would break in, Marco played on his ego and offered a different option. What about a full blown con? It might take a little longer in the set up, but the results proved hard to beat. No one got hurt. Jimmy bit. He liked the idea of the hustle.

They met a few nights later for drinks and dinner. Marco, dressed again like Ed Bentley, with a nicer shirt and clean Dockers explained how the con would unfold. He introduced Jimmy to Marissa, the woman that would play his mother who was all decked out in her Millie Raconti costume. Jimmy let them know that he knew a guy who could gain them access to the empty house next door. Thinking about it now, Marco realized he should have asked Jimmy a few more questions—to get a better read on the guy since they were going into the con with him playing a leading role.

How had he let that slip by? He used to be more careful, less trusting of strangers. Was he getting too old for these cons? Was it time to retire?

Now, as Marco sat in his plush living room with floor to ceiling windows overlooking the Atlantic Ocean, he worked through various scenarios to consider all of his options. Marco knew his best option was to let go, move on. Whenever the con gets too complicated, it's a signal to stop and pull out. There's always another mark, another con on the horizon.

But this one was different. Uncut diamonds not seen for decades. Diamonds from a time when larger, higher quality stones were more plentiful. The temptation to own them overwhelmed him. There has got to be another way.

Marissa sat silently across from Marco, watching him. She knew this man, intimately in a non-sexual way. She knew when to remain silent. Over the years their union had proven productive, affording both of them, as well as Dom and Sophia, a lifestyle most people who started out begging on the streets could only dream of. She wanted to help, offer suggestions, but her reading of Marco telegraphed a clear signal—be silent. This was not the time.

Dom had remained in Williamsburg. He sent regular texts on Rachel's comings and goings. And about a new wrinkle, a guy named Daniel. He showed up with Rachel when she returned from Bethesda. He looked familiar, like someone Dom had seen before, but Dom couldn't place him. Who was he?

Marco—as Mark Rogers—had talked to Rachel feigning an out of town business trip when she was too busy to see him. He could pick up the phone and call her anytime. And he wanted to talk to her again, hear her voice, see her. Strange that he had developed feelings for her that went beyond seeing her as a mark. *What was that about?* He had rules about getting involved with marks. She was different. She was interesting. There was something about her that set her apart. Before he called her, he needed a plan.

"Marissa, what if you go up to Williamsburg, befriend her. We could concoct a story, get you close."

"How would I get close enough fast enough? Don't you think she'd get suspicious of another new stranger in her life trying to buddy up to her? From my impressions, the one thing she isn't is stupid." Her tone perhaps a bit too matter-of-fact, Marissa softened it a bit as she asked, "Marco, is it time to opt out?"

"No!" he barked. His eyes pierced through her like knives, his frustration and anger evident in his tone of voice. When he saw her flinch, her reaction registered deep in his heart. There was love there.

"I'm sorry." Taking in a breath, he rose and walked to the wall of windows and stared out at the ocean. "Yes," he continued more softly. "You're right. It's definitely time to let go." Moments passed. She could tell he was trying to come up with something.

"I just can't stop. There is something about this one…diamonds…" he whispered almost breathlessly, "we'd all be set for the rest of our lives. No one would ever have to go out again. We could stay here and enjoy all that we have."

"Marco, my love." Marissa rose and joined him at the windows. She took him in her arms, hoping he would find comfort there. "We've been at this for years and the years have brought us wealth none of us ever imagined when we started. Our skills have proven very useful, and your investing skills brought us all of this." Pulling back so she could look at him face-to-face, she continued, more forcefully, "There is a time to continue...and there is a time to stop. Perhaps now, it's time to stop, when we are ahead...and safe."

Chapter 24

Rachel had been gone all afternoon leaving Daniel to fend for himself. She opened the door from her garage into her home to find soft music playing, candles ready to be lit on a table set with crisp white linens, her best china, and a smiling man handing her a glass of white wine.

"We're having caesar salad. Did I tell you I make a wicked caesar? Followed by herb poached salmon with asparagus risotto, if that meets with your approval."

"When did you do all this...the shopping...the table" exclaimed Rachel as she looked around her home. "I'm impressed. I love a man who can cook."

"I was hoping you'd say that! Here's to us..." Daniel raised his glass to touch hers. "May this be the beginning of something special. L'chaim!"

"Yes. I'd like to think this is the beginning of something special too." Her smile was infectious.

"We have time before dinner. Let's take a walk." The suggestion surprised Rachel. Taking the wine glass from her hand, he gestured his head towards the door. She understood his meaning immediately. He had information to share and he wanted to share it in private.

"That's a lovely idea. A walk before what sounds like it is going to be a great meal works for me. Then again, after all the years I cooked, any meal I don't have to cook is a great meal! Let me get my warmer shawl."

Outside Rachel slipped her hand through Daniel's offered arm as he led her down to the sidewalk.

"This is a one mile circle," she said. "That will certainly build our appetites."

Walking in silence for a few minutes built suspense until Rachel couldn't stand it anymore.

"Okay. Out with it. What did you learn? What do you want to tell me out here that you didn't want to say in there?"

"Well, you certainly get to the point fast, don't you."

"Hey, no time to waste. Spill it."

"Okay. First, you were right about the house next door to your aunt's. It is for sale. I talked to your realtor, Janice Stone. She told me it got pulled off the market for a few months but went back on just after your aunt died. And that guy Jimmy? His prints connected to a small time hood— theft, B&E mostly—some jail time. His body was found in a dumpster on Staten Island. Gang wannabe initiation maybe. Wrong place at the wrong time. Probably never know for sure. No lead on the woman yet. We know she wasn't his mother."

"Jeez. I knew it. He gave me the creeps. The woman was nice. I could see how my aunt would like her. What did you find out about my house? Am I being watched?"

"After you left this morning I did a sweep of your place with a RF detector. You were right. Someone is keeping tabs on you. Your home is bugged. Three audio bugs—one in the kitchen, the bedroom and the living room. Still need to check your car to see if there is a tracking device on it."

"Oh, God. I feel so violated. Where are they? How come

I didn't see them? Not that I'd really know what to look for."

"You know that glass cube on your kitchen counter where you have pens and pencils? There's one there—inside a pen. There's one in the base of that blue ceramic lamp behind your sofa and there's one in your bedroom phone handset."

They walked on in silence. Daniel could see Rachel was processing what he had just said.

"Didn't find any cameras so I think it's safe to say that you are not being watched just listened to. We can do a little redecorating if you like and get rid of them. Which would let whoever is behind this know that we know. Or, if we want to play along a bit—see where all of this is going—we could leave them where they are. Only thing, what you say inside your home—what we say—what you say on the phone—has to be stuff you wouldn't mind the neighborhood gossip overhearing."

"When I talked to Sara the other day I did mention the diamonds. That was the morning after I called security. So maybe that was when the bugs got planted—while I was out having dinner. That chance meeting with Mark Rogers is looking less and less like an accident."

"Yep, it sure is. There is no Mark Rogers. No business. No Rogers & Associates, Security Investigations"

Rachel stopped in her tracks. "You've got to be kidding me!"

"His business doesn't exist. Nothing registered at that location."

"God…*God*" Rachel's face paled. Daniel had her full and complete attention.

"The only thing at 3005 Atlantic Ave in Virginia Beach is a huge stone Neptune statue—sort of a landmark at the waterfront there. There's a website and a call center set-up to answer the phone. Whoever this guy is, you need to be wary of any future chance meetings—or any meetings for that matter."

Daniel witnessed what he would later describe to Cooper as a teutonic shift in Rachel's demeanor. When she had first mentioned Mark Rogers, she seemed interested in him. Just now, when Daniel told her what he had learned, her body language told him that she'd turned a corner. Her shoulders squared. She straightened—suddenly seemed taller. She wasn't angry or upset. More matter of fact, like she somehow knew—had known all along—that he wasn't real. Any trace of victimhood was gone, replaced by an inner strength that he had noticed the day they first met at her aunt's home.

"Okay. Got it." The matter-of-fact, coldness of her tone—pure detachment—told him that an internal protective switch had flipped on. "Did I mention he called the same day I learned about Adam's injuries? Don't think I did. Anyway, he said he'd get back in touch with me when he came back from a business trip. Don't suppose that would be a good idea at this point?"

"Seriously? Ya' think?" Daniel laughed and he could feel her playfully poke an elbow into his side. They walked on a bit before she stopped and turned to him.

"Do you think my aunt's house might have been bugged? If it was, whoever is doing this now heard me talking about them. I showed Sara the diamonds after the funeral. They know I have them."

"If they've bugged you down here, it makes sense they might have planted a few in your aunt's house. We'll probably never know for sure." Daniel brushed a stray hair away from her eyes. "We can take precautions to keep you safe."

She caught his hand in hers. "There's more, isn't there?" her voice more solemn now.

"Yeah. Cooper's been doing some checking for me. The lawyer, Ben Collins. It seems several of his elderly clients have passed away in recent months. Nothing odd really. Old is old and when your time is up, it's up. But that they were all clients of Ben Collins got me thinking."

"There's that detective gut again!"

"Yeah. Funny when it goes off," grinned Daniel. "Can't shut it down until I figure out what's bothering me. Anyway, Cooper has been interviewing some of the relatives. One death stood out. Cooper talked to a grandson. When Cooper asked about his grandmother's passing in a general sort of way, the guy was adamant that she had not been sick. Kind of like what you said about your aunt. And then the guy claimed that money was missing from his grandmother's bank accounts. The guy even hired an accountant to dig into his grandmother's financial records. Cooper's like a bird dog when he gets a whiff of something that doesn't smell right to him. We're alike that way. It's why I like partnering with him. Anyway, he's still interviewing family members of other deceased."

"Wow. That's a lot more than I thought." Rachel considered Aunt Lil. She hadn't been sick either. Just died. "What do you think's going on?"

"I think Mr. Collins may have his fingers in the cookie jar, so to speak. Did you notice if any money was missing from any of your aunt's accounts, especially the ones Ben Collins could access?"

"Don't know. I can look."

"Do that. We hear from a pretty reliable source that he has a severe gambling problem. And that he owes a few people some cash—the type of people who expect to be paid—with interest."

"That can't be good. Aren't those the type of people who don't keep records? And hurt you when you don't pay up?"

"Oh, they definitely keep records, just not the type that we can easily get our hands on. Hopefully, Cooper will come up with something solid that we can take to a judge for a warrant. I'd love to get our forensic accountants to take a look at Ben's books. Especially any trust accounts that he has power of attorney for. I've got a feeling that comparing what is supposed to be there with what is really there—the inflows and the outflows—could prove very interesting, to say the least."

Back at her front door, Daniel confronted her.

"Rachel, I want to catch these guys. I need your help. How good an actress can you be?"

"I don't know. I've got my moments when I fake it with ease. You know, easy stuff like telling someone her outfit looks fabulous when it really doesn't, or telling someone that her cooking is great when all I want to do is throw up. Then there are other times when my face totally gives me away."

"Well, they can't see your face—only hear your voice— what you say. So let's make a pact. We keep our conversations away from the diamonds, Aunt Lil's death, my investigation, anything that might give someone listening any help. Nothing gets said in the house about any of this unless we want to plant information and see where it leads. Okay?"

"I'm in. And when I need to say something or ask you something, I'll suggest a walk. That will be my signal to you."

"Sounds like a plan. When I leave we can make adjustments to minimize the chance that someone might be listening."

Daniel took Rachel's key from her to unlock the door. As he opened it, he couldn't help but wonder if he didn't just witness a hint of sadness cross Rachel's face at the mention of him leaving.

Opening the door, Daniel said, "Come on, woman, we have cooking to do."

Rachel laughed and followed him into her small kitchen. "What can I do to help? I'm a good cook but I know when to relinquish control and allow someone else to take the lead. So, orders please."

This is going to be fun, thought Daniel. "First things first, my dear. Allow me to refill your wine." Grabbing the bottle from the refrigerator door, he added more wine to both of their glasses. "Can't have thirsty cooks."

"Thank you. And I'll flip the switch for the fireplace to take the chill off and get some music going."

"Sounds like a plan. I've done most of the prep already. I'm thinking we'll have the caesar first. Then I'll poach the salmon and you can stir the risotto."

"Works for me. It all sounds yummy. Point me in a direction. Tell me what you need me to do."

In his mind and heart Daniel's answer was clear. *I need you to fall in love with me.* Turning away from her so she wouldn't see his expression which he was sure telegraphed his feelings, he asked whether she had a wooden salad bowl.

"Yep. In the back pantry. I'll get it. It doesn't get used much."

Whipping up the caesar dressing gave him the busy work he needed at the moment. Dipping a piece of romaine into it he held it to her mouth.

"Here. Taste. Strong enough? Too strong?"

"Wow, that's good." Rachel sipped her wine and watched him toss the romaine and sprinkle the parmigiano-reggiano. He filled the plates and carried them to the already set table as she followed.

"Let me get the candles lit," Daniel said as he pulled back Rachel's chair for her.

"Fresh pepper?"

"Not for me," said Rachel as she dug her fork into the fresh greens. "This is delicious. I can't wait for the rest. You are certainly one hell of a cook, Detective Daniel Berger."

"Thank you. I aim to please."

Within moments the salad was gone.

"You were hungry," said Daniel as he stood up and moved back to the kitchen with the empty salad plates in his hands.

"That was really good. Nice and garlicky—just the way I like it."

"Now, you've got work to do. Risotto is serious stuff. Needs to be stirred constantly to release the starches in the rice for that creamy texture. Are you up for the challenge?"

"Ready, sir. I've never made it so just tell me what to do."

"I'll get it started and then work on the salmon. That way there's a good chance both dishes will be done at the same time."

"Where did you learn all this?"

"I like to eat. I used to work in some really fine restaurants when I was in college. You wouldn't believe what goes on in some kitchens. Kind of turned me off to eating out. So I watched what the chefs did and I'd try it. Some dishes worked. Others, not so much. Trial and error. And I threw away the errors. Learned a lot."

Rachel could tell that this was a man who knew his way around a kitchen. The aroma of onions and garlic sautéing filled the room. He added the rice, stirred it and then added some white wine.

"Now, just stir gently. When the liquid evaporates add some more broth. And keep stirring." Handing off the wooden spoon, he continued, "Do you know how many cooking shows are on TV?"

"Not really."

"Tons! You name the cuisine and there's a show for it. So at night, when I can't sleep and need to unwind, I watch Giada De Laurentis cook Italian, Bobby Flay grill, Ina Gartner, Tyler Florence. All of them. Alton Brown's shows taught me tons about food and preparation."

"And I'm an appreciative recipient of your education."

"Stir!"

"Yes sir!" Her smile made Daniel's heart leap. *Now that's a smile that could launch a thousand ships,* he thought. *It sure launches me.*

They sat, they ate, they talked of their past lives. Rachel talked about David, her son Scott and daughter Jenny. David had an invisible, golden thread connecting him to both of their children. He was the magician in their lives. Had answers, direction for them. He was a mensch—Ozzie Nelson and Ward Cleaver smeared with schmaltz. When he died the thread broke. Aunt Lil had been there for her…told her to take the love she had had for David and spread it around…give it outward to others…then it would come back to her in spades.

She learned more about Anna, their two sons and the life Daniel and she created together—the horror of her loss. She died when the towers went down. He died that day, too, burying himself in his work so he would not have to face life without her. Daniel had been alone a long time, she realized, throwing himself into his work, as if work could ever replace the love he lost.

"Daniel, this was wonderful. The food…I can't remember the last time I had such a good dinner. I can't thank you enough."

"It is my pleasure. I love cooking and love when someone eats with as much gusto as you did tonight. I love a woman with a good appetite."

"You go sit. I'll clean up."

"Nope. We cooked together. We ate together. We clean up together." Lifting empty dishes from the table, he led the way back to the kitchen.

"You rinse and I'll stack the dishwasher. Only two pots and we're done."

"Not quite. There's dessert."

"More food?" asked Rachel.

"Yep. I'm a chocoholic. Nothing fancy here. I don't bake. Saw chocolate mouse pie slices in the freezcr case and the woman standing next to me said they were—how did she put it—'to die for.' Hope she's right."

Sitting next to this man who was no longer a stranger in front of the fireplace, enjoying the soft music playing in the background, eating dessert and sipping wine seemed so right. When they had first come back to the house after their walk, Rachel could not imagine what they would talk about if they didn't talk about the diamonds or the surveillance bugs or Mark Rogers or her aunt. Daniel held up a pen from the glass cube container so she would know which pen had the bug. Now, hours later, even the few lulls in their conversation were comforting. She felt as if she had known this man all her life. With aching clarity, Rachel was very sure of one thing. She wanted to know more of him now.

Putting down her wine glass, Rachel shifted her position to face Daniel.

"Daniel, I… I don't know what I would have done…how I…"

"Shhhh."

Putting his wine glass on the sofa table, he reached out to push back that same lock of hair again falling in front of her eye. His fingertips continued down, gingerly caressing the side of her cheek. The tip of his finger lingered under her chin as he lifted it up towards him.

His kiss, ever so light and soft, brushed her lips. Then another one on the tip of her nose, her forehead. She responded to his next kiss with an intensity that surprised him. Delighted him. He could feel her heart pounding against his chest as he warmly embraced her.

Daniel stood and held out his hand. "*As Time Goes By,*" he said. "This is my favorite song. Shall we dance?" Slipping her hand into his, with one graceful move, Rachel was in his arms.

"Yes, I know. We've danced to this song before. Remember? At that little Italian place."

"Yes, I remember," he muttered.

How could I forget the first time I held you, he thought.

"I'm a sucker for the old films. Casablanca, Robin Hood. They don't make them like that anymore." He pulled her tighter to him as they moved together as one.

"What's yours?"

"My what?"

"Favorite song?"

"*When you Wish upon a Star.* I'm all Disney. Raised on it. You know, the happiest place on earth."

He felt her take a deep breath and nuzzle even closer. Daniel couldn't help but notice how well she fit into that special space when dancing between shoulder and face. Not too tall. Not too short. She was just right for him. He was unconvinced in this moment how any physical place could be happier than where he was right now—holding this wonderful loving woman in his arms.

Daniel responded. Holding her ever more tightly, they were barely moving now. Pulling back, their eyes met.

"Maybe we shouldn't…" Daniel started to say, thinking he was heading into unchartered waters perhaps too quickly.

"Yes, we definitely should." Rachel assured him. "You

need to know…it's been a long time…. I'm…nervous…and very out of practice."

"Let's just take it slow…long time for me too… no expectations…see how it goes."

Daniel's inner detective was eager to explore every inch of the amazing woman he now held in his arms. Feeling her heart beating as he held her close made his own heart seem to burst from his chest. Mesmerized by her scent so close now. The final notes of *As Time Goes By* alerted him. The end of their embrace was arriving. What now?

The music ended. She didn't move away. Daniel's hand traced the neckline of her blouse. Gentle fingertips slipped downward. Her nipples hardened beneath his delicate touch. Feeling her shiver slightly, he moved her arms around his neck and tightened his hold. His next kiss was strong and long and intimate. Rachel responded with a passion she had long forgotten, a marvelous, exhilarating tingle down to her toes.

"You are truly beautiful…" he whispered in her ear as his tongue traced its edges and he nibbled and kissed her.

His tenderness brought tears to her eyes. Swallowing, she lifted her chin and reached up, initiating another kiss, fearing any words she might attempt to utter would spoil the moment.

"You sure can cook," was all that slipped out.

Chapter 25

Cooper quickly realized that his investigation had legs. Each conversation with a relative of one of the recently departed elderly clients of Ben Collins had striking similarities.

"No, my grandma had not been sick."

"Yes, my aunt did have sufficient funds to handle all her needs."

"Yes, there had been trust accounts set up for emergencies. All handled by the elder Mr. Collins before he died, now handled by his son, Ben."

Things were missing. Relatives remembered specific pieces, collections that were no longer there. An amethyst ring, a ruby pendant promised to a beloved granddaughter and other jewelry, stamp and coin collections—items that relatives vividly remembered were nowhere to be found when things started to be packed up or split between family members.

Cooper's last conversation was the most disturbing so far. Mr. Joshua Renfeld lost his beloved Emma. She had not been sick, but he had been in a rehab facility for a few weeks after hip replacement surgery. Emma came to be with him every day. They'd been married for sixty years. She'd started to tell him that she couldn't wait for him to come home because she thought she was losing her mind. Things were going missing. She couldn't remember where she put her favorite bracelet, the one he had given her their very first Chanukah. She couldn't find his gold pocket watch. She was sure it was on his dresser, but when she went to get it to bring it to him, it wasn't there.

And then one day she didn't come. He asked the nurse to call her. No answer. The nurse sent the police. They found her at the bottom of the basement stairs. Only one problem, claimed a very distraught Mr. Renfeld to whoever would listen. Emma, his beloved Emma, never went into the basement. There was no reason for her to go down there.

Brad Cooper was listening, intently, especially after he learned the name of Mr. Renfeld's lawyer—Ben Collins.

Cooper sat next to Mr. Renfeld after one of his physical therapy sessions.

"I just don't know what I am going to do without her, my Emma. Did I tell you she was a great cook? Made the best latkes. No one made latkes like my Emma."

"Yes, Mr. Renfeld, you told me and I am so sorry for your loss. Good latkes are hard to find. Do you remember any of the other items she said were missing? I know you said a bracelet and your gold pocket watch. Anything else?"

"Not that I can remember," answered a very frail, sad looking man. "You know we were married on New Year's Eve. Back then, you just didn't live together like they do now. Kids! What do they know about love? Anyway, it was cold and we just wanted to be together so we got in my car— a Ford. And we drove down to Maryland. You didn't have to wait. You could just get married. And we did. That was sixty years ago. The best years of my life. She…she was my life. My son, he was just here. Did you meet him? Aaron, nice boy. A doctor. He's going to take me in—says I can't live alone anymore. What am I going to do?" Mr. Renfeld turned away from Cooper. Tears swelled in his eyes.

"I know what I'm going to do, Mr. Renfeld. I'm going to get you answers. I'll be back in touch," promised Cooper. "You can count on me."

Walking down the hall of the rehab center, Cooper couldn't yet fathom that kind of love. He yearned to feel that connected to another human being, to be that committed to someone else. Most of his relationships ended almost before they began. The life of a cop, and now a detective, is not easy for a girlfriend, let alone a spouse. Cases override family plans. Stress builds up. Divorce runs rampant.

As he left Mr. Renfeld, a deep seated rage against the unknown fired in his belly. Was this a dreadful accident? Did his wife avoid the basement like her husband claimed? Or was there something more sinister at work? Had a crime been committed? And since one of the main characters in this unknown was Ben Collins, Brad Cooper was betting on the latter.

Chapter 26

Friday, October 25

Rachel could still smell Daniel. Breathing in, she was totally captive to his scent. She could still feel his touch. Lying in bed and wanting to be close to him, Rachel wrapped her arms around the pillow he had rested his head on and hugged it to her chest. He was here, with her. Closing her eyes, she hit her mental replay button.

As a romantic finale to a wonderful evening, they had shared breakfast in bed. Sipping coffee and munching on croissants, reading the newspaper, watching morning TV—the things millions of people do every morning without really thinking about them took on a new specialness.

Would her morning routine ever be the same?

Last night as they came to bed Daniel had released her, pressed his finger to his lips in the *shhhh* motion. He removed the phone handset, took it into the bathroom. Closing the door, he came back, encircled her in strong arms and lifted her onto her bed. Talk about the stuff romance novels are made of and women everywhere imagine their men doing.

He said he was off to check in with the local police—a courtesy he claimed he should have done when he first got to town. He also needed to check in with his office, make some calls, do some follow-up with Cooper. She suspected that what he really needed was some space and time to sort out his feelings. If truth be told, she was grateful for some time to herself. He'd be back in a few hours and they'd figure out what they would do for dinner.

She was alone. Alone, but not lonely. What surprised Rachel the most as she lay there was her realization that she felt so complete. At some point she would have to come to terms with the magic of the last night. Right now she was wallowing in the spark of how alive she felt. Her body was on fire! *Is this a prelude to a new happiness to come?* She hoped so.

Two more days, Rachel thought. *He's leaving in two days. Then what? Back to her retirement life of lunches, mah jongg, movies and more lunches? Seriously? Sure, I could do that. Or could I? Do I want to?*

No! I want more. And more is six foot two…has short, steel gray hair and the type of butt that jeans were made for. More wears plaid shirts as comfortably as a button down. And more makes my toes tingle when he smiles.

The Skype bing on her PC brought Rachel back to the here and now. Retrieving the PC from the night stand, Rachel cuddled back into bed.

"Beth. How are you? How's Adam?"

"That's why I'm Skyping. He's doing better. He recognizes us. The doctors say it's going to take some time—and a lot of physical therapy. They'll fit him with a prothesis in a few weeks. And then he'll start learning how to walk again. He'll stay here for a few more weeks and then transfer to a VA facility closer to home. Or we'll get him private care.

"That's great news. It's so good to see you. I love this technology."

"Yes. Me too. So much better than just calling. It sounds silly, but we really feel lucky. Remember that contractor we used to redo the kitchen? I called him to ask about how to remodel Adam's old bedroom and add a ramp and stuff that he'll need to get around. Told us not to worry. He'd take care of it. He's doing it all for free."

"That's awesome. You've got a long road ahead of you. How are you holding up? How's Jacob?"

"Jacob's a wreck. His son…that's all he keeps saying…his son…like I didn't have anything to do with him. Adam's our son…both of ours…and I'm as much a part of this as he is." There was silence for a moment. "I'm sorry. I didn't mean to say that."

"Of course you didn't mean it. And you can say anything you want when you talk to me. You know that."

"I know. Jacob is so angry. All of his anger about the wars—he lumps them all together—he goes on rants to anyone and everyone who will listen. I get most of it," Beth sighed. "We're all going to need help to get through this."

"You know I'm here. Whatever it takes."

"I know. You've always been there. I just needed to talk to someone not wearing scrubs for awhile. And, you are definitely not wearing scrubs right now. You're still in bed! Did I wake you?"

"No. I've been awake for awhile."

"How are you doing? Fill me in. Talk to me. Help me get my mind off of all of this."

"I'm fine. Better then fine really."

"Really? You sound different. You look…well, you look like the cat that swallowed the canary. Spill it. What's up?"

"Remember that detective I mentioned—the one that

showed up after you and Ellyn left. The one I introduced you to last week at the hospital."

"Yeah. Sort of. These last few weeks have been a blur. Can't remember his name right now. My mind is mush."

"Daniel. His name is Daniel. I had told him about some of the stuff that I thought was going on at Aunt Lil's house. Anyway, to make a long story short, he followed me back here."

"Really. Now that *is* interesting. I've been out of touch too long. So what's going on, girl?"

"Well, that night he took me out to dinner before I left Brooklyn after my aunt died. Did I tell you about that? Probably not. I ran into him at this street fair and he invited me to dinner that night. One thing led to another and I told him about some of the odd things Sara and I experienced at my aunt's. I mentioned them that night. He called just before I left to come meet you—and then he showed up—in Bethesda."

"What odd stuff?"

"Remember the neighbors—Jimmy and Mille? Well, Jimmy was making me and Sara really nervous—kept showing up. And we looked in the window at their house and there was nothing there—and it was also for sale."

"Slow down, Rachel. I'm having trouble keeping up. Nothing in their house? Like they had no furniture?"

"Right. And Daniel has been looking into them and it seems they aren't really related. And the guy is dead."

"What? Who's dead?"

"Jimmy."

Rachel went on to share all the details of the last few weeks with Beth. Jimmy's body in the dumpster, the deaths of old people, Beemer guy, and the fear of being watched. She stopped cold.

"Shit…shit!"

"What's the matter?"

Looking at the still empty phone cradle, she breathed a sigh of relief. "Nothing. Beth, I've got to go. This has been great. I'll be in New York in a few days—." Again, Rachel caught herself and stopped talking. Realizing she almost told Beth about the diamonds and her meeting with Leo, she shifted gears.

"Sara and I made some plans for some girl time. I'll call you when I get in. Maybe you and Ellyn can join us—at least for lunch—if not for a mahj game."

"Sounds good. Bye. Love you."

"Love you too, Beth."

Hanging up, Rachel was furious with herself. Forgetting about the bug in the phone was just stupid. *Stupid! Stupid! Stupid!* She had to be more on her guard. Walking into the bathroom she still didn't see the phone. Her eyes landed on the linen closet. She opened the door. There it was—on the shelf with the towels. *Thank God Daniel's smarter about these things.*

How loud was I? Could the bug in the living room have picked up what I said? Shit! I can't do this. This has to end— and end now.

A momentary flicker of annoyance crossed Daniel's face.

"An admirer?" His question telegraphed that the beautiful bouquet of yellow roses he was holding out to her was not from him.

"Awkward." Rachel's voice gave the word a sing-song lilt.

"They're from Mark Rogers." Rachel blushed as she read the card. "He's back in town." Rachel raised her shoulders and sent Daniel a silently questioning, "What do I do now?"

"I think I saw a vase under the sink," offered Daniel as he took the bugged pen from the holder. Looking around, he took the easiest way out and stuck it in the refrigerator.

"What do you want to do?"

"I want to run away to a deserted island in the sun and forget all of this…all of this…but you." Rachel took the flowers from Daniel's hands, placed them haphazardly on the counter. Her heart knew this was the man she wanted to be with. The best she could hope for was that the feeling was reciprocal. Rather than bluntly asking the question, she wrapped her arms around his neck. Her message was clear and he returned it in kind.

Thank you, God!

He retrieved the pen from the fridge so whoever was listening wouldn't get too suspicious.

"Let's get these beautiful roses in water and then do what we were planning to do before the door bell rang. Go out to dinner. Where are we going again?"

"Down to Colonial Williamsburg…Berretts…good seafood…great crab cakes…and I asked for a quiet little romantic table in a corner when I made our reservations."

Once Rachel and Daniel were safely ensconced in their corner table with a clear view of the dining room and all of its inhabitants, Daniel's detective alter ego took the lead.

"Do you think this Mark guy, given what we know now—that he and his company are not who they are trying to be—do you think he could be the one bugging your place?"

"I've thought about that. He just keeps popping up, doesn't he. You've invaded my brain, thank you very much. Got me questioning things that I used to think were innocent."

"Good. I'm glad I can be helpful." Daniel's smile was

infectious and they both found themselves laughing as they picked at their salads.

"I really don't know anything for sure about Mark Rogers. What I do know…what I think I've figured out is what I'm going to do with a portion of my inheritance from Aunt Lil. I talked to Beth this morning after you left."

"Talked?"

"We skyped, though I did totally forget about the bugs…which made me so angry. I always hate it in movies and books when the girl does exactly what the hero tells her not to do. And then I go and do it. Too stupid."

"Hero?"

"Don't flatter yourself. You know what I mean."

"Yeah. Just liked the sound of it. Anyway, don't beat yourself up. You've got a lot going on."

"I was so relieved when I realized that you left the phone in the linen closet. Can't believe you thought to do that last night. Detective brain! Anyway, this has to end. I want my privacy back. I want my life back. And I'm thinking I may be able to do some good as well."

She could see she had Daniel's full attention. Taking a sip of wine, Rachel continued laying out her plan.

"You know, Aunt Lil always used to say, take care of yourself so you can take care of others. Like the thing the flight attendants always say, put your oxygen mask on first, then help your children. When I was talking—skyping with Beth this morning—she was telling me about what's ahead for Adam. He's going to be released in a few weeks with new legs."

"That's great, Rachel. He has a long road ahead of him. I know a lot of guys who have traveled it—some make it through—others have a really hard time. Some—well— some don't make it at all. Do you know how high the rate of suicide is among injured vets?"

"No, but I thought of all those young men and women we saw at Bethesda—how they gave so much—lost so much. Beth's pain is so great right now. I want to help—and I've figured out a way that I can. Thanks to Aunt Lil I'm going to become an angel of sorts. I don't have it all worked out yet, but my plan is to start a fund—calling it the Raphael Fund at this point. Raphael was one of the seven archangels who brings healing powers from God. Do you know much about mystical Judaism?"

"No. I'm Jewish—had my Bar Mitzvah—and then like a lot of kids sort of left the religion. Never got into the Kabbalah or anything like that."

"Well, I've been doing my research. The name Raphael literally means God heals. Healing is what these men and women need right now. They have so much healing to do, physically and more important, emotionally. Emotional scars run deep."

"Wow. That's a big undertaking. Honorable, generous...and huge. Do you have any idea what you're getting yourself into?

"Yes and no. What I know—the only thing I'm really sure of at this point is that I can help Beth. I can help Adam. I've known him since he was a baby. Before he was born really." Rachel played with her hair as she thought about the enormity of what she was contemplating.

"I know it's huge. I need a lawyer...someone with experience setting up trusts or foundations...or whatever these things are." And making eye contact with Daniel, allowing a wicked little twinkle to reveal itself, she added, "and not Ben Collins!"

Peals of laughter whirled around their table. *Laughter lightens everything,* thought Rachel.

"When I get back to the city tomorrow, I'll make some calls. I know people who know people. I'm sure I know someone who knows a lawyer who handles these types of things."

"Tomorrow? I thought you were leaving on Sunday."

"Yeah. I'm sorry. Brad called. We're swamped. Murder waits for no one. I've got to get back."

"When I was talking to Beth this morning, I told her I was planning to come up in a few days. What if I follow you up? We can play leap frog on Route 95."

"If I remember correctly, the last time you played leap frog with a stranger on Route 95, it took an unexpected turn into—well, at this point, we're still not sure what."

"But the difference here is that you're no stranger."

"True. What if you just come with me? You can always fly back—or I can drive you back whenever you want."

"Tempting offer, Detective!" she teased, playfully flirtatious. "Let me think about it."

"Anything I can do to sway your thoughts?"

"Hmm…let me think about that too. I'll sleep on it tonight."

Chapter 27

Saturday, October 26

Lying with early morning light filtering in through the slats of the plantation shutters, and with Rachel breathing deeply tucked into the crook of his arm, Daniel replayed the magic of the previous evening, of their budding love. *What could be better,* he thought. She stirred, snuggling closer.

They had made magic again last night. He could still feel Rachel's soft lips against his skin, her gentle kisses moving along his cheek, down his neck and back to his lips. Her hair cascaded over his face as she mounted him and traced the outline of his neck with her tongue, lingering over each nipple. He rolled on top of her. Pressing closer, her warmth enveloped him as her hands moved up and down along his back, gently caressing him. His lips were on their own intimate journey of discovery. Feeling himself inside her, them moving rhythmically together, her body trembling and then calming. He wanted to know all of her and his love intensified with each touch, with each kiss.

Protect and serve was the mantra he lived by and this

amazing woman lying next to him was the only person on the planet he really wanted to protect, serve, be with. Her head gently rested on his chest. His kiss brushed her hair. Jasmine and cherries surrounded him.

Feeling luckier than he ever thought possible, Daniel considered his options. Being a bad news first sort of guy, the worst option came quickly to mind. All of this was fleeting. He and Rachel would soon each go their own separate ways. Not his first choice.

The best outcome—a future with Rachel. His body seemed alive and awake as he considered what life could be like with this strong, yet vulnerable, woman. He eagerly wished for this future. Wishing would not make it so. How to make it happen?

Loose ends didn't work for him. Right now, he was all about tying up what he perceived to be loose ends. The problem was that there was really no legitimate case so he had few resources. Mostly favors. He was investigating on his own time, calling in favors from friends. His gut was telling him that Rachel was the linchpin. What he wanted for her was safety, calm, happiness. What he saw was challenge, angst, and in his own odd lexicon, stranger danger.

Old people dying, maybe before their time, maybe not. A lawyer, connected to several of the dead old people, with sticky fingers. Perhaps. A woman, grieving for a lost aunt gets her home bugged. Why and by whom? Who was the guy she met on the road and what does he really want? Too many questions remained unanswered. Way too many.

For now, he delighted in the silence. She stirred. Daniel drew her closer to comfort her.

"Shhhh, my princess. You are safe," he cooed softly. He gently stroked her arm, soothing her to sleep as he stood watch.

"Good morning," came breathlessly from the sleeping beauty beside him.

"And good morning to you. It's early. Go back to sleep." Daniel could see what he believed to be a smile of contentment cross her face. She cuddled closer.

"Only a few minutes more," Rachel murmured, eyes still shut. "I've got things to do, places to go, people to see before we head out tomorrow. Thank you for agreeing to stay one more day."

Resigned to the need to get moving, Rachel slipped away from Daniel, wrapped herself in her old blue robe, thinking that it was time to replace it, and headed to the bathroom. She started the shower and turned to find herself back in Daniel's arms. His hands undid her robe's sash and slid around her waist to rest on her lower back.

"Frisky, aren't we." She arched her left eyebrow and melted into his touch.

"I love when you do that. Great muscle control. And oh, so sexy." He leaned in, placing a gentle peck on her brow.

"Your breakfast order, ma'am?"

"Just coffee and maybe an English muffin if I even have any. Which I don't think I do. I've been gone so much, I'm not sure I have much of anything left in stock. Let's just go out for breakfast. I've got a hair appointment and other stuff to do. We can meet back here later and decide about dinner."

"Okay, out it is. I'll still make a pot of coffee to get us going."

"What's on your agenda for the day?"

"Not sure yet. Think I'll do some more looking around. The only part of Williamsburg I've seen so far has been the historic area. I want to see what else is here. I'm sure I can keep myself entertained for a few hours. Coffee and a full breakfast is a good start. I'll shower after you."

A mischievous little cat smile lit up her face. "You could shower now…if you like."

"Ah…My mama always told me to accept invitations from beautiful women." Daniel's lips came down on hers as his arms pulled her closer. Rachel wrapped her arms around his neck and stroked the back of his head. Her efforts were rewarded as Daniel moved his hands around to cup her breasts, his thumbs toying with her nipples. She felt him harden as he pushed his body closer to hers.

"After you, ma'am," quipped Daniel adding the flirtatious flourish of an arm sweep and a gentlemanly bow, as he pulled open the shower door.

"Gracias."

"Ah…beautiful and bi-lingual."

Rachel graciously accepted her increasingly unorthodox behavior. So out of character. So deliciously fun. Sharing these last few days with Daniel, sharing her secret stash, totally unguarded, released an unbridled passion that surprised her. Now, a romantic rendezvous in the shower. This was the fantasy of movies, what other people did, not the ever so proper, Rachel Resnick.

Rachel shivered. Daniel nibbled at her shoulder as he lathered it with the powder blue net sponge.

"Are you cold?" asked Daniel, reaching for controls to increase the hot water.

"No…I'm fine…really, really fine."

If her friends could see her now, Rachel thought. *Oh, my God, what would Sara think. What would Jenny think?*

Her thought train was heading down a track she didn't want to ride. The hell with what anyone thinks. This man unlocked a door inside her that she never knew existed. In an amazingly short period of time, he brought her unfathomable pleasure. No duty. No obligation. Just pleasure. Just enjoy.

Her hair appointment went smoothly followed by a morning of errands. Returning home, she was surprised to see Ben Collins standing at her front door.

"Hey. How are you?" asked Ben.

"Fine. What are you doing here?"

"Had some business in Newport News. Went faster than I expected—have several hours before my flight so I thought I'd stop by on my way back to the airport to see how you're doing."

"Come on in. I'll make us some coffee, or would you prefer a glass of wine?"

"Wine sounds good." Rachel pulled her car into the garage and Ben followed behind her.

"I'm surprised to see you down here. I didn't think lawyers worked outside of their own jurisdiction. Red or white?"

"White please. Just doing a favor for a friend. What a lovely home. How long have you been here now?"

Rachel grabbed a bottle of white wine from the refrigerator and pulled glasses from the cabinet.

"Thank you. Five months next week. It's been great. I am glad I decided to rent first—you know, get a feel for the area. I love it here. I'm thinking of buying a lot in a new section of this community that is opening up next year. It's down by the James River and there is a lot I have my eye on that borders right up to the water. And I've started to look at house plans."

Even after all she had learned about Ben Collins, Rachel still found him easy to talk to. She realized information was flowing from her lips perhaps a bit too freely. Her eyes landed on the bugged pen on her kitchen counter.

"This place works for you. You're looking really good— not stressed at all. I know you've had a rough few weeks taking care of your aunt's affairs. Anything I can do to help you?"

"No. I'm pretty much done with everything. The house actually sold already. Can you believe it? The realtor said it was because I priced it right. I'm still sad when I think of Aunt Lil but I know she is in heaven and things in my life are getting back to normal—a really nice new normal."

Rachel dug in a drawer for the corkscrew.

When she turned back to face him, horrified eyes locked on the gun. Rachel's face drained of color. She reached out to steady herself, holding onto the island counter to keep from falling.

Take a breath, thought Rachel. *Regain your footing.*

"I don't understand, Ben. A gun? What's the gun for? What do you want?" Her fear at the sight of the gun made her voice shrill. Bile burned in the back of her throat.

Stay calm. Don't panic. Yeah, right.

"The gun is my motivator. What I want…I suspect you already know what I want…what that idiot Jimmy wanted…what your new friend—detective what's his name—probably wants. The diamonds, Rachel, I want the diamonds."

Rachel couldn't move. Paralyzed by fear—her feet felt nailed to the floor. Her mouth gapped open. Her heart pounded.

"And please don't insult me by claiming ignorance here. I know about the diamonds and I know that you have always known about them—and are now the proud new owner of them."

Rachel could see beads of sweat glistening around Ben's hairline. She wasn't expecting Daniel back for a few hours. There was never a cop around when you needed one. Stall for time. Maybe he'd come back early. Hope springs eternal.

"What the fuck!" gasped Dom as he heard what was happening inside Rachel's kitchen. While most of the goings on inside the pretty blue and white cottage at 200 Willow

Lane had been mundane conversations punctuated with gestures of emerging love, this latest interception made Dom grateful the bugs he planted were working.

Marco, we've got a problem was the short text he sent. His cell rang within seconds.

"What's up?"

"That lawyer guy from Brooklyn, he just pulled a gun on Rachel."

"Shit!"

"What do you want me to do?"

"Intervene. Make sure she does not get hurt but be discrete. Do what you need to do and only what you need to do to end this without calling undo attention to yourself."

"And just how do you suggest I do that? The guy has a gun," protested Dom.

"Protect her!" demanded Marco. "That is what I want you to do." And in a calmer voice he continued, "Dom, you know that I've become very fond of Rachel and I don't want her harmed. The game is done. I'm pulling the plug. But, right now, I want Rachel safe. Understood?"

"Yeah. I'll do my best."

"Good. I know she'll be safe with you doing your best. No one does their best better than you."

A rapping on the glass of the kitchen door cut the tension. Ben and Rachel turned to see a new face.

Dom smiled and shouted out a 'Hey Rachel' greeting through the door like they were long lost friends. A white styrofoam cup danced between two fingers as he quickly added, "Mitzi needs sugar."

Her savior had arrived. She didn't know who this man was, but she wasn't about to turn him away. The only thing she knew for certain was that he was not her neighbor. Her neighbors, Todd and his partner, Mitch, were traveling through Europe for another month. There was something familiar about this man with his swarthy complexion, bulging muscles, dark brown eyes and silly grin. She knew him from somewhere. She'd remember later. What mattered now was that he was here and she needed his help. What could Ben do now? There was a witness—a wrinkle in his plan. He couldn't kill them both.

Out of the corner of her eye, she saw Ben quickly lower the gun and move behind the kitchen counter, slouching onto one of the stools. She didn't miss a beat. Opening the door and taking the cup from the stranger's hand, she said, "Sugar you say? I think I can handle that. What's Mitzi baking?"

"Cheesecake."

Approaching Ben from the other side of the kitchen island, the stranger extended his hand and said, "Hi, I'm Mel."

Ben had already slipped the Ruger LC9 into his pants pocket, thankful he had chosen a gun so easy to conceal. His window of opportunity had closed and he knew it. He only wanted to scare Rachel, not kill her. Killing two people was out of the question. He stood to shake hands with Mel.

"Hi. Ben Collins. Nice to meet you." Ben noted a certain strength and challenge in Mel's eyes.

"Any friend of Rachel's is a friend of mine. Well, ours— mine and Mitzi's. Hope you'll stick around. Mitzi's cheesecake is legendary. I'll bring over two slices later when it's cooled. Topped with some strawberries and it's a slice of heaven on a plate."

"Thanks. Don't expect to be here that long. I've got a plane to catch."

"Oh, too bad. You're missing great cheesecake—a true delight," said Mel. "Where's home?"

"Brooklyn. I'm a lawyer. That's how I know Rachel. I'm her lawyer…or at least I was her aunt's lawyer. You know, settling her affairs."

"Rachel, we were so sorry to hear about your aunt. Our deepest sympathies. If there's anything we can do," said Mel.

Sincerity dripped from every word. *Whoever he is,* thought Rachel, *he's good.* She took her time filling the cup with sugar. Finally, she could stall no longer and held it out.

"Here you go." She needed this man, whoever he was, to stay. "Can I interest you in a glass of wine? Ben and I were just about to open a bottle. Or some coffee?"

"Wine sounds good," said Mel as he slid onto one of the kitchen stools right next to Ben. "Mitzi's been hounding me about my drinking so I try not to indulge too much in front of her. She'll figure we got to talking so sharing a glass with you two sounds mighty fine."

The hard stare from Ben sent chills up Rachel's spine. Remembering back to her first encounter with Ben, she wondered how she could have ever thought this man handsome and even someone she might want to spend time with.

Don't panic, thought Rachel. *My actions are putting this guy in danger, but they are also giving me time to figure out what to do. And who is this guy? And why does he look familiar?*

"Berger." Daniel answered his phone as he leaned on the fuel pump waiting for his tank to fill. His trip around town, scoping the place out proved fruitful. He could see himself living here.

"Detective, get your ass back to Rachel's fast. She's in trouble. She needs you."

"Who is this?"

"A friend. Another friend is running interference…slowing trouble down…but he may not be able to do all that's needed. Get going." The line went dead.

Stopping the pump, Daniel replaced the hose, screwed in the cap, jumped into the driver's seat and headed out. He wished he could go full throttle, sirens and flashing lights. But he was in his own car and the best he could do was speed.

Not knowing what was happening, he considered the worst outcome—he'd be too late to save Rachel. He'd already lost his first love. Buried memories. Now, thank you God, he had another chance. Long time between loves—and he was not about to lose Rachel —not while any breath remained in his body.

Hell, what's the worst that could happen? Getting pulled over by the local cops was a small a price to pay for Rachel's safety. He'd explain who he was and why he was speeding. Surely they would join him. Cops stick together. And if there were any repercussions? Well, hell, it was time to retire anyway. He hit the gas and allowed his years of training and driving in New York City traffic to take charge. Amazingly, he attracted no other law enforcement attention. *Donuts must be fresh,* he thought. Chiding himself for berating his fellow officers, he was relieved no one stopped him.

He slowed as he went through the residence entrance gates. Approaching Rachel's street, he saw an unmarked black van parked a few houses away from Rachel's home. Empty. Probably someone working in one of the nearby homes. There was a car with Virginia plates in her driveway.

Strange, thought Daniel. *Who could that be?* Rachel hadn't mentioned expecting anyone and they were leaving in the morning to head back to New York. *Who would show up unannounced?*

Daniel parked one house over from Rachel's. He popped his trunk, loaded his service weapon, chambered a round, and checked that the safety was on. He pocketed an extra magazine just in case. Not knowing the full extent of the trouble, he grabbed a few other small tools that he thought could come in handy. Unknown danger demanded both caution and preparation.

She'd given him a key. The most natural thing to do would be to park in the driveway and enter through the front door like nothing was wrong. What would he find? Would that compromise her…increase the danger?

He could go around back—try to see through a window or through the patio doors. What if whoever was causing the unknown danger saw him? Hesitation was the enemy. His training took over. He needed intel. Size up what he could and then decide how to proceed.

Walking around to the kitchen window, Daniel pulled a slim silver tube shaped instrument out of his jacket pocket. He twisted its handle, extending a telescopic shaft to its full three foot length and exposing a thin red cable at one end. Then he screwed a small screen-like attachment to one end, connecting its red cable to the one from the handle. Positioning the shaft to the side of the window, this small camera gave him a bird's eye view inside the kitchen.

Daniel could see three people around the kitchen island. Rachel stood with her back to the window. He was surprised to see Ben Collins and a man he did not recognize sitting on the stools across the counter. This answered the car question, but created two new, more pressing ones. *What's Ben doing here?* He didn't have a clue, but considering what he had been learning about him, seeing Ben Collins in Rachel's kitchen did not foster good vibrations. *Who's the other guy? Must be the interference the caller had mentioned.* Whatever was happening, for all outward appearances, the situation seemed calm and under controlled—for the moment.

Decision made. Front door entrance. *Act like you know nothing. Won't be hard. Don't know jack shit.*

"Rachel, I'm back," called Daniel as he opened the front door.

"We're here—in the kitchen," said Rachel, working to keep her voice from cracking. *Thank you, God!*

"Wow, looks like we've got a full house," said Daniel as he turned the corner into the kitchen. "Ben Collins. You're the last person I expected to see in Williamsburg."

"Had some business in Newport News. Stopped by to see how Rachel was doing on my way to the airport."

"Hi. I'm Daniel Berger." Daniel held out his hand and looked inquisitively at the stranger.

"Um…Mel…Rachel's neighbor. I'm just borrowing some sugar. Wife's baking." The facial expression and the low key, almost country bumpkin demeanor just did not match the man Daniel was shaking hands with.

"Nice to meet you, Mel. So, catch me up on the news from New York, Ben. What's been happening? Feels like I've been gone for ages. This place sure can be calming. I've barely been gone a week."

"Nothing much. Same old. Same old." Glancing at his watch, he added, "Think I'll skip that wine, Rachel. I best be hitting the road. Get to the airport. These days you never know how long security is going to take. I wouldn't want to miss my flight. Come, walk me to the door." The final phrase came out more like an order than a simple request.

Getting him out of her house was her wish come true. Moving past Daniel, Rachel played the gracious hostess, even as she was screaming inside. There would be time to tell Daniel everything, but she knew that her eyes were sending him strong signals. She could feel Daniel come up behind her—close enough not to be too obvious—close enough to give her a sense that she was safe. He was here— watching over her.

"Rachel, let's make sure we get together the next time

you're in New York." Ben squeezed her arm with so much force she was sure it would leave fingerprints.

"I'm not sure when that will be. I'll call you Ben."

She opened the door and Ben stepped over the threshold—out of her house.

Slamming the door, Rachel ran into Daniel's arms. She was shivering, verging on hysterical. Daniel held her close and stroked her back to calm her.

"Deep breaths. What was that all about?"

Rachel broke free, but did not answer immediately. She was a woman on a mission, on her way back to the kitchen. Too late. The kitchen door was open. Mel—or whoever he was—was gone. Only a white styrofoam cup filled with sugar remained on the kitchen island.

"Want to tell me what's going on here?" asked Daniel.

Rachel started shaking again and could barely catch her breath. Taking her hand, Daniel led her into the living room. Moving her out of the kitchen, away from the immediate location of the altercation was standard operating procedure. Detective brain.

"He just showed up. Was at my door when I pulled in the driveway. I didn't think anything of it at first. Said he just wanted to see how I was doing—all sweet and concerned about my well-being and he was in the area…and…" Her spasmodic sobs grew louder and louder as she continued blurting out the events of the last half hour. Breath hard and fast—out of control.

"Here, sip this." Daniel offered her a small glass of Armagnac, hoping her favorite brandy would calm her. A million thoughts raced through Daniel's mind.

"Okay, take a breath—a big one. Now exhale and continue." *Funny,* thought Daniel. *I've calmed down victims hundreds—no thousands of times—but this time with Rachel—someone I love—it feels so different.*

The warm brandy slid down her throat, soothing her frazzled nerves. Color returned to her cheeks.

"Then he pulled a gun…a gun…in my house…and demanded the diamonds…I don't know how he knew about them, but he did. We've got to call the police."

"I'm the police, remember? I'd rather not get locals involved if you don't mind. I know where to find him. I'd prefer to take care of him in my jurisdiction—where I have more control over the outcome. Okay?"

"Okay." Calmer now. "Maybe he's the one bugging my place?"

"I don't think so. Do you think your aunt might have told him about the diamonds?"

"I don't know. I never remember her talking about them to anyone, but I wasn't with her every minute. We'd talk on the phone or Skype. She often sounded lonely, and he was her lawyer, so she might have confided in him—or his father." Rachel felt a wave of sadness and guilt wash over her. *Dying alone without family or friends around you is no way to go.*

"She hadn't mentioned them to me in years…only alluded to them once after David died. He said you wanted them too…that that was the only reason you were here." Her eyes full of tears cut him to his core.

"No, Rachel," Daniel whispered, kneeling in front of her, "I don't want them. I am here because of you…because of how I feel about you. I'm in love with you."

Rachel seemed to be searching his face. He could see her wrap her mind around his words and embrace them as truth. A major hurdle had been crossed and he was sure he had passed with flying colors.

"Who was that other guy?"

"I don't know. He looked familiar. I know I've seen him before. I just can't place where. He just appeared and started knocking on the door…and I let him in thinking his being here would keep me safe for a bit…praying you'd come back early…and you did…you came back."

"Yeah. I got a call. Don't know from who…but whoever you are," said Daniel looking up from Rachel, speaking more loudly into the room. "Thank you. I owe you big time."

"I feel so violated. What am I going to do?"

"*We*, Rachel," Daniel said emphasizing the word we, "*we* are going to make sure this never happens again. That is what *we* are going to do."

He wrapped his arms around her. "And Rachel, as God is my witness," he said, pushing her away from him so he could look into her eyes, "I want nothing from you. I only want to give you my protection, my care and my love. If you'll have me."

Of three things Daniel was sure. He was sure that the events that just transpired would have no encore. He knew that he could protect her. He was sure of his love for Rachel. What was once only a distant dream was now alive—flesh and blood.

He was also damned sure of one final thing. It was time for Ben Collins to meet his maker, figuratively speaking. And though Daniel could not be a party to his actual murder, from what Cooper and he had learned about Ben Collins' less than trivial pursuits with his very sticky fingers, he was sure he could help the DA make a case that would put this guy away for a long, long time.

Marco hung up from Dom, breathing a sigh of relief. Everything was okay. The detective had arrived at just the right time. The situation was diffused. The lawyer left empty-handed. And Rachel was unharmed.

His feelings for her surprised him. *What's that about?* She wasn't one of his people, like Marissa, Dom and Sophia. Yet she stirred something inside him that had him rethinking his current situation. Maybe it was time to unlock other suppressed feelings? Like Marissa, he was tired of the life and wanted out. They all had more than they could possibly spend in one lifetime. Dom had a growing family that he worshipped. Sophia kept talking about moving to Italy. And he sought out Marissa's company constantly. He loved their long walks on the beach and their quiet dinners more and more. He loved her. Maybe it was time to explore their relationship more openly.

This con was over. He was pulling the plug. He texted Dom to remove the bugs from Rachel's home. He had his out. He could let this one go on principle. Rachel had called earlier to thank him—well, thank Mark Rogers—for the flowers and apologize for not calling sooner. She told him she'd been out of town comforting a dear friend. She told him all about Beth's son and his devastating injuries. She told him about her visit to Walter Reed. She told him about all the wounded. She told him she cried.

Finally, she shared her plans. She was returning to New York to set up a fund for wounded warriors and their families. These brave men and women needed so much and her inheritance from Aunt Lil was her opportunity to help. She did not go into details about her inheritance, only that it was more than she or her family would ever need.

He guessed the rest. The diamonds. And he remembered. He'd been a soldier once—Vietnam. It had not ended pretty for so many of his buddies. And his homecoming was nothing like what was happening today. No parades, no bands, no one waiting at the airport, buying you meals and drinks, patting you on the back, thanking you for your service. They were scorned, spit upon. Vietnam was not a popular war.

So many went without the care they needed, care they had earned with their blood, care they richly deserved. If that was where the diamonds were to be used, though she did not specifically use the word diamonds, then he could let this one go.

"A penny for your thoughts."

Marco smiled. That playful lilt could only be one person.

"Marissa, I was just thinking of you." Turning away from the ocean, he felt his heart skip a beat. Amazing grace. Dressed in slim white capri pants, a shimmering gold silk camisole top under a golden lace shawl loosely hung over her shoulders, Marissa was a vision of elegance and sexuality. He felt the pulse in his loins, a longing too long denied. She was real. She was here.

A twist of fate had brought Marissa and Marco together on a cold winter's night in a back alley in Greenwich Village too many years ago to count. Seeing him shiver, she had invited him to share her cardboard refrigerator box to get out of the cold. They shared a thin blanket, a small bottle of cherry brandy and huddled together to generate body heat. Marco thought her Eurasian features exquisite that night and every morning, afternoon and night since then. Their friendship was born and its bonds had proven to be unbreakable over the years. But it was never a friendship with benefits.

"Oh, and what were you thinking…about me, that is?" she asked with a coy wink and a trace of mischief in her voice. She sauntered up and planted a kiss on his cheek.

"I was thinking that maybe you and I…" His voice trailed off.

"You and I what?" Marissa's brows pinched as her face twisted into more of a questioning expression. Her curiosity piqued. She and Marco had a long history together, but her senses were picking up something new, a different vibration coming from him now. Maybe their history was about to change. She was hoping any change would be one that united them.

"What?" She watched him carefully, observing a minute flare of his nostrils. She detected emotional upheaval, emotions fighting inside this man…fear…envy… ambition…guilt…rage…shame…lust…joy…love. He was clearly in turmoil. She could almost see the wheels turning in his mind. Eventually, he'd tell her. He always did.

"What troubles you so?" Marissa's soft touch on his forearm made him tremble. She was having trouble reading him, a rarity after their long years together. He was a complicated man, but someone she could always read. She looked deeply into his eyes willing an answer.

"Nothing…don't concern yourself." He covered her hand with his own. "And besides…I was thinking that maybe you and I…" Marco hesitated and Marissa could see him shift gears, "should take a walk on the beach and talk."

Her discerning gaze caught the falsity of his words. A walk on the beach was not what he originally wanted to say. This last con has clearly taken a huge toll on him, too. Maybe he did develop feelings for Rachel. Not like him to care about a mark, but there was always a first time. Something was different. Marissa knew that now was not the time to push.

Restraining herself from jumping to a premature conclusion, Marissa replied, "Sounds good."

Her own nerves were terribly frayed after this con. Jimmy had been difficult to work with. He was wound way too tight for this line of work. And his tongue wagged too loosely. The tension between them increased with each of his failed attempts to find the diamonds. Nothing had worked like it was supposed to.

Maybe it was a signal that the time had come to get out of

the business. They had profited handsomely from manipulated opportunities. They all had more than enough money to last several gluttonous lifetimes. Not that any of them were spendthrifts. People of the street rarely were. They knew how hard money was to come by and how easily their lives could return to ruin.

Arm in arm, Marissa and Marco made their way onto the beach. The sand was warm to the touch. No pretense needed here. Safely ensconced in their own private corner of the world, Marco and Marissa strolled down the beach, kicking up the water as it met the shore. The tide was coming in.

"I've got two tickets to Paris ready to go. We can leave tomorrow. In the city of lights let's see if we can make a little magic together," said Marco. "What do you say?"

"I accept."

Chapter 28

Monday, October 28

"Terrific. I'll pull together what we have so far and have it ready for you when you get here. This son-of-a-bitch is going down." Brad Cooper was nothing if not enthusiastic about his work.

Daniel gave Cooper the short story version of the events at Rachel's. They had concocted a plan to flesh out whoever was bugging her house by sharing details of her plans for her inheritance. They needed to know who this guy was and what he was capable of doing in the future. They would wait and see where that led.

The evidence that Ben Collins was somehow involved in the deaths of several elderly, while circumstantial, was mounting. The guy was a lawyer, but even lawyers get into trouble. And this guy was in a world of shit. His best bet would be to make a deal with the DA, lose his license to practice, maybe offer some useful information about the inner workings of Big Al's operation, if he even knew anything, and then disappear.

Two hours later found Daniel and Cooper entering the law offices of Benjamin R. Collins, Attorney at Law. The whir of a shredder grabbed their attention. Rushing by the secretary, they burst into Ben's inner sanctum. He was a shredding fool.

"Stop immediately," shouted Detective Daniel Berger, in a booming, authoritarian, powerful voice. He wanted to do more—be more aggressive after the gun incident at Rachel's—punch Ben's lights out—but his professional judgment forced him to hold these feelings in check. He was working on a longer term solution—something that would change Ben's world forever, not a few cuts and bruises that would heal within days.

Startled, Ben looked up. The papers he was holding scattered in all directions when he dropped them. "Detectives, what can I do for you?"

"For starters, you can stop doing what you're doing. That's what you can do for us," answered Cooper.

"This?" Ben questioned waving his hand across the remaining pile of yet to be shredded documents. "I'm just cleaning up some old files. That's all."

"We've got some questions that you may be able to help us with," stated Daniel, not wanting to spook him too fast. "The ME has alerted my office to a series of recent deaths of several elderly people. You're shown as the lawyer of record for each person."

"Elderly people die all the time, Detective. That's what happens."

Ben backed away from the shredder. He slowly returned to his chair, straightened his tie, and assumed the veneer of a successful lawyer behind his desk. He could sense his options diminishing.

"I don't mean to sound harsh or callous, here. But it's a fact of life. You get old and then you die."

"Yes, we know only too well that death is a natural part of the life cycle," said Cooper. "What concerns us is the number of recent deaths connected to you. They're falling like flies on rotten meat."

Daniel winced at Cooper's tacky analogy. "What Detective Cooper means is that there have been more than the usual number of deaths recently…and they all seem to be connected to you in some way. Care to shed any light on this for us?"

"Well, Detectives, perhaps I can help you. Many of my elderly clients were really my father's clients. I think I mentioned this the last time you paid me a visit. When he died I took over his clients as a courtesy. And I guess, now they are also meeting their maker, in a manner of speaking."

"What can you tell us about these clients?" Daniel passed a list of ten names across the desk.

Ben read down the list. He could feel his stomach tighten as his eyes went from name to name to name. His face drained of color. Sweaty palms had him putting the paper down on his desk lest his hands start to shake. His mind raced. Each name represented a trust account he had the authority to access. And he had accessed each one of these along with several others.

"You know I can't really share anything with you. Attorney client privilege."

Using this tired line seemed like a good idea. Ben knew it would not slow these detectives down especially after witnessing Detective Berger and Rachel together in her home. That had been a surprise he had not expected. Ben hated surprises.

"That privilege has been waived by Mr. Samuel Solomon, the son of the late Bernice Solomon," said Daniel, pulling another document from his inside jacket pocket.

Holding it in his hand, he continued, "A Mr. Bernard

Golden came to us, expressing some concerns about the death of Bernice Solomon. It seems though they never married, they had been long time companions, partners in life for many, many years. After speaking with him, we contacted Mrs. Solomon's family and shared Mr. Golden's concerns. Got permission from her son, Samuel, to investigate how her estate was handled. And since the son is her sole surviving heir, and the concerns center on the estate, and you were the lawyer of record handling the affairs of that estate, we'd like to see the files please." With that, Daniel handed the document to Ben.

"And, in fact, we have court orders for the files of all the names on that list. Detective Cooper, if you would be so kind." Daniel loved the flourish. More importantly, he loved catching sleazy people like Ben Collins—people who thought they were smarter than everybody else, that they wouldn't get caught. They screwed up their own lives and then they took advantage of other people to fix their mess. This time was worse, in Daniel's opinion, because Ben had preyed on innocent, trusting elderly people to cover up his mess.

Cooper produced and handed over nine additional documents. "We've probably got a few more coming within the next few weeks, but these files will give our forensic accountants a head start."

"Is there anything you'd like to tell us?" asked Daniel.

"No, nothing I can think of. Give me a minute," Ben said as he got out of his chair and headed for his office door. "I'll just have my secretary pull these files for you. Won't take but a minute." Working hard to appear calm, cool and collected, Ben walked out to talk to his secretary.

How did these guys get those names? What did they really know? And how? Was this all a huge fishing expedition, the NYPD bluffing or did they really have proof to back up the warrants? Too many unknowns.

Cooper got out of his chair and stood in the doorway watching Ben talk to his secretary. He turned to Daniel and whispered, "What do you think?"

"I think you need to work on your metaphors. Flies on rotten meat. Jesus!"

"Over the top?"

"Way over," laughed Daniel.

"I'll work on it. But what do you think about him? Think we got his attention?"

"Oh yeah. We definitely got his attention. He knows we know something. He also knows that his life as he has known it is over. In the toilet. It's only a matter of time before we put the pieces together. He only needs to be properly incentivized to get his more cooperative juices flowing. Once the forensic accountants get a whack at those files, and we can show him we have a convincing case against him, he'll come around."

"I like that—properly incentivized—has a nice ring to it."

"What he has to realize is that dealing with us will be better for him in the long run. With us, he gets disbarred and jail time. Disappointing someone you owe money to, like Big Al. Shit, that'll get you killed."

"Yeah. We've just gotta hope the forensic guys can connect the dots," said Cooper. "They're good, but I suspect this guy is good too at covering his tracks."

"We'll get him. One way or another," replied a confident Daniel. Unrelenting persistence—a mind not at rest—was his calling card when people tried to hurt those he loved. And he loved Rachel. Slow and steady, let one piece of evidence lead to the next, each one piling on, supporting and strengthening his case.

Ben Collins was back. Cooper stepped aside as he entered the room, his arms full.

"Detectives, here are the files you requested. I'm sure you'll find that everything is in order."

"Thank you, Mr. Collins."

"We appreciate your cooperation in this matter. We'll be back in touch shortly," said Daniel as he took possession of the files and then handed them to Cooper. Being nice, being polite always seemed to spook guys like Ben Collins more than rough stuff. Finesse worked with the Ben Collins of the world.

Chapter 29

Monday, November 4

Daniel and Rachel had been back in New York for a week. Details to set up the fund had moved quickly. Rachel, Sara and Uncle Stan had met for brunch yesterday. He agreed to broker the sale of several uncut stones. This morning she was meeting with a lawyer to complete the paperwork for the Raphael Fund. They planned to return to Virginia after Thanksgiving.

Daniel's case against Ben Collins had not proven to be as strong as he had hoped. The meeting he was about to have with Ben would either end the entire affair or shift it into new territory.

"Thanks for agreeing to meet with me, Ben," said Daniel as the two came face to face at the corner of Fifth Avenue and Fifty-ninth Street. I thought a walk in the park rather than meeting at your office or mine would be a nice change for both of us, especially considering it's a beautiful fall day—and we won't be seeing many more of these this year."

"We can agree on that. It is a beautiful day. And thanks

for returning my files. My secretary said they were all in perfect order."

"You're welcome."

The two men walked on for a bit in silence. Daniel thought of an old ploy—that he who spoke first had the most to hide—the most to lose. He was willing to bide his time, let Ben's nerves get the best of him.

"So, where do we go now, Detective? Did you find what you were looking for?"

"Our forensic accountants noted a few irregularities, but not enough—nothing the DA is prepared or willing to act on at this point. We've still got some loose ends we're working to clear up. Things that don't make sense, you know."

"Let me save you some trouble," offered Ben, feeling more relaxed now then he'd been in weeks. His come-to-Jesus moment had passed. Turning to face Detective Berger, Ben continued, a more confident man then he was a week ago when he was served with the warrants for his files.

"Here's the thing, and there's no getting around it, Detective. You've got nothing on me. If you had found what you were looking for in my files—anything to connect me to some perceived wrong-doing festering in your creative imagination, we'd be having this conversation at your office, in an interrogation room, not here in the park. And if you think you can imply some slight of hand with the accounts of my clients who have recently died, we can chalk it up to the simple fact that I'm a lawyer, not an accountant.

"And, furthermore, if you think by implying something sinister that you are scaring me into revealing something about any of my extra-curricular hobbies that might take place in that neon infested hole we know and love as Atlantic City…let me be clear, you don't scare me half enough to divulge one iota of anything about anyone. So unless there is something else, this meeting is over."

Bold man on a beautiful day, thought Daniel.

"I just want to make sure you understand that you have options…options you may not have considered yet. We may not scare you—and believe me when I say that scaring you is not my intention."

They walked on in silence for a few minutes.

"Rumor has it," said Daniel taking a different tact, "that you owe a considerable sum of money to someone who should scare you—someone who does not offer the kind of options I can offer you."

"Ah, rumors—the lifeblood of the human species. Detective, your options would have me looking over my shoulder for the rest of my life," chuckled Ben sarcastically. "Your options would have me worrying every time I start my car. Worrying about things that could go bump or boom or bang in the night. No, thank you. I'll pass."

"We can protect you, you know."

"Funny, I used to use that line when I worked for the DA. And witness protection is not my idea of living. I'll take my chances with the devil I know."

"If you change your mind, you know where to find me," said Daniel. Wanting to send a different sort of message, he added, "And if I'm not at the precinct, I'm probably with Rachel Resnick. We've gotten rather close since her aunt died. I'm feeling rather protective of her, if you catch my drift."

"Caught, Detective. Definitely caught. And just so you know I'm not a total shit, I wouldn't have hurt her. I'm sure Rachel told you I pulled a gun. It wasn't loaded."

"Then a word of advice. Buy some bullets. Never point an unloaded gun. It could get you killed. The next time you pull a gun, be prepared to use it."

The two men sized each other up for another minute.

"See you around, Detective."

Ben turned and walked off towards Fifth Avenue. Daniel sat down on a bench and watched him go. He kept his eyes on him—watched him buy a coffee from a street vendor and hail a cab.

One cool cucumber. He was right on all counts. They didn't have enough to arrest him. Money moved around in various accounts of his clients, gone for a few weeks and then replaced. Was it a crime? Yep. Embezzlement is definitely a crime. Enough to prosecute? Ben Collins was one lucky man, with very good friends in very high places. Daniel was told to drop it.

The ME hadn't found real evidence to connect any of the elderly deaths to foul play at the hands of Ben Collins. Most of the victims had not even been autopsied. Almost a perfect crime. At least until something materialized to make it not so perfect.

And did it really matter? To Rachel, yes. It mattered to her. And she mattered to him—so it mattered. But the ME was also convinced that Lillian Steinmetz had died of natural causes—a heart attack. Nothing was found in any of the extensive toxicology tests that he ordered run on the blood sample he had pulled. The ME would bury those costs in the minutia of its huge departmental budget.

"Got a minute, Detective?"

Startled, Daniel shot off the bench like he'd received a jolt of electricity.

"Jim Greene, FBI."

Dressed in the traditional FBI uniform—dark suit, dull tie, he had the look. Clean cut. Boy Scout. *This guy missed his calling,* thought Daniel. *He should be on a recruiting poster for the FBI.*

"Why do I get the feeling this meeting isn't a coincidence?"

"Detective, you and I both know that there's no such

thing as coincidence in our line of work. Let's just say we share a common interest, Ben Collins. What's your business with him?"

"Just that…my business."

"Come now, Detective. We're both on the same side. You know, truth, justice, the American way and all that."

"Yeah, right. Play nice," said Daniel oozing sarcasm. "You go first. What's your interest in the esteemed lawyer?"

"He's a friend of ours, a new friend to be precise. Approached us just the other day. Has agreed to do us a favor…a favor that we would prefer not to see get sidetracked or disturbed."

"Ah. Doing you a favor you say. A friend of the Feds. Now, that is one interesting friendship. What's the favor?"

"Sorry Detective. Need to know only on that part."

"I see. So you want information from me, but you don't think I really need to know your details. Interesting."

"We all have a job to do," laughed Greene. "So, what's your interest in Ben Collins. I take it you're not social friends—and this meeting in the park is off the record."

"Ben and I, we're friends—of a sort. Know some of the same people. Just swapping stories. A friendly chat. Nothing more." Looking at his watch, Daniel said, "Gotta go. Let me know if I can be of any assistance—you know—help you help Ben with his favor. Nice meeting you."

As Daniel walked away, pieces of the puzzle were beginning to coalesce. The FBI connection surprised him. He knew Ben had some major gambling debts. He was in deep. His visit to Rachel in Williamsburg and the gun he pulled on her—totally out of character for a smooth, classy lawyer like Ben Collins. When he realized he couldn't get the diamonds he took the only other way out. Contacted the Feds. And it answered the question about why Collins did not jump at the options he had laid out barely an hour ago.

Ben Collins already had his WitSec invitation. Doing favors for the Feds was dicey and had its own inherent complications. And Daniel could guess what the favor entailed. Wearing a wire to bring someone down—Big Al perhaps. Daniel also knew that the Fed's ship could be one very leaky boat. Hopefully, Ben would be alive after the favor was delivered so he could cash in his WitSec chip.

Always know your motivation. That was a simple way to live—and Jolene was a simple person deep down. Maybe not in her tastes in clothing, or lifestyle, or men, but in all other aspects of her life, especially her work. Jolene did not like to complicate things. The KISS principle—keep it simple, stupid—worked.

Motivation also helped Jolene get into the appropriate character. Who did she need to be right now to complete her mission? The eager prostitute turning a trick for the right price? The high level, sophisticated lady of the evening, dressed to kill, who could easily walk into the finest New York establishment without a question being asked or an eyebrow raised?

No. Right now she just needed to be Jolene—sweet, cuddly Jolene. The woman Ben Collins trusted with his life. And she had proven her trustworthiness time and time again to the many men in her life.

Uncle Al trusted her now too. To do his bidding. Plug the leak.

"Let's walk a bit, Ben. It's a beautiful night, probably one of the last we'll see for awhile." Jolene slid her arm through his as they walked up Fifty-eighth Street heading towards Fifth Avenue.

"Works for me. Did you enjoy your dinner?"

"Yes, Le Cirque was all that I hoped it would be. The lobster risotto was to die for. So yummy. I could have licked the plate. But Ben, it was so expensive. Are you sure you can afford that?"

"Too late now to worry about that, babe. It's done. And I'm so glad you enjoyed it."

"Pleased beyond compare. And I'm enjoying my new necklace even more." Jolene's fingertips touched the princess cut two-carat diamond Ben had surprised her with, now nestled in her neck dimple.

"It's so beautiful. So much extravagance for little old me. I know you've been so stressed lately…and I always thought it was about money. That's what stresses most people, you know."

"I'm sorry I've not been the best company lately, but I plan to make that up to you." Stopping, he pulled her around to him and held her tightly. His lips found hers.

"Everything is fine. My problems are in the process of working themselves out. And I'm through with gambling. Done. Finished. I've learned my lesson. No more for me. I'm quitting cold turkey."

"That's good. I like you better this way," Jolene cooed. Walking arm and arm, they continued down Fifth Avenue toward the Plaza and Central Park.

"Let's get away for a few days, babe. South Beach maybe? What do you say? Ready to put on a nice bikini and enjoy some warm fun in the sun?"

"That's sounds like just what the doctor ordered. I need a day or so to clear my calendar."

"Good. Just tell me when you can leave and I'll have my secretary make the arrangements."

"Look, there's the Plaza. Let's go into the Champagne Bar. I've got to use the Ladies Room and then we can toast our get-a-way."

Walking into the Plaza was always a magical experience. No costs had been spared with the recent highly publicized renovations. Jolene returned from the Ladies Room and joined Ben at a small table in the Champagne Bar just as he was hanging up his cell phone.

Two crystal flutes were already at the table as was a small order of caviar and strawberries. The bottle of Dom Perignon was in the sommelier's hands awaiting her return. As Jolene sat down, the sommelier popped the cork. Perfect timing. *Timing is everything,* she thought.

"So good," she said after her first sip. "Thank you so much for a wonderful evening."

"Well, you deserve it. But there's been a slight change of plans, my love. It looks like our little get-a-way will have to wait a bit. That was a client. I need to head out of town tomorrow morning for a few days on business. Our trip will have to wait until I get back. I'm so sorry, love. Let's not let this spoil our celebration. Okay?"

"Oh Ben. That is so disappointing. Promise me we'll go just as soon as you return. Promise me." Her pleas and pout cut him to the core.

"Yes. We'll go just as soon as I get back. And stay at the finest hotel and eat at the best restaurants. Excuse me for a second. I think I need to make a pit stop, too."

Ben walked away from the table, leaving Jolene in full pout. He'd known she would not like his news, but better to let her know now so she could get her anger out of her system. That way they could still end their evening with some heated love-making.

Once he was out of sight, Jolene got down to business. First, some refreshment. Dipping the tiny spoon into the caviar she plopped a huge dollop onto a toast point and eagerly gobbled it. Fresh caviar sent her taste buds to heaven.

Opening her tiny purse, she discreetly pulled out a skin toned latex glove. Slowly and carefully to avoid any tearing, she pulled it onto her right hand which remained just below the table edge in her lap. Then she gently lifted a small gel capsule from her silver pill case being careful not to squeeze it too tightly lest it burst. With minimal movement she reached across the table, selected a strawberry and plopped the gel cap and the berry into Ben's champagne glass. The bubbles encased both. Removing the glove and placing it back inside her purse, she patiently watched as the gel cap dissolved and disappeared.

Dropping a strawberry into her own glass, she sipped the champagne and noted how well the strawberry's essence brightened its flavor just enough to mask any other flavor issues the dissolved gel cap might create.

He'd be well into his business trip, or whatever his trip was all about, before the effects of the ricin filled capsule began to show. Ricin was a slow poison, designed for patient people, extracting revenge without a need to witness the affair. Tracing it back to her would be next to impossible.

Ben was going on a trip all right, only this one was not of his own choosing. And not at the behest of his newfound friends, the Feds, either. By the time anyone realized what had happened, she would be long gone. She almost felt sorry for the cops who eventually landed the case to unravel who had done what and when.

"To us," said Ben as he lifted his glass and sat down.

"Yes, to us. To our trip of a lifetime."

No return ticket necessary. Bye, bye Ben.

Chapter 30

"So, how's it going? You've had a crazy few weeks." Sara lifted a tray of deli salads out of her car and smiled at Rachel who held a tray of small sandwiches.

"Crazy yes, but it's also been…well, it's been great."

"You're beaming!"

"Even with all that's gone on, the truth is, I've never been happier. I feel alive, like this door opened inside me."

"And is this door named Daniel by any chance?"

Rachel's smile was all the answer Sara needed.

"I know I haven't known him very long, but it feels like I've known him my whole life. Or maybe like I wanted to know him—have been waiting to know him. You know what I mean?"

"Yeah. But you weren't ready for him before. And knowing guys, he probably wasn't ready for you. Had you met thirty years ago, I bet you would have just passed each other by. Now, you're ready for each other. Let's face it, you are not the Rachel you were when you were married to David."

"From your lips to God's ears. That girl is so gone. She was afraid of her own shadow, worried about every little thing—never felt good enough—wanted to please everyone else—did what was expected—the all around good girl. I remember so many times my insides were screaming and all I did was walk away in silence. I mean we had a good life, raised two kids and all. But something's different now."

"You're different. Look at all you've done. You sold your family home. Left everyone you know and started a new life in a new place. Talk about chutzpah. That took courage—more than I think I could even muster."

"Seriously?"

"Yes, seriously. Rachel, that meek, passive woman who did as she was told, what was expected, has blossomed into someone who can stand on her own two feet. Before you were predictable. I could set my watch by you. There were times when it seemed to me like you were apologizing for your very existence. Now—anything goes. Screw the routine. As your friend, I'm loving the new you. These last few months have been major for you. Not only since the move, but all this stuff when your aunt died—with Ben Collins and Beemer guy and Daniel—you didn't fall apart."

"Oh, I came pretty close a few times, especially after the gun thing."

"Close doesn't count. And I think having a gun pointed at you is a good reason to fall apart. But you recovered quickly and now look at all you've accomplished—at the people you're helping."

"When David died I felt like strings got cut. No one was yanking my chain anymore—telling me what to do, when to do it, and how to do it—making me feel like I wasn't good enough. All of a sudden, I felt free."

"I remember when we met. You were so uptight. Shit, I'm amazed we ever became friends."

"You were the one thing I wasn't prepared for—a gift really. You said what you thought and you didn't take shit from anyone. I learned a lot from watching you. Not that I could ever be quite as out there as you are. Your honesty—I always appreciated that about you."

"Really? I'm surprised I didn't scare you away."

"Scared me, yes. Away, no. I just wanted to be more like you—say what I meant without fear that my words would come back and bite me in the ass. And now, I don't really care if my ass gets a bite or two. Living up to other people's rules and expectations is exhausting. It's not living. I'm so done with that."

"Good. The new you suits you. By the way, did you ever hear from Beemer guy again?"

"No, nothing. It's like he fell off the face of the earth right after the gun incident with Ben. And Daniel said he checked my house right before we came back up here and the bugs were gone so I'm guessing all that was somehow connected."

"And Daniel?"

"I don't know where this is going, but I'm enjoying the ride. He makes me feel like I matter. But he doesn't smother me too much. I think it's a guy thing—wanting to feel useful, helpful, protective. When it gets too much I shoot him that raised eyebrow thing I can do and he backs off laughing."

"As long as you're both laughing."

"We are. And now, thanks to your uncle, any money worries I may have had are blown away. They're gone. Jenny, Scott—everyone I care about is more than taken care of and I can take care of others like Adam, too, and still have plenty left. Talk about falling into a pot of shit! I'm sad my aunt had to die for all of this to be possible, but I feel her presence overseeing everything I'm doing. Like her hand is guiding me. What more can I say? I'm happy."

"And you deserve it. You deserve to be happy. You're

radiant. So whatever you and Daniel have got going, it's a good thing."

"Yes it is."

A door slammed behind them. Turning in the direction of the sound, they saw Daniel and Scott coming down the porch steps.

"Hey, we're hungry in here. Where's that food?" asked Daniel.

"We're coming," said Sara.

"So's Christmas. We figured if we didn't come out here and grab the food, none of us would ever eat. You two can stay out here for as long as you want, but I'm taking these with me." Scott took the tray of sandwiches out of Rachel's hands.

"There's another tray in the back of Sara's car," said Rachel. "And the desserts are in the bag on the floor behind the driver's seat."

"I'll grab the desserts," said Daniel. "They're the best part of the meal."

The papers were signed. The Raphael Fund was born. Sitting in Beth's living room, surrounded by the people who had a hand in making this possible Rachel's heart was bursting with joy and love. She was sure Aunt Lil was smiling down on the small gathering. She would be pleased. Her life diamonds were serving their intended purpose, assuring new life.

Adam Ingram was comfortably ensconced in a special chair that would give him more flexibility of movement as his body healed and he got used to his new limbs. All of Adam's therapy was covered beyond what the military offered. Twenty-four hour in-home care, support for Beth and Jacob, whatever was needed arrived without question.

"L'Chaim." Raised glasses clinked.

"This is so good. And, Sara, you are a big part of what we've accomplished here," said Rachel.

"Thanks, but all I did was introduce you to Uncle Stan. This is all Aunt Lil's doing."

"And we can't thank you enough," said Jacob. "You've done more than you know."

"I've done nothing compared to Adam's service. And I met with the administrators at Walter Reed yesterday. I've a long list of people who will also benefit from the Raphael Fund."

"And invested wisely, the fund will grow and be available for a long time to come," added Daniel. "Rachel has a great investment company working with her to insure that the fund continues to grow."

"That's important, that the fund grows so we can help as many people as possible," said Rachel. "Uncle Stan found buyers for three of the stones who were willing to pay top dollar. Leo Schwartz cut one of the stones. We sold the three gems he created for an astronomical amount of money. Did I tell you he knew my aunt?"

"Yeah. How amazing is that," said Beth. "Small world. Even smaller back then. And you said, they were in love?"

"Yeah. So sweet. But it just wasn't meant to be. You could see Leo thought my aunt was very special when he saw the diamonds. He was going to move heaven and earth to help me."

"Daniel, whatever happened to Ben Collins?" asked Ellyn. "He seemed so nice when we met him."

"Looks can be deceiving. He's really slick. Teflon Ben. Nothing seems to stick to him. His secretary said he was out of town on business and couldn't be reached. Odd really. I'll keep digging quietly, but I was officially ordered off continuing any investigating of his antics by higher ups."

"Interesting," said Sara. "How high?"

"High enough. Let's just say, I'm ready to retire and I want my full pension so I don't plan to make any waves. He'll get his…one way or another. The universe is funny that way. You know, what goes around, comes around."

"What about that woman? What was her name, Millie?" asked Ellyn.

"Nothing so far. No print match in the system for the partial we did find. Whoever she is, she's good. Very thorough. Wiped the house clean. We'll probably never know who she is. Then again, I've been surprised before."

"So, just what are you planning to do as a soon to be retired New York City Detective?" asked Sara.

"Good question, Sara. Things are up in the air right now. I won't be officially off the job until spring, probably early June. I've got some decisions to make. I may be looking to move south shortly, get out of the city—you know, someplace with a slower pace." Feeling Rachel squeeze his hand told him all he needed to know.

Rachel thought about the last month. It had been one hell of an October, one she would never forget. God works his wonders in strange ways. Her aunt dying put her in the right place at the right time to meet Daniel. Her grief morphed to joy every time she looked at him. They were starting to make plans together. *What would that be like long term—being with someone special—someone who made her toes tingle?*

She found herself wondering about Mark Rogers. Would she ever see him again? If she did, what would she say? Daniel had told her about the call he got the day Ben pulled a gun on her—from a mysterious someone telling him to get back to her place because she was in trouble. *Had the caller been Mark? Was Mark his real name? Had he been after the diamonds? Was Millie connected to him? What caused him to stop his pursuit?* All unanswered questions that someday might get resolved.

She leaned back on the sofa, the fingers of her right hand intertwined with Daniel's. Closing her eyes, she remembered what Aunt Lil used to say. *Happy is a gift you give yourself. You can be angry, sad, miserable or happy. Choose happy. Life's easier happy.*

Book Club Discussion Questions

1. Coming into a large sum of money can be challenging. We all think we know what we would do and how our new-found wealth would affect us. What would you do if you won the lottery or inherited a huge sum of money?

2. We all have our own stories about personal growth and change. What aspects of Rachel's retirement journey ring true for you? How was your initial foray into retirement / a new location / a new job a learning opportunity?

3. All of us have people in our lives that influence our actions for good and bad. Which people in your life influence your behavior the most?

4. What did you think of Rachel's plans to start the Raphael Fund? If you were writing the story, what would you have had Rachel do with the diamonds?

5. Have you experience a friendship like Rachel and Sara's—one that requires no words? What has it meant in your life?

6. Think about your comfort zone and the areas where it prevents you from exploring new opportunities. What would it take for you to break out?

7. Relationships matter. Which relationships between the characters stood out for you? Whether family or friends, which relationships in your life have enabled you to become all that you could be?

8. What one thing could you do that would have a positive impact on your life? What stops you from doing this?

Gotcha!

Coming in 2016

My newest story, *Gotcha!*, examines the depths of a parent's love.

Her daughter has been missing for five years. It's a cold case. But Carolyn Conrad can't let go. She knows Amelia is still alive—out there somewhere—desperately needing her help. Carolyn takes matters into her own hands when faced with the unthinkable—losing her daughter forever. Using her strong research talents laced with a little deception, Carolyn methodically unravels a sex trafficking ring and journeys into its murky underworld to save her daughter. Catch up with some of your friends from *Bamboozled* along the way as their lives intersect with Carolyn's quest to find Amelia.

Thank You...

I am so appreciative to everyone who has journeyed with me during the writing of *Bamboozled.*

Thank you Carolyn Koppe. You have been my muse during this process. Our walks and talks helped me flesh out my characters and plot lines. I truly appreciate your time and energy and your belief in the story that I wanted to tell. Thanks to Bernie and Judi Newman for their help with my Jewish questions. My heartfelt thanks goes to my beta readers Kimberly Miller, Missy McKenna, Lucy Oakleaf, Lynne Lerch, and Mish Kara. Your insights and suggestions were so helpful. Ann DeFee, you have been a wonderful inspiration during this entire process. Your guidance, help connecting with resources and support along the way has kept me putting one foot in front of the other to complete the book. Whenever I called, you were there with answers. To my editor, Leslie Wainger, your comments helped me smooth out plot lines and add depth to my characters. Thank you Dar Dixon for a great cover. You are a joy to partner with. Your patience and kindness through all my small tweaks and changes made the process so enjoyable. Thank you to Amy Atwell and her team at Author EMS. Your formatting skills are priceless.

John, your love and support is what every woman wants from her husband and what I consider myself so lucky to have. You are a blessing in my life.

Meet Jane...

After spending 40 years in business and education, I've left that chapter of my life for a new adventure as a romance novelist. Talk about change! The interesting part for me is that my stories continue to explore how adults navigate their life journeys which are always affected by the choices they make. Through story I want to offer my readers a new way to think about change, empowering them to make choices aligned with their innate talents and gifts, thus generating rich and rewarding lives.

My most recent professional book, *The Change Intelligence Factor: Mastering the Promise of EXTRA-ORDINARY* (2013) is available at Amazon. In it, I marry the dynamics of change with emotional intelligence and offer you an easy to follow formula for success. After identifying three critical change factors, I show you how to leverage key emotional change skills into high powered change intelligence drivers that lead to outstanding personal and professional results.

Come visit me at www.janeflagello.com.

20314087R00183

Made in the USA
Middletown, DE
23 May 2015